Ans	_____	M.L.	11/00 (____)
ASH	_____	MLW	_____
Bev	_____	Mt.Pl	_____
C.C.	_____	NLM	_____
C.P.	_____	Ott	2/08 (Bill)
Dick	_____	PC	_____
DRZ	_____	PH	_____
ECH	_____	P.P.	_____
ECS	_____	Pion.P.	8/06
Gar	_____	Q.A.	_____
GRM	_____	Riv	_____
GSP	_____	RPP	_____
G.V.	_____	Ross	_____
Har	_____	S.C.	_____
JPCP	_____	St.A.	_____
KEN	_____	St.J	8/07 Donald
K.L.	5/08	St.Joa	_____
K.M.	Roy 12/06	St.M.	_____
L.H.	_____	Sgt	_____
LO	_____	T.H.	_____
Lyn	_____	TLLO	_____
L.V.	_____	T.M.	5/07
McC	_____	T.T.	6/08
McG	_____	Ven	_____
McQ	_____	Vets	_____
MIL	_____	VP	5/09
	_____	Wat	_____
	_____	Wed	_____
	_____	WIL	•
	_____	W.L.	_____
	_____		
	_____		_____
	_____		_____
	_____		_____
	_____		_____

Riders of the Plains

**Center Point
Large Print**

This Large Print Book carries the
Seal of Approval of N.A.V.H.

Riders of the Plains

Max Brand®

CENTER POINT PUBLISHING
THORNDIKE, MAINE

The text of this Large Print edition is unabridged. In other
aspects, this book may vary from the original edition. Printed in
Thailand. Set in 16-point Times New Roman type.

ISBN 1-58547-758-3

Library of Congress Cataloging-in-Publication Data

Brand, Max, 1892-1944.
    Riders of the plains / Max Brand.--Center Point large print ed.
      p. cm.
    ISBN 1-58547-758-3 (lib. bdg. : alk. paper)
    1. Large type books. I. Title.

PS3511.A87R52 2006
812'.54--dc22

2005033852

CONTENTS

Chapter I

THE CONTEST

This was the day of Ross Hale. The whole county knew it. When he got up that morning—and he had slept very little the night before, you may be sure—he looked at himself in the mirror and decided that he would now take off ten years of his age and grow young once more.

He put on his best suit, scowling when he saw how shiny it was at the elbows. Then he went out and hitched his only team to the buckboard. It was a sorry pair, incurably thin, incurably down-headed, hardly fit to drag their feet along the road with the old buckboard trailing them, though Ross Hale forced them to carry him across the hills when he had to ride range.

Ross was desperately ashamed to go in for the great occasion in such a guise as this; nevertheless, he was mildly comforted by the knowledge that every one understood. The whole county knew the wager that had been made between Ross and Andy Hale eleven years before, and the whole county was burning with excitement now that the decision was about to be made.

Eleven years before—to tell all briefly—the wives of Ross and Andy Hale were caught in a fire that broke out in the house of Andy. They were burned to death in spite of the great effort made to save them. And the two brothers were left in exactly the same condition. They were of the same age, for they were twins; they were widowers; and they had each a boy of the same age.

In the winter that followed, when they talked over what the world might hold for each of them and for their boys, they laid their schemes, in their own ways, for the development of the young lives. To Andy Hale there was only one existence under the stars that was worth while. His argument ran something like this:

"Nobody but a fool would want to live in the city, if he could get away from it. No, everybody with good sense prefers to live in the country. Why? Because he ain't so crowded, in the country. He's got elbowroom and breathing space. And that's the reason that he goes out from the cities. Well, if he goes to the country for that reason, where in the world will he find more elbowroom than right here in this county? Where will he find better mountains or more of them? Where will he find better grass for his horses and his cows? Tell me, partner?"

And Andy Hale, who was so exactly suited by this world which he found around him, decided that he would raise his son to follow in his footsteps and do exactly as he had done. He took pains that young Charlie Hale should attend the same tumble-down shack of a school where he himself had learned his letters. He also took care that Charlie did not remain in the school a minute longer than his father had remained before him.

"What made a man of me is going to make a man of my boy!" he announced to the world at large—and particularly to his brother, for there was a great contest on between them.

The views of Ross Hale differed materially from those of his twin brother. Ross could not tell just what was wrong with the range. He did not mind riding range; he was a cowboy of sorts—so good with a gun that he could have made a living as a professional hunter, if nothing better had come to his hand. On the whole, though he thought that this life might be well enough, he dimly recognized the faint horizon of another universe, a sort of Milky Way that streaked thin across his sky. And that other universe was the world of mind and soul.

In just what fashion the human brain might expand and flower, Ross Hale did not know. But he knew that he was extremely eager that his son should wander through the unknown spaces where his own feet had never trod. So he came to the great decision that young Peter Hale should be sent to a school where he could be prepared for a great Eastern university.

He consulted the rich rancher, Crowell, on the subject, and Crowell, in his usual positive manner, said:

"There is only one place in the world where an American boy may be properly prepared to enter a great American university. That place is Huntley School. Furthermore, there is only one great American university. But that I need not tell you, because if your boy attends the Huntley School, he will be sure to know the name of the only real university before he gets out of the doors."

The matter was thus settled for the rancher, but when he began to look into the matter he found that this was a staggering thing. Education was not a gift, in the Eastern States; it was something which had to be paid for, and often paid for through the nose. However, Anthony Crowell had spoken. And upon such matters no man on the range would dare to question his opinion, however little Crowell apparently knew about cows, poor fellow! Thus, it never came into Ross' mind that he might be able to provide for his son more reasonably.

He had to clean up his savings in cash at the bank in order to provide for the very first year at Huntley School. But he made the provision, and after that, he could not resist the desire to redeem the money he had already spent by completing the work which he had begun. And each succeeding year was more expensive than the one before.

Since he could not afford to spend two hundred dollars on a trip East to see his boy, he could not afford to spend the same amount of money in bringing his boy West to see him. Therefore the years slid along, one after the other, with more and more money departing from the pocket of Ross Hale, and never a glimpse of his boy, Peter, in the flesh.

Peter himself, even when he was only fourteen, realized that he must be a heavy drain, and he wrote home to say that there were various ways of picking up quite a bit of pocket money and arranging matters so that when he got to the college age, he would be able to provide his own board and lodging—if his father could only manage the tuition fee. This letter gave a ray of hope to the rancher. He carried it to his educational oracle, Mr. Anthony Crowell. The latter said instantly:

"Education serves two purposes, Hale. In the first place it gives a youngster mental discipline and it pours a certain quantity of facts into his mind, together with the knowledge of how to go about collecting new facts about new subjects, even after he has left school. But on the other hand, education gives a boy a prolonged childhood. It gives him a longer season during which the burden of the weary world is removed from his shoulders, Hale. He plays out in the sun without a bit of thought for the shadows that are to come. His body grows straight and his muscles grow strong. And his mind opens its gates and gathers in impressions. But if you make a poor lad work his way through school, the weight of the world is introduced, and it crushes flat that play existence which should fill the school from wall to wall. School is not for work only. It is primarily a social experience and a place where the boy can remain a child until he is actually forced to take on the duties of a man—until he *yearns* to take them on, Hale. That's the great thing."

Ross Hale did not understand a great part of this speech, and what was clear to him was really hardly more than that Anthony Crowell did not advise allowing a boy to work his way through a school. This was enough. Of these matters, Ross Hale knew nothing, and he was such a frank and honest man that he never dreamed of pretending an opinion in matters where he was not learned by experience.

He went back home and wrote to his boy in the very spirit of the lecture which had just been read to him. He wrote, in effect:

Spread your elbows at the board, and do not regard any reasonable expense. The ranch is doing very well. I want you to have a good time, along with your studies!

Then he went down to see his brother, Andy, and sold him the southeast forty-acre field which Andy had been yearning for all these many, many years.

The resolution, which Andy and Ross had taken, of developing their boys according to their own views, had put Andy on his honor. He had changed his old way of living; ceased being a happy-go-lucky, free-swinging individual, without that understrain of seriousness which had always been a shadow in the life of his twin brother. But when he saw Ross settling down and making great sacrifices for his boy, Andy changed his own way of life, little by little. A certain number of years hence—so the agreement between Ross and Andy went—they were to produce their sons to Will Nast, the sheriff. And they would then accept the verdict which the sheriff might pronounce as to which was the finer man and the more valuable citizen.

This was a contest upon which a great deal depended. There was no doubt but that Peter Hale would come from his education a fine lad, and Charlie Hale would need a great deal to compete against him and keep from being disgraced. So Andy Hale did two things. In the first place he seriously impressed on his boy the necessity of doing all things well that are expected from a cowpuncher and a range rider. In the second place, he set about building up a respectable property, for his dream was that, at the end of the probation period, Charlie might appear as the prospective proprietor of a fine bit of land and cows. That would give point and emphasis to all the qualifications which Charlie might possess as a cow-puncher.

So Andy, from being a free spender, became a most thrifty and saving soul, and as the years went on, his place began to show all the effects which industry and care and forethought could present. He had good fortune also, and what he turned his hand to prospered exceedingly. His cattle were free from sickness and plagues. When he tried his hand at crop raising, he got bumper returns of wheat and barley. And he always managed to sell at the top of the market and buy everything at the bottom.

"I dunno how it is!" said Andy Hale, marveling at himself. "Everything seems to turn out well!"

There was one touch of learning in Ross Hale. He used it now: "You've sold yourself for the touch of Midas!" said he.

13

Chapter II

PROSPERITY FOR ANDY

Andy did not know what the touch of Midas might be. But he gathered from the sneering tone of his brother that it was something rather disgraceful, and he returned a hot answer. Humility was not the chief virtue of Ross Hale, and so one word led to another until they parted from each other in passion and never again returned to the former kindly footing.

No doubt, Ross Hale should have been big enough of soul to look upon the waxing prosperity of Andrew without jealousy, but he could not control himself. About this time, too, Andrew took a second wife, and for some reason Ross felt that this was an indubitable token of the other's prosperity. For, after all, wives cost money. And Ross Hale felt that his brother was getting money to burn. Moreover, on his way to and from town, the road passed close to the house of Andrew, and Ross could see, with almost every trip, some new token of the comfort of his brother.

There was either a new bit of fencing, or else a new brand of cattle among those in the fields—for Andrew had taken to buying up the run-down and starveling stock of the neighborhood. Perhaps there was a new coat of paint on house or barn—fancy wasting paint on barns!—or the roof of some brand-new shed piercing the horizon. And Andrew's ranch was beginning to extend itself, too. Andrew needed more land,

and yet more land! He was renting great acres of alfalfa among the irrigated little valleys among the foothills and he was carting the produce of alfalfa to his ranch. Then he bought up, in the dreary winter of the year, half-starved stock from far ranges, where the winter offered wretched pittance to the grazing cows. Yet these cattle, almost too thin to be driven to his ranch, soon grew plump. They were wretched poor strains, most of them, but they sold at so much a pound, once they were fattened, and Andrew always knew just when to take his stock to market to get the top prices.

His fields were expanding, therefore, to meet his requirements. He did not buy rashly, but a little here and a corner there, when one of his neighbors was in a desperate need of hard cash. Clever Andrew was so well established by now that the banks in town were fighting to get his business, and they were more than willing to lend him money, all the money he could use, at six percent.

"Some day it'll be the ruin of him!" said Ross Hale darkly and bitterly, "usin' money like this. Because the money shark'll swaller him! It ain't gunna be for the lack of my advice to keep him from it!"

He dressed himself in his best clothes—that he might pass the inspection of the wife of Andrew—and rode over to offer that advice and, incidentally, to see if it were true that Andy was laying out the foundations for a barn which would hold three hundred tons of hay. It was true; he found Andy assisting the workers to sink the foundations. Part of those foundations had been dug already and laid, and the building was to be built upon—concrete piles!

Ross Hale stared with wonder and sharp envy gnawing at his heart. Standing there he spoke out his heart to his brother and gave his warning against the money sharks, as he had conceived it. Andrew listened with an intent frown, at first, then shaking his head and smiling. At last he laid his hand upon Ross' shoulder.

"You mean me the best in the world, I hope," said he. "I wouldn't think that it was just envy of me that brung you over here, Ross. You mean me good, and that's why you warn me. And lemme tell you that sometimes you're right, and there's more than one man that's working for a bank and not for himself. But not me, Ross. No, not me. I've learned something and I tell you that, so long as I got my wits about me, I'm gunna keep right *on* borrowing from the banks. Why? Because I need capital which I ain't got. I want to go out and buy when the season is right. When I hear that there's a bunch of a hundred worn-down, dying cows some place, I want to be able to ride right out and pay down the cash and snatch up that band. I can't do it with my own money. I could only bargain for a *corner* of that whole herd. Well, the bank lends me that money at six percent interest, but maybe I make hundreds of percent in the meantime. I give you an example: Last November I heard of a batch of eighty dogies down in the Sawtrell Valley dying of hunger—no way to save them.

"Well, I borrowed money from the bank to buy them. Now look at what happened! Ten months later I sold off that batch. Eight of them had died. Too far gone for me to save them from starving to death. But seventy-two of them pulled through.

"The result was I cleaned up near twenty-five hundred dollars, old son! I paid back the bank a few days ago. Besides, I sank the twenty-five hundred in the vault, but not for long. I'm going to have that coin out again! It'll rot in the bank at a miserable rate of interest. I'll soon want that money out and working in my hands!"

This was all a little bit beyond the ken of Ross Hale. He knew, however, that transactions that looked simply gigantic to him were as nothing in the capable hands of his brother, and he felt that time had transformed Andrew into a new and formidable force. To dare to gamble on such a scale—to clear twenty-five hundred dollars in cash in a single, simple transaction, and clearly to regard that transaction as a mere nothing—this was like handling fire, to Ross Hale! He stared at Andrew with awe, and the spite of malice could not be kept a little from his eyes.

"Well, Andrew," he said, "I dunno that I understand all of these ways of doing business. But I wish you all kinds of luck."

"Thanks," said Andy, "and lemme give you a mite of advice—which is that if you want to make money out of Durhams you had ought to—"

"Curse the Durhams!" said Ross Hale. And well he might curse them for disease was wasting his herd strangely and swiftly.

"Well," said Andy kindly, "you take care of your own business. How's things with Peter, though?"

A broad grin of triumph twisted the mouth of Ross Hale, and his eyes shone with triumph. He tried to make his voice casual and unimpressive. "I just heard from him, sort of indirect. Some one that knows him, sent me along this clipping, but Peter himself, he wouldn't say nothing about it!"

And he took out a newspaper clipping, already well worn in the creases and the seams, telling the tale of how Huntley School, in its great annual football contest with Winraven School, had triumphed gloriously with two touchdowns to one, through the heroic work of young sixteen-year-old Peter Hale. His burly shoulders had burst through the line from his place at tackle, blocked a punt, and carried the ball to a touchdown. Again he had broken through and tackled a back, so hard that the fumbled ball was picked up by a fellow Huntley man, and so the second touchdown was achieved. There was not so very much about the game, but there was a great deal about Peter Hale. His name was in the big, flaring headline. And there was a whole long paragraph at the beginning of the story, telling about the manner in which stars are born and made.

This missive was read through twice, from beginning to end, by Andy Hale, and his lips pinched a little as he handed it back.

"Curse it, Ross!" he said frankly. "I really dunno whether to be proud of having that boy for a nephew, or to envy you for having such a son. Still, I ain't ashamed of my Charlie, only I don't think that he's any such headliner as all of this!"

And he turned his head to mark Charlie in person, big and bronzed, healthy and laughing and handsome, as he galloped his big, fast cow pony around the corner of the barn.

"He's sixteen, but he does a man's work," said Andy Hale. "Maybe he don't speak trimmed-up garden English, like your boy most likely does, but he can tell which side his bread is buttered on, and he knows how to ask for more! I ain't ashamed of my Charlie, even if he ain't made any touchdowns!"

However, Ross Hale felt, when he rode back home that night, that he had scored a great triumph. True, he had sold the corner lot to Andrew. But he had been able to sit in the sun of Peter's glory and lord it over the others. And that was enough! In the meantime, if he had to ride back to a cheerless house and to a cold kitchen, he felt that it was worth the agony. And that night he entered his damp bedroom and went to sleep well acclimated to his fate.

Chapter III

NOT IN THE LINE-UP

The scholastic reports were not so flattering as the athletic ones. In the fall, Peter roamed across the gridirons and did great, flashing things. In the winter he was a member of the ice-hockey team for the school. In the spring he was on the baseball nine; and in the hot summer days he was straining his back over an oar in the Huntley eight. All of these things he did surpassingly well, and now and then a flattering note came like air from heaven to the eye of Ross Hale, far off in the mountain desert.

In his studies, Peter was just a bit above average—below that, at first—but making slow, sure progress. He had his stumblingblocks. Terse and uncommunicative as his letters always were, they once contained a wail on account of Latin, the bane of his soul. And immediately afterward a greater curse entered—clad in strange garments—Greek! Between them, they were nearly the undoing of poor Peter, but he managed to struggle through.

When he came into his seventeenth year everything seemed much better to Peter. Studies went more easily. On the athletic field he was triumphant, and in his eighteenth year, he completed his course in a blaze of glory—football captain—crew stroke. He stood on a peak even in brilliant Huntley School.

Then came the fall, and the heart of Ross Hale swelled

with anticipation. He could not help writing to Peter:

Look here, Pete. I know that college is a place where you go to get an education. But I tell you what—I like to hear about you doing good in athletics. I can't understand what tackling a Greek verb may be like. But I can understand what smashing up a football line may be. I'm proud of your studies, Pete, my boy, but I'm a lot prouder of what you're doing in athletics—and most particular on the football field. Folks are reading a lot about you here in the papers—maybe you understand what I mean!

How hard it would have been for Peter really to understand! He could not know that another vast chunk of the old ranch had been sold to Andrew Hale, and that the remainder had been heavily mortgaged. And still there were three mortal years during which this education affair must be carried on!

The first college year brought more glory to Ross Hale. It was only freshman football; the Crimson would not take a player on the college eleven until his second year. But in that freshman team, Peter Hale roved up and down fields, breaking the hearts of opposing teams! They had made him an end. Eighteen years old, and a hundred and ninety pounds of him, but so lightning fast that he was always first down the field under a punt. And he was forever smashing through the other line to get at the ball carrier—to say nothing of the moments when he looped far out and speared passes out of the air, then zigzagged down the field, ripping the enemy apart as lightning divides the startled sky!

Track and crew also held his attention. And he carved a name for himself in each. The heart of Ross Hale swelled big with expectation of the next fall, when his boy would stand in the varsity eleven. Then real fame would come to him!

The fall came, and there were no press notices about Peter Hale—only this strange line in one paper:

The Crimson is not so strong in advancing the ball as it was expected. Simpson failed in his studies and cannot represent the Crimson on the gridiron this fall. Above all, the brilliant Hale, of whom so much was expected after his grand work on the freshman team, has been thrown out by a severe accident.

That was all.

It made Ross Hale ride half the night to get to town and send off a telegram:

Are you badly hurt, and when can you play again?
                                                        FATHER.

He did not get a reply for two days. The answer read:

Out for a month or two. Nothing serious.
                                                        PETE.

That somewhat allayed the anxiety of Ross Hale. Still, an accident which put a boy out for a month or two must be a rather bad one. He waited a week. Then he rode over to tell Crowell what was worrying him.

"Why," said Crowell, "don't you know what happened to your boy?"

"Good heavens!" said the rancher; "you talk like it was serious, Mr. Crowell!"

"Serious?" echoed Crowell, with a strange glance. Then he added hastily: "Now, I suppose it might have been worse!"

"Yes," said the rancher, "it'll only keep him out for a month or two."

"Is that all he wrote to you?" said Crowell.

"Yes," said Hale.

Crowell murmured something and looked hastily away. He seemed a little moved. But Ross Hale rode back to his ranch and went on waiting.

Late October came—November—and still there was no word of Peter in the lineup!

Well, it was a crushing blow, but there were still two years left of Peter's varsity career, and perhaps it was all for the best. He would be bigger and stronger and better able, in every way, to make football history in the following fall. Therefore Ross Hale steeled himself with patience and endured for another year. Small consolations came to him along the way. Sweetest of all was the news in the early summer that Peter had done well—extremely well—in his studies. The strangest part was that Peter had not appeared in the varsity crew—or in the varsity nine!

"I am saving myself for football!" wrote Peter.

But the junior year brought not a bit of better luck. October came, and still there was no word of Peter in the college lineup. So Ross Hale wrote to the coach— to the famous Crossley himself—asking: "Why doesn't my boy make good, after the fine start which he had? Doesn't he measure up to your varsity standard?"

In due time—but that was November and the big games were already played for the year!—there came a bittersweet letter for Ross Hale. It was quite long and it was all written out in the hand of the great Crossley, himself, and signed with his very own name at the bottom of the last page!

It said in part:

Peter is good enough to play for the varsity. He is head and shoulders above any man on the team as it stands at present. It is a dreadful blow to us that we can't play him. But his leg was never properly treated, and it gave way during practice again.

However, even if Peter were never to play a game of college football, you have a right to know that we who really watched him in action in his freshman year understand that he was a great athlete, one of the very finest, I think, that I ever saw break up a football line. In addition, he has a heart of oak. But you are his father, and doubtless you know that for yourself.

For my part I should like to add only this: That

sometimes great disappointments, even in little things, will ripen a man and make him truly worth while.

There was much more to this kind letter. But the major fact remained that Peter had not played football this fall again. And Andy Hale said with a smile and a shrug:

"Pete don't seem to be tearing them up quite so much this year, Ross!"

"Wait till next year and you'll see him break all records!" said Ross savagely.

Yet with the coming of the next fall there was still no word of Peter Hale in the lineup.

A poor team had taken the field for the great Crimson, and it was passing through a most disastrous season. The big fellows trampled it under foot, and the little fellows rose up and battled it on even terms. Surely, surely, there was room on such an eleven for Peter Hale. His anxious father, reading Eastern sporting pages with an anxious heart, waited and waited, swearing to himself that life would be worth while if Peter could only stand in the Crimson line for a single period, for five minutes! But it was not to be. No college letter would come to Peter!

A dreadful winter followed. Twice Ross went to the banks, and twice the banks refused to talk to him. They had heard the old story before, and there was nothing in it to interest them. They did not care how great an amount of interest he was prepared to pay. He sold off almost all of his remaining stock. For his own part he lived on milk and bread and what rabbits he could reach with his rifle. He had furniture for two rooms—the kitchen, into which he had moved his own bed, and Peter's room, kept exactly as it had been in the old days, when Peter left his home.

But the rest of the house had been denuded. It was true that it did not bring much when it was sold to the second-hand stores; yet it brought something. Even so, he could not get enough, it seemed.

"I am afraid, from the size of your last check, dad," said a letter from Peter, "that you haven't been having as much luck as usual on the farm. Now, if you will say the word, I can easily raise enough money to see me through commencement week."

But Ross Hale had begun this thing eleven years before and he would see it through. He took his last dollar into a poker game and came out with a couple of hundred. Every penny of it he sent East. This would see his boy through. It was the last stroke and it crowned his work. Now he had only to sit back and reap the fruits of his labors!

Chapter IV

THE GREAT MOMENT

Now you understand why it was that the entire county knew that this was the day of Ross Hale. They knew, for one thing—for the papers had proclaimed it—that young Peter had graduated with honors, which seemed to mean a great deal more than football, at the Crimson, although not to sporting editors.

And here was a note from the great Crossley to Ross Hale.

DEAR MR. HALE: If we have missed your son mightily on the football field during the past three seasons, you now see for yourself that he has been doing a work that is a great deal finer for himself and for our college than anything that he could possibly have performed upon the football field!

I wish you joy of him. He is true blue—true-blue steel. There was never a finer fellow.

What a letter from the busy Crossley; how much heart in it; what an outpouring! It raised the head of Ross Hale into the clouds, and he almost forgave Peter for having failed in the football—owing to injuries, of course. The great Crossley himself had pledged his word that that was the reason! And did he not have that letter to show to the doubters?

The whole county was willing to believe—all except Andy Hale. He had reason to doubt—for it would not be long before he would have to let his boy stand at the side of big Peter Hale in front of the sheriff. And if Will Nast's eyes had not suddenly grown dull, were they not apt to see something in the great athlete, the man who spoke so many languages, who read, at least, in two dead ones! He wondered how Charlie would stand this comparison?

Big and strong Charlie undoubtedly was, and straight in the back, and broad in the shoulders. At bulldogging a yearling, where was there his superior in the county? He had a good business head, too, and one day he would have all of his father's rapidly growing estate to handle. Yet, in the eyes of Will Nast, would he be as valuable to the community as this startling Peter Hale, into whose well-being half the life and all the prosperity of Ross Hale had been poured?

Such an effort was worth a great crop. And it seemed as though one had surely grown from it. There were thousands of students picked from all parts of the country—hand-picked. And yet this Peter Hale had distinguished himself among them all. He had been great in athletics; he had been great in his studies—or far, far above the average, at the least.

As for Andy Hale, what was it that *he* had invested? In preparing an inheritance for his son, he had simply discovered the means of occupying himself more fully and happily than he had ever been able to do before. Ross Hale had completed his active life; he shrank, a weak and exhausted soul, from the business of life. But Andy was ready to attack life with more fervor than ever. He had used every one of the past eleven years to push out his boundaries. And if he had begun the work in the interest of his boy, was it not true that in the end he had been completing the task for his own sake? But it was certain that he dreaded the day on which Peter Hale should reach his old home. And of all the people who streamed toward the station to await the incoming of the express, there was not one downhearted spirit except that of Andy.

As for Charlie himself, his smile never varied on his brown face, and his eyes remained as bright and as clear as ever they had been. You would say that malice could not live in the heart of such a man. If the people looked with a pleasant expectancy down the track where the front of the express would soon show itself, they looked also with a very definite satisfaction at the son of Andy Hale.

Everyone knew the terms of the contest. And they felt a jealous interest in its outcome. They knew that Charlie Hale had had what every Western boy was apt to expect, except that he had a little more of it. He had been trained on a prosperous ranch under a clever father. He had a sharp head for business, a keen knowledge of cows, their ways, and how to make money out of them, and he knew how to use the range to the best advantage, summer and winter. In addition to this, he was big and handsome; rode well, shot straight, and feared no man. Peter Hale would have to be a fine fellow to take a mark above his Western rival!

Ross Hale, driving toward the station, found that the platform was already crowded, though it was well before train time. Still others were coming in haste to join the throng, but a way was made for him.

For instance, since there was a crowd of buggies and buckboards at the nearest hitching rack, Tom Ransom backed his rig out and gave the place to the father of the returning hero. And when Ross Hale climbed up the steps to the station platform, way was made for him, so that he walked through to the front. He paused here and there—to take a cigar from one friend, to shake hands with another, and to exchange a word with a third.

He felt the admiration in the eyes which were fixed upon him. They were quite willing to overlook the shabbiness of his clothes, as if they felt that this were proof of the sacrifices and the efforts which he had made to complete his boy's education.

Now and then they looked from him to Andy Hale, and their faces darkened perceptibly. It was not that any one could have a word to speak against Andy Hale, but, compared with the sterling example of his brother, it was felt that Andy had almost sold his soul to the devil. He had preferred to make money; Ross Hale, on the other hand, had preferred the mental welfare of his boy.

To be sure, Charlie Hale was as fine a looking fellow as could be found on the range; his hand was as strong and his heart was as steady—but to compare him with his cousin from the Eastern school would be a very silly thing, indeed.

Weaker and smaller men than Andy Hale and his son would perhaps have felt all of the implied criticisms in these glances, and melted from the crowd, but they endured it all with smiles. However, it should be remembered that prosperity, when it passes the common point, cannot be tolerated with complacency by others. The commonest cow-puncher could see that in the past eleven years Andy Hale had lifted himself fairly out of their ranks to a position in which the bankers smiled most cordially upon him, the officials of the county asked his opinion, and that opinion was liberally quoted by the county newspaper—where reputations were made and buried also!

Here was old McNair with his keen blue eyes and his bulldog jaw. He grinned at Ross Hale and wrung his hand with the paw of a giant.

"Look here, Ross," said he. "You got the finest boy in the range, and I got the prettiest girl. How about making a match between them, eh?"

It was a sad thing to say in the very presence of his daughter. But Ross Hale noted that though crimson flooded her throat and her face, it was rather with confusion than anger that she quickly turned to her father and shook her finger at him to keep him quiet.

"Darn it, Ruth," said McNair, louder than before, "you *are* the prettiest girl, and I'll see no man that dares to say that you ain't. But they won't make such fools of themselves to say that! Eh, lads?"

He looked about him with the eye of a bull but he met with smiles only. What would have been an intolerable speech from any other man, could be endured, coming from the lips of McNair, because he was a known man. For that matter, Ruth McNair was a known girl, too, and it would be hard to bring from any man in that crowd a speech that would offend her in any way.

31

If she had to turn away to hide her color, Ross Hale passed on with a keen sense that the sun was warmer and more gently golden that he had ever known it to be. The very smell of tar from the tracks seemed to him more bitingly delicious than any fragrance of flowers.

Presently, there was a faint humming of the rails. He looked east along the line above the hills, where the trees met with the pale blue of the sky, and he saw a streak of white smoke. It blended in with the glistening clouds in the sky. Then the whistle screeched twice, and here came the front of the engine, swaying around the long curve into view, and then straightening out, staggering with speed, as it sped on for the station.

Now the train was slowing. The brakes went on with a screech. Voices began to be raised around him, excited voices frankly and freely speaking, because they had the thunder of the engine and the roar of the grinding wheels to drown their noises. The more they talked, the more excitement grew. A buzz and a stir filled them, and all the Sumnertown people pressed a little forward on the station platform.

The great moment had come, and Ross Hale, as he saw the train slowing toward a halt, tried to see through the windows, but found that his eyes were misted over. The gasp and whisper of the crowd—which was all that was left of their rattling excitement of the moment before, sank still lower and went out. Silence swept through them, and it was as though a great searchlight had fallen upon Ross Hale and his boy.

Chapter V

THE RUINS

Here was "Doc" Murray, the rich rancher, swinging down from the steps of the train and looking about him with a joyful wave of the hand and a cheery word here and there to various faces which he recognized among the crowd as though he thought that this impromptu reception was being held in his honor. But there was no heed paid to rich Doc Murray. He suddenly recognized that he was not the center of the picture, but that he was obscuring it! And he shrank suddenly to the side and away into the crowd, turning a bright scarlet.

Ross Hale smiled. He had waited a long time for this moment; he had invested eleven years of purgatory in the labor, wrecking his life and using up his farm. There was nothing left to him except a shell of his old existence. So if a few others had to suffer a little at the instant of his triumph—well, how could that be helped? And was it not really fitting, in a way?

Here was another and another dismounting from the train, blinking as the keen scrutiny of the public fell upon their faces. They glanced from side to side, as though frightened by this unexpected publicity. Then they scurried away. How lucky it was that his boy was to dismount last of all! How lucky it was!

He was not the first to see Peter. But he heard a little gasp from several people around him. Then, by a great effort, he controlled himself, clearing his eyes with a slight shake of the head. Above the crowd he saw the face for which he had yearned these many, many years! There was a set smile upon the lips. And he thought that he had never seen such a pale face in an athlete.

As he came closer, the people before him gave way. And was it possible that an expression of pity was in their eyes as they glanced at Ross Hale on this most glorious day in the world?

They separated before him, and he had a clear view of Peter standing beside the train, while his baggage was handed down for him—standing beside the train with his wide, powerful shoulders bulging over the support of two crutches. Down to the waist he was a veritable giant of a man; below the waist he was distorted, grotesque—with an iron brace running along one leg. He moved and trailed the lower half of his body with a lurch.

Poor Ross Hale suddenly recalled the past three years. He remembered how the brilliant young athlete from Huntley School had mysteriously dropped from the football ranks. And he remembered certain passages in the letter from the famous coach, Crossley. Well, that was enough.

Slowly he went toward Peter, and as he walked, it seemed to him that he was making eleven steps, and each step meant a year of torture which he had under-gone for the sake of this moment. And each year was now blazing with an incredible brilliance of torture in his soul.

He had failed; he had failed; he had failed! Here was his hero, his breaker of the ranks of men, his demigod, his Peter—a mere shattered wreckage crawling home from a ruined life!

Ross felt no pity for Peter; he felt no pity for him-self. Muttering something—he hardly knew what—he calmly stooped and picked up the bags which Peter had brought with him. Then he strode away through the crowd, and that crowd melted away on either side.

The very first man to retreat was Sheriff Will Nast, who was soon to be called upon to make the decision upon the value of each of these two young men. Others went in haste. Voices were raised with a sham cheerfulness. People recalled a thousand-odd bits of business, anything that might furnish them with a decent pretext for turning and hurrying away.

Yet they did not go unnoticed. Here and there a deep, quiet voice spoke, as Peter Hale noticed and rec-ognized one face and then another. He paused to speak with each and to shake hands with each. He had a clever way of shifting all his weight and his right crutch onto the left arm and the iron-braced left leg. Then, balanced a little precariously in this fashion, he had his whole right hand and arm free for shaking hands.

People thought that he looked very white and sick. His eyes were quite hollowed and shadowed. But his voice was perfectly cheerful. He had something to say to each one whom he knew, and so he came with a surprising ease through their midst and out to the steps at the back of the platform. By this time, there were few people left. Every one had started off at full speed. Consequently there were not so many eyes to see the little calamity that followed.

Peter, fumbling for the steps with his crutches, hardly noticed that one of the concrete steps had crumbled away. There was a grunt; the crutches plunged down through thin air, and the heavy body of Peter lurched to the ground and rolled in the dust.

Two or three ran to help him up. But he managed himself with a surprising adroitness. He had not lost the crutches, and now one had a chance to estimate the immense strength that must have belonged to him once. One could believe those old tales of how Peter had crushed through opposing football lines and come at the ball carriers with an incredible, cruel force, merely from seeing the lightness with which his long, powerful arms heaved him up out of the dust and the cinders and balanced him erect upon the crutches again.

His father, looking back, saw the commotion and its cause but he did not hurry to the rescue. He felt an insane desire to throw back his head and burst into laughter, and he felt that if he ran to Peter, he would run with laughter that must not be heard!

Besides, there were plenty of others to brush the dirt from Peter's clothes. He thanked them gravely and calmly. It seemed to Ross Hale that his son had no shame and accepted the ministrations of the others with a pleasant smile, like one accustomed to the pity of the world. Ah, well, after this day the world might just as well end!

Only one thing was amazing—that the blow could have fallen so suddenly. One instant, he was like a king, above the rest of the people of Sumnertown and of Sumner County. The next instant, there was the cause of his elevation reduced to a horrible mockery of manhood!

When the hulk of a man reached the buckboard, his father stood by. He would not offer help until it was asked, although he wondered how Peter would go about getting into the vehicle. But the moment was not so clumsy as it might have been, for Peter, balancing himself on the iron-braced left leg, put his crutches away in the back of the buckboard. Then he grasped the upper rim of the front wheel tire with one hand and the side of the seat with the other. He gave himself a swing and a lurch, and there he was, sitting in the seat, breathing a little hard with quivering nostrils.

It did not seem like a very great thing, except to one who knew something about the limitations of human strength. But Ross Hale knew. He had been crippled once for nearly eighteen months by the kick of a refractory mule which he was harnessing by the semi-light of a lantern, before dawn. And he knew what it means to take the drag of a heavy body upon the arms alone! As Ross gathered up the reins and climbed into the buckboard, he rebuilt for himself the picture of Peter Hale as he might have been—as he once *had* been!

Once strength of foot had matched the strength of hands. Then he had been a veritable giant, indeed. Oh, to have had him only once come back here that the people of Sumnertown might have seen him in his glory—merely that they might contrast this glory with the wreck that it had come to now! But even that small mercy had not been granted to him, and he had read the disgust in the faces of the people who turned away from that station platform—disgust and pity commingled—than which there are no lower passions!

They would not forget; they had heard the lies for three years by which they were promised stories of the giant's prowess. This, they now felt, had been merely an artful deception practiced upon them by the father and the son—a stupid piece of artifice to keep from them the irrevocable fact—that the life and the body of Peter Hale were ruined things!

Ross put the whip to the ragged, downheaded team of mustangs and drove them out of the town in a whirl. But they passed over the first mile before he could look at Peter, and then it was only a side glance, which showed him his son sitting with a high head and a glance fixed calmly on the road before them.

Presently Peter said: "This goes even harder with you than I had feared, father."

"Harder?" repeated the rancher. "Harder?" And then he laughed, but the sound was choked off and died in the pit of his throat.

"You see," said the level voice of Peter, "when I saw that you were so dead set on having me do something on the football field—why, after the accident, I talked it over with the coach and the doctor. They agreed that it might be a good thing if I didn't give you the great disappointment. They agreed, at that time, that there was one chance in ten that my legs might be untangled from the knots that they were in. So I took that chance—like a coward! And having started with fear, in that manner, I've never had the nerve to speak to you about it since. I've written those misleading letters to you. I've even let poor Tony Crossley write lies to you. Bless Tony for it, though! He meant the best in the world!"

It was an echo from a far and glorified world—in which the son of Ross Hale called the great Crossley—whose picture had appeared in papers a thousand times—by his first name. Ross Hale sat quietly, without answering, and digested the bitter sweetness of this fact through the remainder of the miles that brought them to the ranch house.

Chapter VI

THE ACCIDENT

As they drove along, with the wheels sagging now and again into a deeper rut and tossing up a whirl of gray dust and a film of white mist, it seemed to the rancher that something else might follow. Something else *must* follow. There were other explanations owing to him, and Peter would at once attempt to make them. It did not matter that they might be hard to make; Peter would surely make them!

But Peter did not speak. He seemed only to be waiting for his father to open up the conversation again. For his own part, Peter was merely contented to sit there and let the time streak idly on, and the miles jog away toward the home ranch.

The early burst of speed had left the bronchos down-headed. Their feet trailed, for the toes of their hind hoofs had been chipped away by constant trailing through the dust of this same road. For how many years had Ross Hale seen them pause to walk up the rises and lurch wearily into a trot again, on the farther slope? How many times had he seen them reel at the same places, and stumble at the same places, and lift their heads with a sudden interest, when they smelled the black mud and freshness of water that always blew to the road from Murphy's windmill and overflowing water tank!

Peter Hale sat like a young Indian, and his father

decided, in bitterness, that perhaps he had not lost so very much, after all. For instance, his Peter was not the handsome youth that he had promised to become. Or was this, too, an after effect of the sickness? It seemed to the broken heart of Ross Hale that the accident that had wrecked the powers of his son had marred his comeliness also. His square, powerful jaw, for instance, might not look so brutally cruel and stern if it had been fleshed over a little. And one would not have noticed the forbidding depth to which the eyes were sunk, if it had not been that beneath the brows they were blackened so tremendously by suffering and long years of gloom.

Yes, Peter had suffered. There was no doubt of that. But it did not lighten the load on the soul of Ross Hale to know this. Certainly it would have been a sad thing if his son had turned out too great a fool even to understand how much he had lost, how much had been taken away from him by the fatal accident!

"Tell me how it happened?" asked the father.

"I was up in the mountains with young Bassiter—Dick Bassiter. That was the summer after my freshman year. You know, Bassiter was in my class, and I'd seen a good deal of him at Huntley School. We were what you might call chums."

"I didn't know that."

"No?"

"No, you never wasted much time writing to me, you know, while you was away all of those years at school!"

He felt the glance of Peter twitch aside toward his face, but knowing that the eyes of his son were upon him, he looked steadily down the sun-whitened road before him. And he knew that his jaw was iron, and the rim of his face was iron, also, as Peter looked at it.

"Well," said Peter in his deep, quiet voice, "Dick and I had always been great friends. He had taken me home with him a good many times, you see? I knew his family. They knew me. We were all pretty fond of each other. One day we were all in swimming in the river—a little river that runs across the Bassiter estate, you know. There's a huge lake—with the falls tumbling in above the farther end.

"Dick's little sister, Molly, was there. She said that she wanted to go in swimming above the falls, so we climbed up there with her. But we saw at once that it was no good. The current was smooth on top—smooth but very fast. It whipped things right in and under and it tore for the falls full speed.

"However, we hardly had time to warn Molly. She had fixed her mind on diving in and the smoothness of the surface deceived her. She plunged in and began swimming, but she'd hardly started when the current took her spinning around and drove her down the stream.

"Dick leaped in after her with a yell. But the current mastered him, too. I saw that there wasn't much chance, because Dick was a better swimmer than I, by a long shot. However, I couldn't stand there on the bank and do nothing. Anything was better than that. So I dived in."

"And the water, it got its grip on you, too?" asked the father darkly.

"I was helpless in it. I couldn't make any headway. I saw the girl shoot down toward the lip of the falls and then catch at a rock and hold herself there. I saw Dick reach for her, and she managed to pull him in to her. They were safe—the two of them. I saw that I couldn't make out to them. So I swung back for the shore that I had just left and tried to make the shallows. It was no good. I couldn't handle that current for an instant. It was as strong as a team of hard-pulling mules!"

He paused, and Ross Hale found his son looking quietly, sternly, at a cloud that floated low in the sky, burning with the fire of the sunshine.

"And then?" asked the father.

"Why, the water snatched me down over the edge of the fall, and when they managed to fish me out my legs were badly done up, as you see for yourself."

That was all. Ross Hale, setting his teeth, waited for the harrowing details. It is an invalid's privilege to take a bitter glory in the troubles which have stretched him in the sick bed. But to the astonishment of the rancher, his son seemed to have reached the end of his tale with this stroke.

He had gone over the edge of the waterfall, and now he cared to talk about it no more. Ross Hale, breathing a little more deeply, turned his horses in at the gate

43

and handed the reins to his boy. He saw the eyes of Peter flick over the yard and toward the house, and he steeled himself to hear the remark which must surely be forthcoming.

But it did not come. One would have said that Peter did not even see that the yard had been denuded of trees. They had all gone the winter before. There had been nothing else to sell, and they had brought in a good, fat price, together with a stiff winter task for him. That money had seen Peter through one crisis of the college career.

However, here was the team going on toward the barn. And there was Peter sitting in the front seat—his son, his treasure, the reward of all of his labors. Ross tipped back his big head, and his laughter was good neither to see nor to hear.

The horses were soon unharnessed, and he noticed that Peter, for his part, managed with a singular adroitness to handle his wrecked body, standing about and working so fast with his hands that he was able to do a full half of the unharnessing and of the tending to the horses afterward.

It gave the father a cruelly sad pleasure to see it. He had not thought to bring back his boy to such labors as these. But now he saw before him the complete wreckage of all his hopes. They came out from the barn. And one would have thought that big Peter's eyes had been ruined no less than his legs. One would have thought that he had seen nothing of the poverty which appeared in the mow of that barn, where not two hundredweight of moldy hay littered the floor; that he had been unable to discover the sagging state of the roof, or the loft door hanging from a single broken hinge.

What the barn was, the entire estate had become; it was a burned cinder of a ranch. All that had once been prosperous had gone to the nurturing of Peter. And what return would he make? Well, that was yet to be learned, for there were ways in which money could be made, and it was true that many a man had been able to pile up a fortune despite worse handicaps than the crippled body of Peter. Yet there was little hope in the soul of Peter's father.

When they stood in the welcome brightness of the sun outside the shadowy interior of the barn, a crow lighted on the watering trough and cried at them. And the despair and the rage which had been growing greater and greater in the heart of Ross Hale now burst out in a childish spite. He snatched out his Colt and blazed away. Both shots went wide—one that startled the crow up into the air, and the other as he rose into the wind.

But as Hale lowered his weapon the strong hand of Peter reached for it and took it. The crow had risen well into the wind and now was flying for the safety beyond the roof of the barn. Peter fired at that black streak.

The crow sagged sidewise and dropped half a dozen yards, shrieking a bitter protest. Then it drove onward once more, but before it reached the barn, the gun spoke again. The black fellow tumbled in silence out of the sky and bumped heavily upon the ground.

Ross Hale observed, and though he said nothing as he took back his gun, he was keenly conscious of the matter-of-fact expression on the face of Peter.

"That gat of mine bears to the right," said Ross Hale, as they went toward the house, across the corral.

"It bears to the right," said Peter. "That's why I winged him on the right side, I suppose."

"You've been trying your hand at shooting, then?" asked the rancher.

"A man has to do something for amusement, you know. And I had no chance at the other sports," said Peter. "So I got me some medals in the rifle and revolver teams."

And he smiled, without bitterness, and straight into the eyes of Ross Hale.

Chapter VII

ONE SORT OF TRIUMPH

Sometimes it requires only a small thing to make us revise our mental estimates of men and events. It seemed to the rancher now that there might be cause in this mere bit of target work to alter his first judgment. But he decided that he would make himself more cheerful. He would talk to his boy of all that he could. And since there were blank and dreadful days, he thought that nothing could be better than to talk of the great moments which Peter had enjoyed on the gridiron.

"Of all the days that you ever had on the football field," said Ross Hale, "what was the biggest and the best for you, Peter?"

"Every day at football was a pretty good day for me," said Peter. "I was big. I was fast. I loved the game. And I had the instinct for it."

Ross Hale glanced askance. He felt a prickling sensation and he was glad that there had been no other person at hand to hear this remark. It would have passed for a reasonably immodest utterance in the village of Sumnertown or on the ranges around that village. But Peter did not seem to be boasting. He was stating a fact.

"However," said Peter, "there was one day which was bigger and better than all of the rest put together. That was the day that Huntley School played its alumni in a practice game—just before the big game of that fall. My last year in the school, you understand."

"Go on!" said Mr. Hale, sharpening his taste for the tale of the deeds of glory.

"You see," said Peter, "I had developed fast. I was eighteen. And I was my full height, nearly my full weight, very tough and hard, muscles very nearly as tough as they ever became. I'd been in athletics all my life, as you might say. And so I was never more fit than I was for that game.

"I was the star of that Huntley School team. That's

not saying a great deal, because it wasn't a very good team. But I was their star. I was their one scoring threat. And I was able to take care of everything that went toward my end or tried to cut around me or inside of me. The teams we had played, used to take good care not to bother me. It was the far half of the line that they used to tackle, and so I got into the habit of scooting back behind the line as soon as the other fellows snapped their ball.

"Then came this practice game. The alumni had a queer team in the field. Some old veterans, with their heads beginning to grow shiny, and pretty slow on their feet. And some big fellows just out of college, strong and fast and hard as nails. But the whole lot of them worked like tigers, and they knew their game. The end who played opposite to me was named Christian. Did you ever hear of him?"

"No," said Ross Hale. "But go on!"

Peter was lost in a dream for a second, and he descended from it to say: "Christian was an 'All-American' end the year before that, and he was as big as I, with five years added age to harden him. And all that extra experience and college coaching were behind him. Our coach said to me, before the game, that he knew the alumni would be too much for our team. But that he wanted to see what I could do individually against Christian. That would be the test in the eyes of the alumni—how many plays they could shoot around my end!"

"Go on!" gasped Ross Hale. "I hope that you

slaughtered him! I hope that you made a fool of him! I hope that you laid him out in the first quarter, boy!"

Peter looked with a mild eye of forgiveness upon his father's passion. "Well, when the game started," he said, "I was keyed up to do my best and I did it. But you remember how I was helpless in the water floating toward the waterfall? It was nearly the same against Christian. He knew everything! And, heavens! but he was hard. They began to send the plays at my end. And when I tried to break through, Christian seemed to be six men, not one. I couldn't manage him, and they began to slash around my end for terribly big gains. I was ashamed. I fought like a wild man, but nothing was any good. In the three quarters they made three touchdowns, and they made them all around my end. The coach was simply white when he looked at me between halves, and at the end of the third quarter he sent a substitute in, and the substitute—a halfback, I think he was—said to me: 'The coach wants to know if you're quitting, big boy?'

"Of course, that made me wild. We had a tied score for the beginning of the fourth quarter. Very lucky tie. We had picked up one of their fumbles; we had blocked a kick and recovered it, and we had intercepted a forward pass. Every one of those breaks had meant a touchdown for us. And that was why we were in a tie! So we went in the fourth period, feeling that we would do or die, but that we *had* to keep that alumni team from squeezing over another score. A tie was all the glory that we wanted.

49

"I noticed that the whole alumni crew was pretty thoroughly done up. Even Christian was pretty thoroughly tired out. He was everything that a good football player ought to be, but he was not in the best of condition, and I was. He had exhausted himself pounding at me and he had made a pretty thorough fool out of me. However, I told the quarterback to try my end, the first time that we got the ball. That was five minutes before the game was to finish. He took the chance. I went in to box the great Christian, and for the first time in the game, I succeeded. By this time I was stronger than he was. Besides, he had shown me his whole bag of tricks, he'd been so bent on making a monkey of me.

"We got three yards on that play. And, of course, everybody took particular notice that we had made that yardage through the great Christian. There was a good deal of yelling from the crowd, and when we hammered at Christian again we got a little more. We made a first down over Christian or around him, and by that time he was groaning with helplessness. But he was too far spent to stop us.

"I had an idea that if the backs would charge straight at Christian, instead of trying to cut around him, we could run him into the mud and gain twice as fast. I told the quarterback what I thought and he told me to come back. We put a substitute in at end in my place, and I went back to carry the ball, which was a shift that they often used with me.

"I called the signals, and my plan was to feint at the

other side of the line, but continually to take the ball myself and whang away at Christian. It worked wonderfully well, too. Not big yardage, because I was simply line plunging. I went through the great Christian again and again, until he was reeling and staggering.

"We hammered him back toward the far end of the field. It was very pleasant for me. I was getting a fine revenge for the way Christian had handled me in the first part of the game. He began to look like a high-school substitute.

"Well, we got down on the three-yard line, and I began to call the signals for the last play. I knew that I could take that ball and smash right through big Christian for the touchdown. And while I began to call the signals I looked across at the stands and saw all the people on their feet. I looked to our side lines, and there was my coach, who had asked me if I was a quitter. He was doing a war dance, now the happiest man in the world. Of course, a good deal of the credit for the manner in which Christian was being used up would go to him and his coaching.

"Then I looked back at Christian and nodded to him, to let him know this was for him also. He was white and shaking and resting one knee in the mud. But though he knew that this was the finish, he didn't flinch. He was ready to fight to the last gasp. I remembered, then, that in his four years at college no one had ever made a touchdown through him. But after that, I thought of something else. I saw the ball snapped back to me by the center. I caught it and started for Christian—and then I let it dribble away out of my hands—"

Peter made a dreamy pause.

His father groaned. "What made you do that?"

"Christian came around to me after the game and asked me the same thing. They had recovered the ball, of course. And that game ended in a tie. Well, I told Christian that when I stood there with the ball tucked under my arm and the touchdown in front of me, I suddenly remembered that this was only a game, after all, and not an infernal gladiatorial combat."

"I don't understand what you're driving at!" cried Ross Hale. "There was a chance for you to make yourself famous, and you threw it away."

"Christian didn't understand, either," said Peter. "I believe he thought that I was nervous when I had the chance to do the big thing. When I said that I had remembered it was only a game, he looked a bit stunned and a bit disgusted. And then he walked away. However, that was my biggest day, though the team thought that it was my very worst one. And the people said that I was off form. Well, let it go at that!"

"Your biggest day? Your biggest day?" cried Ross Hale. "And what about the time when you scored three touchdowns in—"

But Peter had forgot to listen, for he was looking back too far into the old days, and it seemed to his father that, for just an instant, a hint of despair showed in the eyes of his son. He was not sure of it. The darkness was gone in an instant. And then they were interrupted by the arrival of Andy Hale.

He came in briskly, with a sort of determined good humor and high cheer, as though he feared lest the condition in which he found Peter might throw a damper on him in spite of himself. He came to welcome Peter home; to invite them both to dinner whenever they would come. He came, above all, to excuse the absence of Charlie from this family call.

"But Charlie is sort of celebrating this day himself!" said Andy. "Because Ruth McNair has promised to marry him!"

Chapter VIII

NO PROFESSION

So Ruth McNair was to marry Charlie Hale!

When Andy Hale had gone, Ross Hale sat in a brown study for some time. "Well," said he at last, "Charlie was well off before, but he's a made man now. He's a made man now—lucky young devil!"

"A made man?" queried Peter in the same calm voice.

"Oh, his father has him pretty well fixed. His dad ain't blowed in all of his money the way that I have. Charlie's father has made his ranch the finest place that you ever laid eyes on, nearly. Maybe I ain't told you about the way that Andy has fixed up his ranch?"

"You haven't written to me about it," said Peter,

53

"but I could guess a good deal from the appearance of Uncle Andy. I could see that he thinks better of himself than he used to!"

"He does, and he has a reason for it, I can tell you! He has a *good* reason for it! He's made that place of his bloom, but what does it all matter—all that work of his—compared with what Ruth McNair will bring him?"

"Is she rich?" asked Peter.

"Oh, her dad has got more money than you could shake a stick at. A lot more money."

"A million, eh?"

"What's a million?" asked Ross Hale, shrugging his shoulders. "No, I don't suppose that he could sell out for a million. He ain't got that much improved land or such a lot of cows as all of that, but he's got enough range to really be worth *more* than that, and he could run three times as many cows as he's got now. Besides, will you look at all of the trimmings that old McNair has got? There's a company back in Denver that wants to buy the water rights to that big creek that goes busting through the McNair place. They don't mean the rights of watering their cows from that stream. That would be different. All that they mean is the right to dam up some of that water and turn it into electricity.

"McNair looked into the thing and liked it so mighty well that he said he would let them build the dam, not for any cash price, but for a share in the company. They put up the dam and do all of the work, and he gets fifty percent of the holdings. And they say that the company will accept the business even at that figure! That alone might make McNair a millionaire. But it goes to show you what sort of a position the man will be in that marries McNair's heir!"

He threw back his head and uttered a faint groan. "Once there was a time, Peter—"

"Well?" said Peter.

"Never mind! Never mind!" replied Ross Hale.

He broke out suddenly: "Why, Peter, your cousin is gunna be, by all odds, the biggest and the most important man in the whole county! You hear me?"

"I hear you," said Peter.

"Curse it!" cried his father. "It don't seem to bother you none!"

"Bother me? Of course not. I'm glad for the sake of Cousin Charlie; that's all."

"Curse Cousin Charlie! Don't the money end of things mean nothing to you?"

"Why should it?" asked Peter. "I could be very happy with a most moderate income."

His father wiped his perspiring forehead and finally muttered: "Well, there's ways and ways that an educated man can do things, and I'd be the last man in the world to deny it. You said that you had got a leaning for the law, Peter. I suppose that maybe you'll start right in being a lawyer in Sumnertown?"

"Start in being a lawyer?" cried Peter. "Why, father, the law course takes three whole years after the regular course is finished."

Mr. Hale reached for the back of a chair and steadied himself.

"Three years—more?" he gasped.

"Yes, at least three years."

"Three years more!" said Mr. Hale, and began to laugh in a very odd fashion. "But maybe you're ready for something else. You never told me much about yourself, son. You never said much about your work, and so how can I know what you're ready for?"

"It's true," said Peter. "I'm afraid that I haven't kept you in touch with my work."

"When I busted my legs, nine years ago," said Ross Hale, "it cost me close onto a hundred and fifty dollars, first and last. Well, Peter, maybe you've fitted yourself for being a doctor, if you can't be a lawyer. Maybe you're ready to start out and make yourself a good living doctoring."

Peter shook his head.

"The medical course is twice as long as the law course," he said. "A man has to spend four years on top of his collegiate work, and after that he has to work in a hospital as an intern for two years. Six years altogether, on top of his college diploma!"

The rancher was almost speechless, but when he had recovered some of his presence of mind he muttered: "Law and medicine takes pretty near forever, then! Peter, tell me if there ain't no profession that this university *does* fit a man for."

"There are technical branches of it," said Peter, "where a man can learn to be an engineer and such things."

"Mining and bridge building and such things! All fine work! I hope that you went in for such things, Peter!" cried his father.

"Never gave them a thought," said Peter. "Most of the boys I knew were taking a general course, and I took one, too."

"What does a general course mean?" asked the father. "A little bit of everything and something of nothing?"

"You might call it that," said Peter, apparently unable to notice the agony and the biting disappointment in the tones of his father. "I don't know what I'm ready to work at, unless it were to be a teacher. I could teach in a high school—Greek or history—or Latin."

"A teacher!" shouted Ross Hale. "A teacher! Teach in a school? My son?"

He broke into a wild laughter and lunged blindly from the room.

His son made no effort to follow him. He waited for a time, with his keen eyes fixed upon the uncurtained, shadeless window, through which the sun streamed. Peter finally gathered himself and set about examining the state of the larder and the provisions of meat in his father's house. He found an empty sugar sack, the last fragment of a side of bacon, mostly fat, a quarter of a sack of moldy potatoes, five or six pounds of corn meal, a little salt, and half a pound of a very cheap brand of coffee.

Peter examined all of these possessions in detail.

When he had examined everything he swung himself dexterously down the hall toward his room. He did not need his crutches for this, for he had a most extraordinary skill in supporting himself with his hands when there was anything for him to press against—as, for instance, the walls of a hall. Then he would swing the iron-braced leg beneath him and so progress with great, awkward, and unhuman strides.

In his own room, he went over everything with an equal care; not a detail was missing. All was as it had been when he left. All was in good order, too. There was no sense of sticky mold and damp about the chamber, as there usually is in a room which has not been lived in for a long time. Instead, there was a sweetness in the atmosphere that proved this room had been cleaned and aired with some regularity. It told Peter everything that he could have asked.

Still he made a slow round of the rest of the old ranch house. It was like moving through the bare ribs of a building which has been wrecked by fire. He could remember this house in the old days as a veritable bower of coolness in summer and of warmth in winter, but this was now all changed, for the trees which had once shaded and beautified the old house were all gone, and he did not need to be told where the bodies of them had gone.

They had been transmuted into text books and tuition fees and all the other items which he had piled up so freely. Other men sent their sons to college. And he had almost forgotten that he was being supported from so small a ranch and by so untalented a money maker as Ross Hale.

The first suspicion had entered his mind when he saw the tumble-down span of horses which waited for him at the station and the faded old coat which his father wore. The sight of the house and the falling barn had been eloquent additional touches. However, all that he saw in the house itself was needed to sink the thought to his heart of hearts.

An ax began to ring behind the house. He went out and found his father busily engaged in cutting up some wood. But it was tough and time-seasoned oak, and the ax was dull, and the arms of Ross Hale seemed strangely weak on this day. Peter took the ax from him without a word.

Chapter IX
PIPE SMOKE

"Can you swing an ax, too?" asked Ross Hale.

"Watch me!"

It was a novel sight to see Peter support himself, driving the iron end of his brace into the ground to anchor him, and then wielding the ax in both hands. From that tough wood the tool had been rebounding impotently while Ross Hale swung it. But now that Peter stood to the work, all was changed. The very first blow fleshed the ax by half the depth of its blade; the second brought out a chip as big as the joined hands of a man. And the ringing of every stroke echoed far off, like the rhythmic explosions of a long rifle.

Ross Hale, watching with wonder, looked up and down, following the flash of the ax, thinking—if this giant had not been maimed—

"Is that enough?" asked Peter.

The butt of the big log had been chopped into stove-wood sizes, and here was Peter, resting lightly on the haft of the ax and smiling. He looked at his father, but there was too much pride and pain combined in the features of Ross Hale. His son was compelled to stare past him.

Through the soft light of the dusk, a twelve-mule team plodded up the road, their heads nodding in a beautifully regular rhythm. Behind them a great wagon lumbered and creaked.

"The quarry wagon!" cried Peter. Suddenly he began to laugh with pleasure. "Don't tell me that that's the quarry wagon, dad?"

"It's the same," said Ross Hale. "What about it?"

"Why, it's eleven years since I saw the last one. I'd almost forgotten that there was such a thing in the world as the quarries!"

"Don't you forget it no more!" said his father. "They're busier than they've ever been before. Only the difference now is that they're getting something better than rock out of them! A lot better. They've struck silver down there. And it's paying them pretty good."

60

"Silver!" cried Peter. "Up at the old quarries?"

"Aye, silver there. And that scoundrel Jarvin—"

"Old Mike Jarvin?"

"Yes."

"But Mike and his whisky bottle—"

"Listen a minute!" called Ross Hale.

Through the evening, above the rumble of big wheels and the creaking of axletrees, he heard the floating voice of a husky-throated singer who bellowed forth an ancient ditty to the effect that a blue-eyed girl was waiting for him in Mayo, and the oceans and the mountains could not keep him from her.

"It's Jarvin!" murmured Peter, still smiling and shaking his head with delight. "I thought that the old villain had drunk himself to death long ago, for sure. But there he is, and he sounds as strong as ever!"

"Stronger, because now he digs the money that he spends out of the ground! And he has the full charge of the quarry and the mine now."

"He has it all?"

"Every bit."

"But what became of old Sam Debney?"

"That's what a lot of folk would be curious to know. But all that was ever seen of Debney was his body, smashed up among the rocks where he'd fallen. And a handy place up above from which he could of fallen— or been pushed!"

"Murder!" said Peter Hale sternly. "Murder, I say!"

"The whole county says the same thing, but there was no proof. We know that old Debney was mur-

61

dered by Mike Jarvin. But what difference does that make so long as we can't prove anything? Jarvin has all the mine. Makes more money every month. Has a bank pretty near filled with it, I suppose, and he's got forty men and boys working for him."

"Forty!"

"Yes, sir, that's what I said. And he pays them off once a month. He's carting the pay roll up with him now."

"A wonder that he isn't robbed."

"Who would do that?"

"Why, the Buttrick brothers or some of the other handy murderers and thieves in this county. We used to have plenty of them!"

"We did," nodded his father, "and none better than the ones that you named first. The Buttrick brothers are as mean and as shifty as any thugs that ever breathed, and the reason that old Mike Jarvin ain't been robbed, and won't be robbed, is that he's got 'Lefty' Buttrick's Colts on the one side of him and Dan Buttrick's rifle on the other side of him. And he keeps on paying them so well that they can't afford to cut his throat. He hates them because he has to pay them so much, and they hate him because he don't pay them more. But he can't get rid of them; he's afraid to. And they won't kill the goose that lays the golden eggs. Y'understand?"

"It's a very pretty picture!" said Peter Hale.

"Ain't it, though? And once a month we hear the singing of that swine rolling up the road, carrying four or five thousand dollars in gold along with him, and the Buttricks, you can be sure, are right along with him, watching the pig sleep and keeping care of him."

Peter watched the tail light of the wagon wind out of view, though the rumbling of the wheels still echoed distinctly. Then he gathered up the wood which he had cut and swung himself with uncanny adroitness toward the kitchen steps. His father marveled, seeing him pass. It was plain to him that Peter, after the dreadful accident which had disabled him, must have bent his mind seriously and scientifically to repairing the damage which he had sustained by using the only substitutes which remained to him, namely, a good set of wits and his giant strength above the hips. He had used his athletic training to prepare himself, and he had used his trained brain to study the problems and the way to master them. Now he went with faultless accuracy up the kitchen steps, supporting a mountainous load of wood such as Ross Hale himself could never have managed.

Peter led the way into the darkening house and stood like a lame Colossus before the stove and cooked the dinner, while his father lurked in corners, trying to make cheerful conversation, only to discover, as other and more ingenious men have learned before him, that even to be able to lie well really requires a certain amount of genius.

Another thought came to Ross Hale, and the longer he observed his son, the more certain he was that Peter knew all the humiliation and disappointment which

63

his homecoming had produced, and yet he refused to allow this knowledge to influence his actions. He remained as calmly aloof as ever—and as cheerful!

The tension increased every moment, until it seemed to Ross Hale that he could not endure it. Finally he decided to make his escape. The instant supper was ended—such as it was—he accepted Peter's offer to do the dishes and went out to walk up and down in the darkness of the night.

Behind him, in the kitchen of the house, he could hear Peter's voice raised in a song that boomed and echoed through the old house. But the father knew there was only a pretended cheer behind that singing. The soul of Peter, in reality, was burdened under a greater weight of sorrow than Ross Hale himself could feel.

The dishwashing and drying proceeded rapidly. When all was accomplished Peter took himself to his own consolation. He could hear the slight creaking as his father's heels ground the pebbles in the front of the house. He himself loved walking, and many an hour, striding back and forth, had once brought peace and good will back to his troubled brain. That pleasure, simple as it was, was now gone from him. He sat back in the big corner armchair in the kitchen, remembering when his grandfather had spent his hours in that same chair, and he took out an ancient black pipe, caked and crusted with tobacco. This he packed with care.

It seemed to Peter that smoking helped him to

realize more clearly what his father had done for his sake. It had been a sort of crucifixion. Not only the body of Ross Hale had paid the penalty, but his soul had shrunk and wasted under the weight of his great effort. That task being accomplished, what a reward was this for the crucified man! He awakened and found himself in no heaven—only the father of a man who might never be self-supporting.

Peter, in his agony of mind, took his pipe from his teeth and closed his eyes and his hands. There was a sharp, cracking sound, a sting on the palm of his hand and the ball of his thumb. He had broken his favorite and only pipe into a thousand pieces.

He did not curse, but, looking at the fuming little ruin that had fallen on the floor, he wondered what other man's hand could have crushed the stout brier root in that pipe as he had done with thumb and fore-finger. Feeling a sudden need for the open air, he went toward the kitchen door. As he did so, he saw the glint of his father's revolvers, where Ross Hale had left them on the kitchen table. Peter stopped and picked them up. They were good guns. In the Hale family, the men had always been proud of their weapons. And these fitted neatly against the heel of Peter's palm. He slipped them into his coat and went on.

Chapter X

A HOLDUP ARTIST

Not even a cat, no doubt, could have covered the distance to the side gate without making some noise among the cinders which lined the path—to keep down dust in summer and mud in winter. But Peter moved on crutches shod with broad, air-cushioned feet of rubber. And these made not so much as a whisper as he reached the gate.

He passed through it with care. Then he swung himself off into the darkness of the corral. His mind was fairly clear as to the purpose before him. If only he could do the thing and be back again before his father got into the house and missed the guns.

In the barn, he took the better of the two horses—at least, it was the one which appeared toughest and most able to bear Peter's crushing weight. He saddled and bridled this cartoon of a horse. Since his accident he had spent many an hour in the saddle, and therefore he knew just how to manage everything. He knew the whole trick of mounting and he knew just how to manage himself, once he climbed into the saddle.

First, when he was settled, he strapped his legs into the stirrups. He arranged the braces on either side, and then he was ready, being able to ride in this fashion as well as another man, and with this danger only—that if the horse fell and rolled with him—well, that would be the end of Peter! He had grown accustomed to taking chances.

With unsteady canter he was carried up the road. As he pushed the tired mustang toward the goal, there was no sign of a campfire on either hand. Perhaps drunken Mike Jarvin had decided to push on all the night toward the quarries, for the impulses which moved Jarvin were ever sudden and wild.

For the greater part of an hour he drove the mustang steadily up the road; then he checked the horse. Straight before him he could hear the roaring of the heavy wheels of a wagon, moving slowly through the night. He jogged his horse forward again, and now he heard the harsh, impatient yelling of the driver who was pushing the long team of mules forward.

A thick cloud of alkali dust rolled up into Peter's nostrils. The wagon itself was a looming form against the stars, for it was loaded high with boxes and barrels that swayed and creaked as the wheels dropped into chuck holes on either side of the worn road.

Then Peter Hale took out a big silken handkerchief and tied it so that the loose flap hung over his nose and mouth and chin. Under the broad brim of his hat, his eyes and forehead were well-nigh lost. He sent the mustang slowly up alongside the wagon until he found a broad, made-to-order seat, heavily cushioned. In the center of it lolled the fat form of Mike Jarvin. And on either side of him were the gaunt outlines of two men who sat with the glimmer of weapons in their hands.

"Hello! Who's that?" snapped the man who sat above the head of Peter on the great front seat of the wagon.

"Message for Jarvin," said Peter.

The guard snarled. "Look back, Dan, and see if there's anybody else in sight."

"There ain't nothing behind, Lefty," replied Dan.

"What you got for Jarvin?" said Lefty as ungraciously as before.

"News from the quarries."

"What?"

"Written out in this letter."

"Where?"

Peter reached up his hand, and Lefty Buttrick dipped his fingers into it. At once the capacious palm closed over Lefty's hand; at the same time he was wrenched from his seat, without even time to utter a cry. The higher the seat, the heavier the fall. Lefty disappeared into the dust with a heavy thump and lay still, as though asleep.

But as Peter put Lefty out of the way he saw the flash of the long barrel of Dan's rifle swinging toward him, and Peter fired beneath that faint gleam of steel. He heard a shriek of pain, and he saw Dan Buttrick pitch downward from the seat.

There remained the frightened shouting of the mule driver, near the end of the steadily nodding line of the mules, and the cursing of big Mike Jarvin, in the seat of the wagon.

"What's up? What's happened? Who's there?" cried the driver.

"Tell him it's nothing, Mike," said Peter. "Tell him quickly, too."

"It's a joke, you fool!" cried back Jarvin. "Skin those mules, will you?"

He added to Peter: "Now, kid, this is a good play. What do you want? A job?"

Peter chuckled. He had heard of the savage cunning and the coolness of Jarvin in a pinch, but this was a little more than he had reckoned on.

"I don't want a job, just now," said Peter. "At least, not the sort of a job that you can give me, I suppose."

"How do you know that?" asked Jarvin. "If you can take care of the two Buttricks, you can do a better job than they did. And I tell you, old son, that you can have the same pay that they had and—"

"Keep both your hands in sight, please," said Peter.

"Certainly," answered Jarvin. "I ain't trying to put nothing over on you, my son."

"Good," said Peter. "You might start in shelling out, however."

"You ain't interested in that job, then?"

"Why should it interest me?" said Peter. "What did the Buttricks get from you?"

"They got two hundred a month—apiece!"

"And you'd pay me the salary of both of them?"

"I'd pay you three hundred a month, kid, of the easiest money that you ever laid your eyes on!"

"Thanks," said Peter. "In the meantime, just unbuckle that belt and hand it to me."

69

There was a groan from Jarvin. "You'll hang for this!" he said.

"Unless I go to work for you," corrected Peter.

"Rob me and then work for me? No, by Heaven!" cried Jarvin.

"I've done my day's work," said Peter, as he gestured over his shoulder in the starlight to indicate that that work lay behind them in the road. "And now I collect the profits, if you please. Hello! There goes your driver, I think!"

A scooting shadow against the pale stubble field, the driver darted to the side, leaving his precarious task behind him.

"Cowards and sneaks, all of them!" said fat Jarvin. "And here I am left alone!"

"You didn't try to get out your gun," said Peter.

"Because I don't wear one."

"You don't wear one!"

"The surest way in the world to get yourself killed, if you live the sort of a life that I follow, is to wear a gun and know how to use it well," said Jarvin. "No, son, I never carry a gun. My worse enemies—and I got plenty of those—know that I don't go heeled. Here's the belt. Count that money over and then ask your conscience if you can afford to keep it. Honest money like that!"

"What's Debney's share of this honest money?" asked Peter. "And will you go to Hades to pay it to him?"

"Debney? Debney?" repeated the fat man. "Well, it

looks like you're not just a plain holdup artist; you're a historian, too, and you know all about the way poor Sam fell down from the rocks!"

"Yes, there was no luck for poor Sam, as you say," replied Peter.

"None in the world, lad. None in the world! Tell me, then, if you're through with me? Or do you want to go through my pockets?"

"You're too fat to keep much in your trousers pockets," said Peter, reasoning aloud. "I'll simply look through your coat, if you'll hand that to me!"

Jarvin stripped off the coat with another groan. "Let me tell you something, young man; I would pay you the full double salary that the two Buttricks have been getting. That's four hundred dollars a month, and all of your keep, besides a chance to make a neat little slice of coin in other ways. The Buttricks squeezed about five thousand apiece out of me."

Peter blinked, in spite of himself.

"Ten thousand dollars!" said he. "And that's a very great deal, Jarvin. As a matter of fact, I may come back to talk to you about this at the quarry. What's in this coat that you hate to give it up so badly?"

"Nothing but bad luck," said Jarvin.

And he handed the coat across, but at the same time it seemed to Peter that something flashed dimly down from the seat and dropped into the road so lightly that it made no sound. Only a faint flash of dust in the star-shine. Peter caught the coat and reined his horse back.

"I'll call on you later, Jarvin," said he. "Good night

and better luck to you next time!"

"You young hound!" wailed Jarvin.

The wagon rolled him on, and the great, clumsy bulk of its load rocked onward, outlined by the horizon stars.

Chapter XI

A FLASH OF HOPE

Then Peter rode in and found the thing that he wanted, without so much as dismounting from his horse. It was a little streak in the dust; swinging to one side, he scooped up a wallet. He pinched it, and a crisp rustling came forth to greet his ears. Peter could not help smiling through the darkness.

He turned his mustang from the road, jogging across the fields and into a clump of trees. There he lighted a few handfuls of twigs, and by that flickering illumination he examined his treasure. The belt was loaded with fat twenty-dollar gold pieces, laid side by side, and it was almost heavy enough to make a load in itself. Forty or fifty pounds, he reckoned its weight, and when he counted the coins he found that there were exactly two hundred and fifty of them. In this division of his capture he had scooped in an even five thousand dollars!

But that was not all. Opening the wallet, he found it neatly and thickly stacked with bills. It was no wonder that fat Jarvin had surrendered the wallet even less willingly than he had surrendered the belt with its load of gold. That little sheaf of government promises to pay totaled a full twelve thousand dollars!

Even Peter was a little impressed. He counted the money again. Then he went through the coat. There was a tangle of papers and notes and odds and ends. He emptied all of these into his saddlebags, to be examined at his leisure. As for the coat, he burned it in the last of his fire, after which he still delayed to stamp out the last embers, then kicked the ashes and the blackened remains of the fire beneath the bushes. He threw some quantities of pine needles over the spot, mounted his mustang, and started back.

He felt it was more or less his duty to look at the spot where he had left the Buttrick brothers lying in the road, but a little reflection convinced him that Lefty, whom he had thrown down with his hand, might have been stunned, but he could not have been seriously injured. And he would recover and give help to Dan. Even about Dan, Peter was not worried. For he had fired low; the slug must have passed through the legs.

So he swung back toward the ranch house. When he got to the barn he was glad to see that his father was not there, pondering over the absence of the horse. Behind the barn, beneath the big, half-rotted foundation beams, he found a nook which served him perfectly for secreting the papers which he had taken from Jarvin. As for the money, he carried it with him as he journeyed toward the house.

He passed the side gate, as softly as he could, and then he journeyed around toward the front of the house, guided by a pungency of tobacco that streaked the air. He saw the shadowy bulk of his father, the glowing spot which marked the bowl of the pipe, and then, pulsing out of darkness above it as the smoker puffed, the shadowy features of Ross Hale.

"Hello!" called the father.

"Hello, dad."

"Have you finished up them dishes?"

"Yes."

"Reckon that you must of made a real polishing job of it, Pete. Took you quite a spell, didn't it?"

"The sink needed a scrubbing," said Peter. "That was all. The night is turning out warm, eh?"

"Fairly warm, maybe, but I wasn't thinking about that."

"About what, then?"

"Nothing."

"Tell me, will you?"

"It's a thing that you can't help in, Pete."

"Why not?"

"Because it's a money matter."

"You've got money to pay, then?" said Peter.

"I've got money to pay. Plenty of money to pay, old son!"

"How much and when?"

"What good would it do to tell you?"

"Because I have friends, dad, who can make a quick turn and scrape up quite a lot of money without

74

hurting themselves any. And they *would* scrape it up for me, I think. Any sum in reason, I mean to say."

Mr. Hale considered this for a gloomy moment, and then a bit of life entered his voice. "I've still got near onto three weeks. Then the bank drops on me, Peter."

"For how much?"

"I'm pretty near ashamed to say. You know how many acres we got here?"

"Six hundred and some odd."

"Six hundred!" cried his father.

"That's what it is, I believe."

"Six hundred! I'd almost forgot that we ever had that much land, Peter. No, I've had to give up a bite here and a mite there. We haven't two hundred and fifty left."

"Two hundred and fifty! Who got the rest of it?"

"Your Uncle Andy, mostly. The Swains got a couple of corners, but Andy come in for most of it."

"By the way, how much land does Uncle Andy own, just now?"

"How much? Well, he's growed and growed. Got about three hundred acres out of me in the last ten years. But he got more than that in other directions. He knows how to make things count, Andy does. Let me see. He got eight hundred from the Cumberwells last year. And the biggest section that he ever took in was the whole Grant place, about six months ago."

"There used to be two thousand acres in the Grant place."

"There still were when Andy bought it in, Pete.

75

Altogether, I suppose that Andy has got about ten thousand acres of prime range land. He could sell off the whole shebang for not a cent under twenty-five dollars an acre, they tell me!"

"And you have only two hundred and fifty left—and that with a mortgage! A heavy mortgage?"

"Dog-gone me, Peter, but I'm ashamed to mention how big it is. Forty-eight hundred dollars, and the bank will have to scramble to sell the old place and bring in that much!"

"There's only a shoestring left, then?"

"Only a shoestring."

"I'll tell you what I'll do," said Peter. "I'll go to town and wire in the morning. I'll guarantee to get you more than five thousand by night."

He heard a faint gasp through the darkness. "You ain't joking, Peter?"

"I'm dead serious. Dead serious. I have some very good friends. Leave the whole business to me."

There was another breath of silence, and then Ross Hale murmured: "Ah, Peter, don't I see how the thing is? They're the gents that have seen you in your prime, ragin' and tearin' on a football field and making the mud fly and raking in touchdowns quicker than most boys can wink. They've seen you swingin' into action, and they've never stopped being your friends, ever since that time, eh? Oh, Peter, what a lot of good it would of done me to see a thing like that! What a lot of good it would of done me!"

And he fell into another silence. Peter could see that

76

even this boon which was suddenly offered to his father could hardly do more than to make him grieve for the things that might have been. However, he felt that he had struck the first blow, and that thereafter the load of gloom would be somewhat lifted from the ranch house and the people in it.

Peter slept that night lightly—a broken sleep. And when the first gray of the dawn was beginning he left the ranch, harnessed the team to the buckboard, and drove hastily down the main road and then a mile down the twisting lane that led to the Vincent place.

It was just the same. Old Tucker Vincent was dead, and now Tucker's son looked just as old and as white-haired and as dignified as the original Tucker had always appeared. The county would not have been the county, if it had not been for the Vincents, because they were a veritable pool, out of which good-blooded cattle and horses were constantly drawn. They were always raising, and they were always buying. And they never produced and they never bought anything but the most perfect stock for the range.

In an hour Peter had done the thing for which he came. He had selected fifty head of stock, and in the place of the two broken-down mustangs there were two sound young horses before him; four more would be driven over with the stock. All these things were paid for in crisp, new bank notes, taken from a sheaf of a comfortable size. Then Peter turned the heads of his team toward town. He made his new steppers streak down the highway till they reached Sumner-

77

town, where he made his brief rounds of the stores. Filling his buckboard with all that it would carry in the way of provisions, he turned back toward the ranch.

As he came up the road past his father's house, he saw Ross Hale on the front porch, smoking his eternal pipe and looking forth at the world through eyes which were misted with weariness. He came running out and shouting when he saw Peter.

"Pete!" he cried. "Go into the corral and tell them fools to drive the cows out, will you? They are tryin' to tell me that you been over at Vincent's and have ordered fifty whole head, to say nothing of four of the finest-looking hosses that ever—"

He paused here, for his eyes lighted upon the new team in front of the buckboard and the heaped packages which piled the wagon.

A flash of real hope and desire to believe darted like lightning across the features of the rancher.

Chapter XII

A NEW LIFE

When matters moved for Peter they moved very fast. It was not many days before the bank had received its money and the little, petty debts with tradesmen around Sumnertown had been cleared away. There then remained nothing between Mr. Ross Hale and a new life except the habit of sorrow which had fallen upon him.

However, he could not be long in being aware of a new existence. For, when he wakened in the morning, he could hear the hammers, big and little, chanting in chorus out beyond the corral, where the carpenters were whacking up a new barn as fast as their hands could raise and put together with spikes of a healthy size. Moreover, he could not fail to take note of the string of ten mules which had been brought into the pasture. Ten well-selected mules, well fitted for dragging the five-share plow through the soil of the farming land in the bottom, the surface of which had not been touched these seven years and more.

There were good tools of all kinds, which Peter had collected at the Leffingwell sale. They had cost nearly nothing, and they could be made to serve as well as new implements. For a true Western farmer will not pay five cents on the dollar for rusted implements. He feels that rust may cover up some mysteriously hidden weakness. Yet, for all his dislike of rust, with the carelessness of the true exploiter of a new country, he scorns to take the small expense and trouble of housing his tools.

But Peter was not proud. He made his offers against the junk man, and he won out at ridiculously low figures. He heard his father itemizing his purchases for the benefit of Andy Hale, when the latter came to call and ask the meaning of the strange signs of life which were being shown on his brother's ranch. Included among the necessary implements, vehicles, cattle, and horses, were the entire fittings of a blacksmith shop—

complete, though secondhand—all the other contraptions necessary to make the heart of an iron worker swell with pride. He had even bought a whole young grove of fast-growing poplars and such shade makers, to be set up in the yard around the old ranch house, so that it began to look as comfortable as ever. Sundry oaks and fig trees were set out where time would make them thrive and they would eventually displace the rank poplars. A load of secondhand furniture had been secured at the last great sale.

Peter, who had gone to the house on his noiseless crutches, sneaked hastily back into the old shed where he had been renovating the secondhand furniture. Therefore he could not hear the concluding speeches of his proud and bewildered father. But these had to do with the erection of the new barn.

"He went over to the Cumberwell place, where all of those barns and sheds have been standing, half finished, since old man Cumberwell died and his kids went East. He bought the whole shebang. Said that that timber was well seasoned and would do him fine, and, besides, it cost next to nothing. He ripped those buildings down and carted the stuff over here. And you can see for yourself, Andy, what's happening!"

Andrew had already seen from a distance, but he went out and examined with a hungry eye for detail. "It's a sort of a secondhand ranch that you're turning out here, Ross," he said gravely.

"It is," said Ross Hale. "But Pete, he says that he ain't too proud to use secondhand things, because, in a way of speaking, he's a secondhand man. But his *brains* ain't secondhand, old-timer. You can lay to that!"

"They ain't." Andy Hale nodded. He had grown more thoughtful than ever. "Every ten dollars that he's spent on these old things would cost more than a hundred to replace with new. This here ranch of yours, Ross, was never fixed up like this before. Not that I ever seen it! But what will you use two eight-mule teams for? Expect to work them all on that little strip of bottom land?"

"Pete has rented the rest of the bottom land off of the Cumberwell place, and he's got an option to keep on with it for five years, if it pays him."

Andy Hale whistled. "More and more!" said he. "But we'll see what this dry farming turns out!"

"Not dry. Pete has brought in a couple of pumps, and he's going to pump water up from the creek and get it onto that land."

At this Andy whistled more loudly than before. "Where's Ruth and Charlie?" he asked. "They came over with me. Where did they go gadding?"

"There's Charlie out yonder, looking at the saddle stock."

"Andy, my boy is gunna give your Charlie a run for his money when Will Nast comes to decide between them."

"Only," said Andy, "I'm cursed if I see how Greek and Latin can help a boy to learn how to do these things!"

"It's the habit of learning that counts, and not the things that are learned," said Ross. "Why, the Greek and Latin may be nothing useful out here in the mountains, but Pete, he knows how to study things. He listens to everything that everybody has got to say. Take advice from a greaser, Pete would. He sizes up what everybody has to say. Besides, he's got some books on cows and cow raising and on irrigation. He talks about rotation of crops and such things until you get black in the face, pretty near, listening to him! But come and see him and talk to him yourself. He'll be asking you questions as fast as you can answer 'em!"

Andy stood for a long moment, lost in thought. "Is this football?" asked he at last.

"I dunno," said Ross Hale, tamping the tobacco firmly into his pipe bowl. "Pete says that it *beats* any football that he ever played, and he sure talks as though he meant what he said. Let's go find him."

"I want to round up Ruth," said Andy. "I want to find her and bring her along, because ever since Peter came back home she's been wanting to see him mighty bad. She's pretty sorry for him, Ross. This'll let her see that a Hale ain't the sort of a man that other folks can afford to be sorry for, even when a Hale happens to be crippled a mite. Ross, I take off my hat to your boy—only, tell me where does he get all of his backing?"

"Back East. He's got friends. Friends that have seen him rip down a football field and make his touchdowns. And they got the confidence that he can make *other* kinds of games pay! And they're right! I couldn't stand a five-thousand-dollar mortgage when Pete come back. But yesterday I sashayed into the bank to see how our credit was standing, and I found out that they would advance us up to ten thousand without no questions asked, right now!"

So the two brothers walked slowly across the corral from the new sheds, where the tools of Peter were now securely housed against the weather.

"But can you run a place with junk?" asked Andy. "I've never seen it tried before!"

"Paint and oil is the main things with Pete," said his brother. "Some of them tools look pretty rusty. But they been cleaned off and oiled, and all of the working parts is sound. The stuff that ain't any good is weeded out. And what's housed is all ready for use. It scares me when I think how much money has been sunk in this place. But I tell you that in these here few weeks the boy has spent as much money as *I've* spent in getting him his whole education. And I'll tell you what— football pays. And so does Greek and Latin!"

"It does, maybe," said Andy Hale. "And you're right that Will Nast will be mighty interested in hearing about all of these here improvements that your boy has been making. Where's Pete now?"

"In that shed. There, you can see him now."

"Aye, and there's Ruth McNair in the shadow."

83

Chapter XIII

RUTH MCNAIR

Both Ross and Andy Hale advanced a great deal more slowly than they might have done had they wished to avoid overhearing that conversation which was in progress in the shed. But as it was they went on almost on tiptoe. Certainly they heard, for a reward, the most harmless chatter.

The girl did most of the talking. Peter put in only a word now and then. He seemed to be asking her advice. It appeared to be a matter of the greatest moment, to Peter, to learn what she might be able to advise concerning the manner in which a table, which he was sandpapering, might be repainted. He wanted to know, also, what suggestions she could give him concerning color schemes.

The result was that Ruth McNair drew closer and closer until, in the end, the rasping of the sandpaper ceased, and Peter sat on his crippled legs, with Ruth McNair sitting before him, her knees clasped in her hands and her head thrown back with enthusiasm while she uttered her ideas. It was all extremely innocent, but it made Andy Hale grow black of face. He took his brother by the arm and led him hastily away.

"What's wrong?" asked Ross Hale blandly.

"You know well enough what's wrong!" snapped his brother. "You know well enough, Ross. It's the thing that's making you grin so broadly just now."

"Got no idea in the world what you mean!" said Ross.

"Ross," said Andy, "lemme tell you that you and me have had times when we ain't been particularly friendly. But that ain't been because of what I wished. Never wanted anything except to have you for a brother and a friend, Ross. But I'll tell you this: Folks that interfere with my best plans is my enemies, no matter whether they wear the names of brothers—and nephews—or not."

He said this with such a solemn air of significance that Ross Hale looked sharply askance at him. "That's free talk and out-and-out talk," said Ross Hale. "But still I'm cursed if I know just what you mean!"

Andy shook his head. "You know as well as I know. Your boy is making a dead set at the girl that's engaged to marry my boy Charlie!"

Ross Hale started violently. "It ain't true, Andy!" he cried.

"It is true. And you jumped when I said it!"

"What in the world could put such an idea into your head, Andy? Peter ain't ever seen her before today!"

"How many times does a man have to see Ruth McNair before he would want her?" snapped Andy. "Ain't she got looks enough? Ain't her father got land and cows and cash enough? Answer me that!"

"Peter ain't a fool!" said his father rather weakly.

"He ain't a fool," answered Andy, "and that's the main reason why I should like to ask you if he ain't able to see that Ruth McNair would make a likely wife for any man!"

"He knows," said Ross Hale, growing a little husky with excitement, "that she's engaged to his cousin. And what chance would a cripple like my Peter have against a fine, upstanding boy like your Charlie?"

Andy Hale snarled with anger. "You may talk your boy down, but all the time you're thinking him up. Now, Ross, I'm the last man in the world to run down your boy. He's got brains and nerve and plain grit and a head that's working all of the time: He don't miss any chances. He's showed that already by the way that he's running this ranch for you. But he's showing another thing, too, that he'll throw no tricks away. And one of the strongest tricks that he has to play with a girl like that is the fact that he's a cripple, Ross. You know that. You take a girl like that, and when she thinks what a grand athlete Peter used to be, and when she sees him so broken down now—but so hard working and so clever and so cheerful—how could she hardly help from wanting to mother him?"

"Andy, you talk through your hat! You listened to one minute's talk between them, and you come to a lot of fool conclusions that ain't got nothing to do with the truth at all. *I* heard nothing out of the way, and I heard everything that you heard."

"You heard him asking her advice, didn't you?"

"What of that? About the colors to use on furniture. A woman knows more than a man does about things like that!"

"Does she? I tell you, Ross, you can't pull the wool over my eyes. There ain't a thing in the world, including color schemes, that Peter Hale needs to learn from a snip of a girl like Ruth McNair. She's got a pretty face and she's got money. But you know, and I know, that girls don't carry around so much brains with them that they can scatter knowledge around them like seed behind a plow. No, Ross, I tell you that Peter is making a dead set at Ruth McNair, and I don't take it kind of him. You understand me? I don't take it kind of him! That girl belongs to his cousin!"

What Andy said was true enough, it seemed to Ross Hale. And the very truth of it made him swell suddenly with anger, so that he snapped out: "When I was down and miserable and done for, Andy, I never got no help from you!"

"What has that got to do with it?" cried Andy. "What has that got to do with this? And, besides, was there ever a time that you *asked* for help?"

"Is it for a brother to ask a brother for help?" said Ross Hale, fairly quivering with a bitter emotion. "You knew that I was down and out. I didn't have a coat to my back, hardly. I was out of elbow with every shirt that I had. There was many and many a time when I come back from my day's work and sat down in that kitchen, yonder, and chewed at a stale crust of bread. I tell you, I've gone down to the bottom of the bread box and took out an old heel and cut away the moldy part of it and chewed up the rest. I've done that. And you knew it! Tell me, didn't you know it?"

"How was I to guess what you was doing, Ross?" asked Andy Hale. "I knew that you had enough money to keep your boy back East in an expensive way and pay for his fine clothes and his tuition and all the rest, that he was spending like water! Should I guess that any man would spend everything on a—"

"You seen me cut down my trees and sell them. You seen me cart my furniture away and sell it. You know that I whittled my land up and sold away more than half of it. You knew that I was covered up with mortgages. And you never offered me nothing!"

"I give you the best advice in the world."

"Hell is paved with good advice. You would of seen me go down the whole way before you so much as offered me a penny!"

"I had my own business. How was I to stay awake at night wondering how you might be getting on?"

"Well, you didn't do it. And now, Andy, you come here whining to me, and you ask me to call off Peter and talk to him rough because he sees fit to talk sweet to Ruth McNair!"

"She's engaged to his cousin. It's criminal for him to start flirting with a girl like that, him with his fine education and his soft way of yarning about things!"

"Curse it!" shouted Ross Hale. "You had your choice. You raised your son among the cattle, and I raised mine among the men. Now let your bull of a son try his own way with Ruth McNair. I tell you that I think you're right! I think that Peter *is* going to go after Ruth. I think that he's going to get her, too. I hope he does! And when he has the McNair millions, I'm gunna ride up to your house, Andy, and laugh at you. I'm gunna laugh so loud that it will start the dogs barking."

Ross Hale was a reasonably hot-tempered man, but he was much more gentle than Andy. Yet there was this difference between them—while Ross had to break out with every thought that entered his mind, Andy ruled himself with a hand of iron and kept his tongue strictly in order.

He ruled himself now, but his face turned white with passion as he listened to the outburst of his brother.

"Very well!" said Andy. "I've heard what you've got to say today. I'm going away and wait for what you may have to say tomorrow!"

And he was as good as his word.

He got his horse. Ruth McNair was brought from the shed and Charlie called in from the pasture. The party went away, leaving Ross Hale wildly excited, filled with vague regrets that he had talked so freely. But he said not a word to Peter. He felt, somehow, that the less he talked with Peter on this point, the better it would be for both of them.

Here was a point on which Andy Hale was hardly so discreet, for he felt that the very ground had been shaken beneath his feet. To be sure, he had accomplished some good things and some big things in his life. No one could say that his ranch was not a triumph. At the same time, all that he had ever done in the past was as nothing compared with this grand opportunity to strike gold by marrying his son to Ruth McNair. And if that chance were lost—it would be like death itself to Andy Hale.

As the girl, handsome, smiling Charlie, and he rode over the hills toward the McNair house, and saw the rolling acres of the rich rancher, all dotted over with little colored spots where the cattle were feeding, it seemed to him that this was a veritable kingdom. Surely there was no youth in the range more worthy of this inheritance.

Who should dare to take the kingdom away from him? Peter, the cripple? Let Peter guard his head well before he contemplated such an attempt!

Chapter XIV

A VISITOR

He determined that he would try one expedient before anything else—to speak to old McNair himself. He left Charlie and Ruth on the back veranda and went out to find McNair sitting on the top rail of the corral, chewing tobacco and squinting at a group of newly purchased two-year-olds.

"I want to talk to you, Mac."

"Talk about cows then. Look at the backs on them heifers, Andy. Sweet, eh?"

"I got a word to say about Ruth."

"What about Ruth? Them cows'll have calves that'll weigh a ton. What about Ruth?"

"Mac, I think that Peter is laying his eye on her!"

"He's a sensible boy, then. She's worth looking at, ain't she?"

"Mac, she's engaged to my son!"

"Why do you bother me about it? Let her marry who she wants to. I'll never bother my head! My old man tried to bother his head about me and my affairs. But heck, Andy, what did I do? Run off with Ruth's ma, not because I wasn't able to live without her, but just to show my old man that I had a mind of my own."

He chuckled. "My gal has got a mind of her own, too. And I'm not going to get her into a foolish way of thinking. I don't want her to marry above herself. That's all. Lot rather have her marry beneath! Don't want some dude to marry her for her money and her pretty face and treat her like a dog so soon as she hadn't nothing left but wrinkles and foolishness, the way that most women get after a time! No, sir. I like your boy Charlie as a husband for her. He'd do very fine. Not too smart; got enough head on his shoulders, though! He can take care of cows, and he could take care of a wife, too. Good cowman ought to make a good husband. Well, I'd like Peter as a husband for her, too."

"Mac, a cripple like that?"

"I say that I'd like Peter for a husband for her, too. He had too much education and he was a lot too smart for her. But when he lost the use of his legs, that made him about even with her. Now it would be safe enough for him to marry her. She ain't bright, but she's brave. She ain't quick, but she's faithful. Like her ma before her. A sweet face and an empty head. Well, that's the kind of a woman that makes the best sort of a wife, and the best sort of a ma, too. I don't like 'em when they start in thinking too much!"

Andy Hale had heard enough. There was nothing to be gained in this direction. Therefore he started talking about the heifers, and, in truth, they were a likely lot. Presently a heavy step came down the path, and the voice of a stranger said:

"Hello, dad. It's about time that we slid out for home, ain't it?"

He turned sharply about. This deep, stern, crisp voice came from his own boy, Charlie, but, nevertheless, it came from a stranger. The voice was altered, and the face of Charlie had turned grave and sober, and the eye of Charlie was filled with alternate fire and shadow.

McNair said: "What's wrong, Charlie. You had a fight with my girl?"

"Not exactly a fight," said Charlie. "We just had a—"

"Shut up, Charlie!" broke in his father. "You let this rest till tomorrow and—"

"I only want to say—"

"You leave it unsaid," commanded Andy Hale. "So long, Mac. I'll see you soon!"

And he quickly hurried away with Charlie.

"You should of let me tell McNair," said Charlie. "It was something that he had ought to know."

"About what?"

"About Ruth."

Andy Hale turned very pale. "Ah, son," said he,

"don't you tell me that you've been doing anything rash!"

"I didn't do a thing. It was her. And she's through with me, dad. Would you guess what done it?"

"It was Peter!" said Mr. Hale.

"You guessed that, eh?" said his son, with a sharp glance at him. "You guessed that, father? Well, it was Peter, right enough. She didn't waste no words. I asked her how could she make up her mind about a thing like this so sudden. She said that one minute with Peter had been about all that she had needed to tell her where she stood. She didn't need nothing more. She knew that she loved him, and wouldn't never love anybody else."

"The impudent young—"

"Don't blame her!" said Charlie Hale. "Don't you blame her. It was Peter. Look at what he knows. Look at the way that he can talk. Make himself as simple as a baby one minute. And the next minute he can talk like a regular governor of a State. It's him that's done the trick to me. He's turned me around his finger. And I'm going to—"

"What?" asked his father hastily. "You're going to do what, Charlie?"

"Get out on the range and ride herd—and—read sign—because that's about the only thing that you ever educated me to do—and—"

He broke off with something that was close to a groan and close to a sob, also. For, after all, Charlie was very young. Then he spurred his horse into a racing gallop and fled away down the road.

His father watched the dust cloud lift and roll away across the willows that followed the creek and the road that wound beside it. Then he shook his head and sighed deeply. It had never seemed to him, in the past, that his son would ever be able to reproach him for the thing which he had received in the place of a college education. Yet he knew that there was nothing but rage and shame and grief in the heart of Charlie. What would Charlie do now—content himself, indeed, by riding out onto the range to forget his troubles? Andy Hale doubted that!

Peter was in the blacksmith shop. Indeed, he spent more time there than in any other portion of the ranch which he was revamping so swiftly and so successfully. He had always had a love for tools. On the ranch, in the early days, he had spent much time in rough carpentering and in watching at the blacksmith shops of Sumnertown. There was always something by way of information to be picked up by a hungry eye. There was always something to be learned by a few adroit questions, here and there. Above all, there was the love of experimentation which never left him.

Then, when he went away to beautiful Huntley School, he had found there a well-developed manual-training department, for the head master believed in such things as handicraft for boys! In that department of the school Peter had chiefly reveled. If he won happy moments on the athletic fields of the school, he won glorious hours of contentment at the turning lathe and, above all, at the forge.

Now everything was equipped on the ranch to suit his crippled condition. In the smithy he could lift himself easily to the swinging seat which stood high up and between the forge and the fire, with the handle of the bellows wheel near and all the clustering tools in reaching distance, while the tempering tub was where he could dip the blackening iron and pluck it out again with a long-handled pincers. He already had made himself more at home in the blacksmith shop, therefore, than in the rest of the ranch.

On the day following the historic visit of Charlie and Ruth McNair, Peter was propped up, swinging his own peculiar sledge. Although he used only one hand for its management, he had the hammer made with a full twelve-pound weight in its head, and with a shortened handle, thick enough to fill his ample grasp. Hammer strokes are not delivered by brute force alone, and those who looked in to see Peter at his work were always amazed by the ease with which he wielded this ponderous tool. The vast shoulders and the long, powerful arms were not a sufficient explanation. Something more was needed, and that was the rhythmic grace with which the work was done.

He was molding a great bar of iron, as thick as his wrist. His face was blackened with soot and reddened with the heat of the fire. The ringing hammer strokes echoed out of the little shop, passing in clangorous waves far over the corral and across the road, where people checked their horses as they rode or drove past, and they said to one another:

"There's Peter Hale in his blacksmith shop. There's nobody like him in these parts. And look what he's done to the ranch, already."

You may be sure that Peter guessed at some of these hearty compliments. How could he help but do so? There was an atmosphere of pity and of respect and of admiration which surrounded him here on the ranch even more strongly than it had surrounded him in his university, where he had been a known man. And Peter, for all the hardness that was in him, was tender enough to recognize and rejoice in these things.

In the midst of the shower of hammer blows, there was a faint alteration in the light to his left. He dropped the hammer and, jerking out a Colt, whirled around in the spinning seat in time to cover with his gun the portly form of Mr. Mike Jarvin, as that gentleman pushed open the little side door of the shop!

Chapter XV

A PLEASANT VOICE

It had been arranged that—when the shop was too choked with smoke that would not blow up through the chimney or through the front door—the side door could be opened, and this would make a cleansing draft. Now the little door was used by Mr. Mike Jarvin to peek in at the big cripple; the instant that he saw the barrel of the Colt leveled upon him, Jarvin hastily dropped something into his coat pocket and hoisted his hands above his head.

"Why, here you are!" said Jarvin. "Here you are, youngster, and it seems that a gent can't drop in on you without having a gun pointed at his head! Be reasonable, young man, and tell me why you take the drop on me like this?"

"Be reasonable, Jarvin," said Peter, "and tell me why you come sneaking in through my side door?"

"Because," said Jarvin instantly, "I wanted to see you at your work without letting you know that I was here."

"Did you?" Peter smiled.

"Yes. We're all hearing a lot about the neat way that you can sling a sledge around. Just point that Colt another way, son, will you?"

"Come closer," said Peter.

"Closer?"

"Do what I say. And mind that you come slowly and keep your hands up. I would hate to harm you, but I'll have to sink a bullet in you, Jarvin, if you make any queer-looking moves!"

"By Heaven," said Jarvin, "I think that you'd murder me!"

"You're overdue!" said Peter. "Long overdue for a murder, Jarvin. How you've managed to escape so long, I can't make out. Nobody else could make out, either, I'm sure. As a matter of fact, I think that I'd collect a vote of thanks, with the sheriff the first one to congratulate me, if I were to kill you, Jarvin!"

"Well, well," said Mike Jarvin, beaming suddenly and broadly. "I suppose that you would, at that. And now, what do you want with me?"

He stepped obediently closer, and as he did so, Peter reached into the side pocket of the big man's coat, bringing forth a handsome gun. He dangled it before the eyes of Mr. Jarvin, his thick forefinger thrust through the trigger guard.

"There you are, Jarvin. There's enough reason to keep you covered. You had this gat in your hand when you stood outside of the little door, yonder, and you hoped that you would be able to push that door open, send a slug of lead through me, and then walk away, though why the devil you should want to murder me, I can't guess!"

"You're wrong, Peter," said the fat man.

"Do you know me well enough to call me Peter?"

"Oh, yes, and you might as well call me Mike."

"Are we old friends?"

"We're going to be the best of old friends before we're through with each other. That's what I hope, Peter!"

"Jarvin, you're a rare old scoundrel."

"An old scoundrel is no worse than a young one, Peter. But leave this rough talk be and let's be friends!"

"Why," said Peter, narrowing his eyes a little, "I'll do as you say, about that."

"Thanks. Only, I wanted to tell you that I didn't

come here to kill you, my son. I simply came here to have a little private talk with you."

"With a gun pointed at my head?"

"Exactly!" exclaimed the fat man, and he smiled with the greatest unction.

"Humph!" muttered Peter. "You are very frank. But go on with this matter and tell me more. I'm interested, Jarvin."

"I came in to talk with you, feeling that it would be a good thing if I had a slight advantage of you, while we was changing words. And I thought that that advantage might as well be in the shape of a gun leveled at you."

"Thanks," said Peter; "but why come at all?"

"I'll tell you," said Jarvin, "a good deal quicker than I had intended to. The fact is, Hale, that I know everything."

The eye of Peter neither darkened nor brightened. It remained calmly fixed upon the face of the other.

"You know everything?" said he. "Good! Very few people have said that before you. They've usually been put in padded cells. But you know everything, then?"

Mr. Jarvin broke into the softest laughter. "I knew it!" said he. "Cursed if I didn't guess that you would take it this way. I knew that you'd be cool and that you'd give nothing away! I knew that! But it's no good, Pete. I admire you for your crust, but it's too late. I've got the lowdown on you!"

"You have?"

"I have."

"You talk like a very confident man," said Peter.

"Come, come. We ain't a pair of kids. I got gray hairs, and you never was less than about forty years old; too old for the good of some folks."

"Too old for the good of some?"

"That's what I said."

"You might give me an example, however."

"I'll give you a couple of them."

"Go ahead."

"The Buttrick boys. You know a good deal too much for them, Pete. Eh? Well, I have you there, eh?" And he broke into huge laughter, his enormous body quivering and quaking with his mirth like a mountainous jellyfish.

When he had ended his laughter he said: "And what do you say to that, Pete? Come, come, you ain't gunna play the dumb man any more, are you?"

"You can put your hands down," said Peter.

"That's right. Be sensible. And give me back that gun."

"I like this gun very well. I may add it to my collection."

"All right, son. You add it to your collection. I won't let a little thing like that stand between us. But now I tell you straight: I know everything and I can prove everything. You hear me?"

"Go on talking," said Peter. "You have a pleasant voice."

"Now, kid, I like you. In the first place, I got a fancy

to any man that can handle the two Buttrick boys the way that you done. A cripple like you! And when I got onto the trail and found out who it was that had done the trick, I wouldn't hardly believe it, all at once. Only, I knew that it must of been an amateur crook, in a way."

"How did you know that?"

"No real professional would of floated all of that money onto the market as quick as you done, Pete."

"Wouldn't they?"

"Never in the world! However, what's fifteen or six-teen thousand dollars to me? I'm too rich to value it; wouldn't value it against the services of a man like you, if you was inclined to work for me, Peter!"

"I'm not inclined, though."

"Think it over, Peter. Think it over. There's plenty of time. I'll come back tomorrow. Or, if you make up your mind tonight, just touch a match to one of the dead bushes on the hill behind your barn. Y'under-stand? I'll be watching and I'll send right down for you. But in the meantime, I've got the cold dope on you. I can prove that you got that money from me—the money that you've been spending on this here ranch. Well, this looks pretty good to me, this ranch work. Except that I've got an idea that nothing good comes out of crookedness; and it won't with you, either. Look at me. I've always been a crook. And I'm never happy except when I'm drunk. Which is most of the time, I suppose! But I tell you this here so's you can think it over when you get a chance. You hear me?"

"I hear you."

"Come up to work for me. Leave this here ranch, where you've sure fixed everything so's to keep your old man happy the rest of his life, and I'll fix you up with a salary fat enough to make you contented. Besides, I can teach you ways of making money faster than you ever thought about before! Come with me, kid, and your happy days are just beginning—that's all! But if you *won't* come with me, I'll put you in the penitentiary as sure as you're a foot high!"

"Unless I shoot you down, Mike."

"You're cold and you're hard. But you ain't a murderer. No, I'm safe with you—though scared. Safe, though darned afraid of you, Big Boy!"

"No other alternative for me, Mike?"

"Why, yes, I'll play fair with you. I wouldn't pin a good shifty man like you against the wall. You collect sixteen thousand dollars and pay it to me inside of a week or a month, and I won't charge you no interest. But where would you get that much cash—unless you stole it again?"

"There are other ways," said Peter, nodding.

"Well," said the fat man, "I don't know what the other ways might be, outside of stealing or inheriting it, or borrowing. So long, Pete. I'm due in another place. Think it over. I look to see that fire start tonight!"

And Mike Jarvin walked out of the little shop. Peter watched him go, whistling softly and thoughtfully to himself, until a shadow slipped across the front doorway of the shop, and he looked up into the darkened face of his cousin, Charlie.

"Your fat friend—whoever he may be—is a fool, after all," said Charlie with a sneer. "He might have known that the easiest way of all is to *marry* money. Am I right, Peter?"

Peter drummed light finger tips upon his chin. "Perhaps you're right, Charlie," said he. "Perhaps you're right. Though I hate to poach on your preserves."

Chapter XVI

ONLY A GAME

The hammer which Peter Hale had raised for the next stroke, descended softly and then dropped into the muffling sawdust which covered the floor of the smithy.

"A little eavesdropping for honest Charlie!" said he.

"A little eavesdropping," admitted Charlie frankly. "And I only thank Heaven that I had a chance to hear the truth about you, Peter. I came here pretty much determined to talk things out with you like a friend, but now I see that I can fight it out with a crook, and that's what I intend doing."

"Fighting?" Peter smiled.

"Not with fists," said Charlie, flushing. "I wouldn't take any advantage of you. But we've heard how you can shoot. How you fanned the feathers out of the crow and then dropped it on the wing. And if you can really shoot with a Colt like that, you've got it all over me! All over me!"

Peter raised himself and stood awkwardly on his steel-braced legs. When he was sitting down one could easily forget that there was anything wrong with him. But when he stood up in this fashion, he appeared the mere wreck of a man.

"Shooting, Charlie?" he asked. "Do you mean that?"

"Why, curse you!" broke out Charlie. "Of course I mean it. Because I won't live without her. You don't want her, except for her money. She's a fool, from your way of looking at things, and you'd never think of marrying her, except that Mike Jarvin has your back against the wall. Oh, what a lot of fools we've all been not to connect the Jarvin robbery with the time when you started spending your money like water! *He* was your rich friends in the East."

"You're right," admitted Peter. "Everything that you say is true. But I give you this warning, Charlie. I don't want trouble with you. You're a fine fellow. A lot cleaner, and a darned sight more honest than I am. I don't want to spoil your life for you, but at the same time I have to tell you that I can't let you interfere in this. I've put my father through eleven years of purgatory. I've taken it into my mind to pay him back with a little comfort and happiness. Your father stacked up money and land for you. Well, there it is for you to take. My father invested money and pain in the attempt to make a fine man of me. And I know that he failed, but I want to keep him from *seeing* that he failed. To gain that point, I'd kill ten men like you, Charlie. I warn you now. You'll have no chance against me. I have no nerves. My hand is as steady now as the hour hand of a clock. And I shoot fast and straight. I've always loved guns. Charlie, if you force this thing through, you're a dead man. If you'll get out of it and let me be, why, we'll fight things out in a different manner. The girl has a right to change her mind about you, if she pleases, hasn't she?"

"She has, I suppose," said Charlie gloomily. "If I thought that she'd be happy with you, I wouldn't step in. But you ain't her kind. You're too deep for her. You're too mean and cool for her. You've knocked her off balance, being so strange to her. But if you step out of the picture she'll forget you and remember me again. You hear me talk?"

Peter sighed, and then a faintly cruel smile touched his lips. "I've stated my viewpoint from the beginning to the end," said he. "Now you may do as you please. You have a gun at your hip, I think?"

"I have. Are you ready?"

"Oh, I'm ready. Though I hate this business, Charlie."

"Curse you and your snaky ways! I'm gunna do a good thing for the world when I rid it of you. Here's at you, Pete!"

And he reached for his gun, a quick and snapping movement, which any good cow-puncher on the range must have approved of highly. It was a vital fifth of a second slower than Peter's answering gesture. That light-triggered gun exploded, and the bullet, flying straight for the heart of Charlie, encountered on its way the Colt which Charlie Hale was jerking up to fire.

The heavy chunk of lead, landing solidly on the weapon, tore it from the finger tips of Charlie and flung it against his face. So he staggered. The revolver landed heavily on the floor, and Charlie dropped upon one knee, his handsome face bathed in crimson, for the front sight had sliced through the skin to the bone.

He was only down for an instant. There was plenty of the fighting blood of the Hales in him. He came to his feet like a leaping tiger and drove straight in at Peter.

And the face of Peter turned cold with a cruel satisfaction as he balanced his gun for the finishing shot. He covered the heart; he covered the head. And then, suddenly changing his mind, he struck with the barrel of the gun and dropped Charlie senseless at his feet.

He leaned and scooped out a handful of water from the tempering tub and dashed it into the face of his cousin. Charlie, gasping and reeling, came unsteadily to his feet again.

"How does it come that I'm still living?" Charlie gasped.

"Because it occurred to me," said Peter in his deep, calm voice, "that this girl and her affair is the business of life to you, Charlie. While to me, she's only a game—only a game. And why should you be crushed for the sake of another—touchdown?"

"Touchdown?" said Charlie. "I don't know what you mean."

Peter did not answer. He had picked up the fallen sledge and he was balancing it deftly in his hand.

The anxiety with which Mike Jarvin awaited the result of the invitation which he had extended to Peter Hale was demonstrated that evening as he walked out in front of the shack in which he lived at the mine. Behind him and beside him were ever the two Buttrick boys, one of them limping, and both of them more saturnine and ferocious than ever, since their disgraceful defeat at the hands of a single robber. However, Mike Jarvin paid no heed to them. His attention was fixed on the black heart of the night in the valley below. It was more than half a day's ride to follow the winding trail that wove among the mountains. But it was a scant span of miles to go as the bird flies or the eye looks. And Mike Jarvin studied that strip of dark shadow until the two Buttrick boys stared, also. And presently, as a yellow eye of fire formed suddenly in the hollow beneath them, they heard big Mike Jarvin murmur:

"By the eternal, the young fool is going to come to me—and throw the rest of his life away."

"*Who* is coming?" asked snarling Lefty Buttrick.

"My lucky day!" said Mr. Jarvin, and broke into a joyous laughter.

Chapter XVII

A PET GORILLA

When big Mike Jarvin saw the answering sign from the deep and distant darkness, he rubbed his fat hands together for a moment and laughed to himself. Then he went back to the shack and kicked at a door. There was no answer.

"Soapy!" he roared.

Still there was no response. So he entered the room and lighted a lantern which hung on the wall. By that light he saw a great mound of a man lying on the bunk beneath the window, as though fallen into a trance, or dead with liquor.

He gripped the sleeper by the shoulder. "Soapy!"

Even the thunder of that rough voice could not wake the other.

"Soapy! Gin!" he shouted again.

Suddenly the other groaned, wakened, and sat bolt upright on the edge of the bunk, gripping the sides of it with his hands, swaying a little with utter exhaustion and the torpor of long sleep.

"Gimme!" said he, stretching out a hand.

How he had got his name it would have been hard to guess, and certainly it could hardly have been from the too-frequent use of soap. Or perhaps it was because his skin was the color of cheap yellow-brown laundry soap. He had a face almost perfectly rounded, above a broad, flat, outthrust chin. Slice the lower part off a globe and you would have a fairly accurate idea of the formation of the head of Soapy. The jaw seemed the widest portion. Everything above it pinched gradually in, and the vast ears thrust out at the angle where the skull began to diminish most rapidly.

Seen from the side view, the same curve was apparent. At the base, that head was still much larger than any other portion of it. The nose was a negligible feature, hardly prominent enough to interrupt the sweep of the contour, except when some emotion made the big, depressed nostrils flare out. The eyes were sunken inside a huge rim of bone, and above the eyes the forehead rounded swiftly back, unconcerned in making space for that region where the brain is usually lodged.

It was a marvelous defensive arrangement. A pugilist would have envied that magnificently built sconce. Where could a blow strike and find lodgment? Only on the jaw itself, and that jaw was so heavily fortified that to strike Soapy there was almost like striking him on the top of his dense skull. To set off these attractive features, there was a dense, close-curling cap of black hair fitting close to his head. It looked like a ridiculously diminutive wig, set on a brown, bald man's head.

The rest of Soapy was made after this same unusual pattern. The arm which he stretched forth in the hope of the expected gin was as bulky as a man's thigh. And the hand, which was big enough to have served for two, was furnished with long, thick fingers, square clipped at the ends.

He was not tall; he was even some inches under six feet. But the number twelve shoe into which his foot had been crowded had not furnished enough room, and therefore it had been cut away at the toes, and the foot bulged through.

"No gin, you blockhead!" said Mike Jarvin, eying the monster with quiet appreciation. "You've slept twenty-two hours, Soapy. Ain't it time for you to wake up?"

"The devil!" said Soapy. "No gin?"

He fell back sidewise upon the bunk, his legs still trailing over the side of it, his body twisted out of shape, but his eyes instantly closed in slumber.

Jarvin raised his foot and ground the heel cruelly into the ribs of the other.

"Soapy! It's a horse!"

The eyes of Soapy opened again, and he sat up once more, wearily, groaning. "Well?" he said.

"A horse, Soapy!"

"Ah-h-h?" growled the mulatto. "Is that it? D'you aim to get a horse that can pack *me* around?"

"I aim at that, you scoundrel."

Soapy stood up, seized a basin of water, and poured it over his head. A careless wipe with a towel removed some of the water, and he now stood up more erect, regardless of the numerous trickles which dripped down his back and chest.

"Lemme know where," said he, "and gimme the coin to get it!" He added savagely: "A hoss to pack *me!*"

"It'll do that," said Mike Jarvin. "But ain't you really slept out?"

"I went three days without closing an eye," said Soapy. "How could I be slept out now? Where do I get the horse?"

Jarvin retreated toward the door. "There's a horse that can carry you," said he, "but you ain't the friend that I want it for."

"I ain't?" said Soapy and caught up a heavy chair, as lightly as though it had been a straw.

Jarvin dodged into the doorway, but Soapy dropped the chair again with a sigh. "All right," said he. "I'll ride that horse back, though. Where is he to be got?"

"He's a chestnut by name of Larribee, and Wisner has him. You can ride across to the Wisner place inside of two hours."

"Well?" said Soapy. "It's a mean ride. What do I get out of it?"

"Here's two thousand, Soapy. You bring back the horse and you can keep the change!"

He laid a sheaf of bills on the table and stepped quickly back into the night. Then he called: "Soapy!"

"Umph?" grunted the other.

"Is that enough to be worth running away with?"

"About five hundred short," said Soapy.

He came out rubbing the weariness from his eyes. There was a loosely arranged circle of shacks, one very much like the other. The miners lived in the inner ones, toward the mouth of the mine. Jarvin's was hardly distinguishable from the rest, but it stood in the

111

most favorable position on the edge of the valley. It was situated in this lookout position, so said the talk of the miners, so that Jarvin could see the devil on the way to catch him.

They said this with a certain amount of good humor, for the enormities of Jarvin were too gross and terrible to admit of real anger. One had either to disbelieve or smile. And except for the occasions when they rose, singly or in groups, and tried to murder him, the miners preferred to smile.

Beyond the shacks, again, there were the stables—the mules and the burros for the mine work were kept here at a minimum of expense by Mike Jarvin. And here, also, were the horses. It was one of the mules that Soapy took. He had tried his two hundred and fifty pounds with unlucky results upon the back of more than one horse, but this mouse-colored mule with the stout legs and the short-coupled back could carry him along at a back-breaking trot for hours on end.

So Soapy rode away through the night. He was so intent that he did not turn back to resent the half-heard remark that drifted after him from a group of the idling miners:

"There goes Jarvin's pet gorilla!"

Soapy heard. He even marked down the voice in his memory with all the care that he could manage. But for the time being he could not turn aside for any smaller pleasures such as thrashing the impertinent. He was bent on seeing a horse actually capable of carrying his own weight, even though the horse was destined to the use of another man.

He passed down a valley, where all that he had to guide him through the thick blackness was the glimmer of a little stream that ran down among the rocks. That was enough for the mule and Soapy. They descended into the plain beyond, and in far less than the two hours his hand was knocking at the door of Mr. Wisner's house.

When Wisner came out to answer the inquiry, Soapy said:

"I hear that you got a five-hundred-dollar horse down here?"

"I got a five-thousand-dollar horse," said the rancher. "What about it?"

"I might buy it," said Soapy.

"You might?" asked the other, eyeing the face and the form of the grotesque.

"Sure," said Soapy. "I got a kid that's fond of pretty horses. Lemme have a look at it, will you?"

Mr. Wisner led the way to a little pasture, and in answer to his whistle a shadowy monster heaved against the stars. Now it stood on the inner side of the fence, reaching its curious head over the bars.

"There's close to eighteen hands of that horse," said Wisner. "Wait till I get this lantern lighted."

In the flare of the light, Larribee tossed his head, but he did not retreat.

"He's a pet, eh?" said Soapy.

"He's a pet. Five years old. Sound as iron. Now

113

you've seen him, what about it?"

"He's too big for the mountains," said Soapy, shaking his head.

"He's been running in the mountains every day," answered the rancher. "He's like a big cat in them. Better than a mule for sure feet. And that's why five thousand ain't too much."

"I got a thousand dollars in cash right here in my hand for you," said Soapy. "What do you say? Take it or leave it?"

"I leave it, and you be—" But Wisner checked the oath.

Another glance at the grotesque face of the mulatto frightened him into a momentary silence, out of which his voice roared again: "A thousand for that?"

"Is he fast enough to run races on a track?" growled the mulatto. "Or can he do tricks on a stage? Or is he handy enough and trained enough for a cutting horse? What *is* he good for?"

"Good to carry two hundred pounds all day long, uphill and down, like it was a feather. Good to never peg out on you. Gentle as a lamb. Afraid of nothing. And you talk a thousand dollars!"

"It's more," ventured Soapy, "than anybody ever offered you for the horse before—more cash, I mean!"

"That's a lie!" replied the rancher hotly. "The fat man, Jarvin, offered me twelve hundred the other day. I laughed at him. The same way that I laugh at you. It's five thousand or nothing for Larribee!"

"It's nothing, then," murmured Soapy. "But I ain't

114

going to be cheap. If somebody else offered you twelve hundred, I'll offer you twelve hundred and fifty. But there's where I stick. You go into the house and talk it over with your old woman, will you? You'll never get more. Who'd give it?"

Mr. Wisner swore under his breath. But he went to the house and came back again at the close of a quarter of an hour.

"Me and the wife have settled it," said he. "We sell him for two thousand, and not a cent less."

"Two thousand!" said Soapy. "Am I a millionaire?"

"You can't talk me down."

"I'll give you one last boost," said the mulatto. "Fifteen hundred. That's my last."

"It ain't gunna do!"

"So long, then," said Soapy, turning his mule abruptly away, toward the road.

He did not ride fast, however. So slowly did he go that a moment later when a voice rang through the night behind him, he could turn and holler in answer. And he knew that Larribee was bought.

Chapter XVIII

THE NEWCOMER

Five hundred dollars was a very neat profit, all things considered, and Soapy was in a fairly blithe humor when he strapped the saddle upon the back of the big stallion. Well above his head rose the withers of the monster. Certainly he was not an inch short of eighteen hands, and as he tossed his head he looked like a dreadful monster in the night.

But all that Wisner had said of the gentleness of the horse was true enough. It went away up the road at a long, stretching canter that made the mule pull back strenuously against the lead rope. And far behind, from the house of the rancher, Soapy heard the broken-hearted wailing of a child.

Well, the stallion might have been a pet in the farmer's household, but he was going toward an unpetted life at this moment, Soapy could swear. For he knew Jarvin, and he knew the friends of the fat man. Only one thing puzzled him immensely, and that was to learn what person in the world was so dear to Jarvin as to be worth the gift of a two-thousand-dollar horse.

He reached the mine again not long after midnight, stabled the giant, and returned to his bunk where, without food or drink having passed through his throat in the last twenty-four hours, he was instantly asleep. For Soapy was so strangely gifted that he could take the necessities of nature in great drafts, instead of from time to time. He could abandon himself to delicious idleness for days and weeks at a time. But during that interval he was simply building up in himself an electric store of power, to be drawn forth and used at will. Perhaps that immense force would be expended in one huge labor, and then he would be ready to rest again.

Soapy had been known to go for five days with no more sleep than he could get while nodding and swaying in the saddle in the hot middle of the day. That five days' ride of the mulatto's had not so much exhausted him, however, that he was unable to prove himself a man of many devices at the end of it. He had trailed two enemies through three hundred miles of mountains, and at the close of the fifth day he killed them both, slept beside their bodies while the clock went round—turned to the mountains, and slept again.

It was known, too, that during the five-day ride he had had not enough to really nourish a single small man through a single day of such labor. But at the end of the great ride the mulatto was not weakened. He was merely made thinner. And the layers of fat which ordinarily coated his body were consumed away as in a fire. It was the fuel by which he lived through such a time of stress.

When the time *came* for eating, no three men could sit at the board and devour pound for pound with Soapy. He ate as a wolf eats and, like a wolf, he slept and was ready to eat again. The flesh seemed to appear sleekly upon his body again, almost as swiftly as huge exertions had been able to whip the surplus away.

So Soapy slept until the dawn peered down upon the camp. Then he rose and went to the cook house. All others were forbidden such privileges. But Soapy was different. Of all the strange charms which this mining camp could hold forth to the mulatto, there was only one, Jarvin knew, which had potency enough to retain the yellow man there. That was his simple privilege of going to the cook house whenever he chose and eating until his raging hunger was satisfied.

It had worked havoc, at first. The despairing cook had seen two or three dinners thrown away down the gullet of the monster, and an outraged gang of miners threatening to strike for better chuck. But after that the cook learned wisdom. On the back of his stove, or simmering in the oven, there was always a vast iron pot filled with beans. A few rough lumps of fat pork— the fatter the better—were thrown into the pot. The mess was seasoned and sweetened with a quart of the cheapest molasses. This was fare which Soapy preferred to almost any other food.

On this morning, when Soapy entered the cook house, he reached for the first provisions which he happened to see before him. That, by unlucky chance, was a great apple pie, intended to make a dozen men rejoice at the noon of that day. But it was in the clutches of Soapy before the poor cook could snatch it from the path of danger.

By the time the pie was gone, however, the cook was prepared. He wasted no time in offering plate and knife and fork. He set out the huge iron pot itself and thrust into it a formidable iron spoon whose ponderous weight had ended more than one incipient kitchen brawl.

Before that yawning and cavernous pot Soapy sat down with a brief-drawn sigh of pleasure, and then the work of destruction began. Twice and again the belt of

Soapy, first drawn as tight as the belt about a monkey's waist, was loosened. And still Soapy devoured and found room for more. The spoon had grated upon the bottom of the pot before he made the first pause, and the cook with a sigh of relief rubbed his hands together and smiled upon his guest.

"More, Soapy?" he asked.

Soapy looked about the kitchen with a wandering eye, but the light of interest had fled from it.

"Look here," said he, lolling back in his chair, "the next time, I tell you what you do—you throw in a handful of lard, will you? These here beans, they're kind of edgy, you understand?"

Lard was cheap. Far cheaper than apple pies in both cost and labor, and the cook grinned as he nodded assent.

"What's the news, Soapy?" he asked.

The giant stretched forth his vast hand. "Gimme smoke!" said he.

The cook obediently produced a sack of the inevitable tobacco. It was accepted, a cigarette made from its contents, and then the sack was dropped into the pocket of Soapy. But the cook made no protest. There was apparently news forthcoming that would be worth a greater sacrifice than this.

In two or three whiffs the cigarette was consumed to a butt. The long, red-hot ash was dropped to the floor and ground under the heel of the yellow man. He made himself another smoke, and already the process of digestion was far enough advanced to permit speech.

"The boss is bringing up a prize boob to trim," said Soapy.

"A prize?" echoed the cook politely, jotting down mental notes.

"Something pretty sweet," said Soapy. "He's got somebody that can be squeezed for forty or fifty thousand, maybe."

"What'll be the gag this time?" asked the cook.

"How can I tell?" asked the negro. "Maybe a fake mine. That's one of the deals that he likes best. Maybe just poker. He's been practicing stacking the deck a good deal lately. Getting his hand in, you might say. Or maybe he'll just tap the sucker on the head and let it go at that!"

"Aye," said the cook, "that's pretty likely, too! Who might it be?"

"I dunno," said Soapy, "but I'll tell you that he's due today. The boss rushed me out last night to get him a two-thousand-dollar horse for a present to this friend of his."

"Two thousand bones!" the cook groaned. "All that blowed in on a horse?"

"You go out to the stable and you'll see why. This here is a horse that's a horse. The rest, they're only imitations of the real thing. So long!" He heaved himself to his feet.

A large cake of gingerbread, freshly steaming from the oven, lay cooling on the window sill. The great hand of the negro gathered it in as he rose to his feet, and half of it had disappeared into his maw

120

before he crossed the threshold.

So it was that expectancy was raised to the fever point at the mine. All of his men were more or less familiar with the scoundrel activities of the boss. They knew that nothing was too small and that nothing was too great to interest his rapacity. They knew that the world was fairly paved with his enemies, but still they had never yet known him to use a two-thousand-dollar bait upon his hook. Great was the excitement to see what the nature of the fish might be for which this bait had been prepared.

Then, in the mid-morning, a horseman labored up the steep. Soapy, stretched upon his back on his bunk, drawing sleepily at a blackened pipe, filled with soggy tobacco, liberally seasoned with perique, had this information brought to him in haste.

"What sort of a looking gent?" said Soapy.

"I put the glasses on him. Looks a biggish sort. And heavy."

"That's him," said Soapy.

He heaved himself onto his feet. The lethargy disappeared. And he, with a dozen others, watched the stranger ride into the circle of the shacks.

"What's he got on his legs?" asked some one in a muttering whisper.

"Hello," called the stranger, "where is the house of Mike Jarvin?"

Soapy, for an answer, hooked a thumb over his shoulder in the proper direction. They watched the stranger swing rather clumsily down from the saddle.

His legs appeared of little use to him. Leaning against the horse, he unshipped a pair of long, strong crutches; then he swung himself across the ground with a wonderful dexterity.

"A cripple, by Heaven!" whispered Soapy. "Doggone me if the boss ain't throwing away two thousand on a cripple. Boys, are we seeing straight? Or who might this here gent be?"

"It's something queer," said the cook. "I got a sort of ticklish feeling in the stomach that we're going to have some surprises sprung on us around here before long! Where's the Buttricks?"

Chapter XIX
QUEER THINGS

The Buttricks were found, of course, with much ease. They came forth the instant that the rumor began, but too late to see the stranger disappear into the house of Jarvin himself. But they made their inquiries, and it was observed that they changed color when they heard the size of the stranger and the breadth of his shoulders. And most of all, the mention of his crutches seemed to have an odd effect upon them.

They retreated to their own shack, next to Mike Jarvin's, and there they remained, though some one, who had a glimpse of them through the window, declared that they were busy furbishing their guns as though in a time of most desperate need.

122

"*They* know him," declared the negro, logically enough. "And then why ain't nobody here ever heard of him? He ain't the sort of a gent to be forgot, once heard of!"

Said the cook: "What do any of us know, except the mine, and the crooked work of old Jarvin? What do any of us know, I say? We keep tight by the mine. He keeps us too broke to do much traveling, and that's why we know him so much better than the rest of the folks in the world does. If they knowed what we know, wouldn't there be a law passed by Congress, or something, to put him in jail, and hang him by his thumbs and toes for an hour a day, as long as he lives the rest of his life? Sure there would!"

It was felt that this remark had not wandered far from the point. But presently all occasion for thought was dismissed. It was a time for observation, pure and simple, for the big cripple was observed emerging from the house of Mike Jarvin.

Mike himself stood in the doorway, smiling upon the back of the newcomer. Then he glanced apprehensively aside to the house where the Buttricks had their quarters.

"It's got something to do with the Buttricks, the coming of this gent," said the cook. "And maybe now we'll find out!"

The cripple was seen going toward the door of the next cottage. He managed himself, now, with only one crutch and yet he swung himself along with wonderful dexterity. Nothing could have been more painfully clumsy than the idea of such a movement, but as a matter of fact, the big fellow handled himself with such smoothness that he seemed to be covering the ground with perfect ease.

"An acrobat, that's what he is," said the cook, who usually pronounced an opinion upon all difficult matters. "You can see by the way that he handles himself that he's been trained all his life to the doing of stunts. I'll tell you what he's been—he's been one of those trapeze artists—you know, in a circus. And he's had a fall that's knocked out his legs. But you see how plumb easy that he handles himself!"

They *could* see and they could wonder at what they saw. Then they observed that the big man had his right hand free from a crutch, free to swing at his side, near the hip, and at that hip there was a well-worn holster of a revolver.

He tapped at the door of the Buttricks.

"Who's there?" called Lefty Buttrick, after a pause.

"It's Peter Hale," said the big stranger. "And I've come to bring you word that Jarvin doesn't need you any longer. He expects you to leave at once and he says that you're paid ahead of time, already. Is that right?"

There was a torrent of oaths from both the Buttricks. They heard what Jarvin had said. But they would not leave. There was an agreement that Mike would give them a month's notice. They'd had no time to look around, and finally, they did not care what message he brought. It was from Mike alone that they would take their orders.

"Sweet, ain't it?" asked the cook breathlessly. "You might say that for a cripple, he's got himself into a pot of boiling water. And how'll he come out?"

Said the deep, quiet voice of the cripple: "From now on it's to be understood here that what I say is the wish of Jarvin. There'll be no going behind my back and waiting for him to give his commands over again. And I'm starting with you two, Lefty and Dan. Do you hear me?"

A fresh current of lurid oaths was listened to in the utmost patience by the big fellow, but when it had ended he remarked:

"I've heard you, and I think that you've nothing fresh to say. Also—if you wish to speak to me face to face, I'm waiting here on the veranda of your house. I won't run away, my friends!"

"Hark at him sing!" whispered the cook. "He's the representative of the boss around here, is he? And he's gunna begin by giving the Buttricks the run? Well, more power to him, I say—but is the world coming to an end?"

"Shut up!" muttered the mulatto. "I want to hear what Lefty Buttrick is gunna say to that!"

It was amazingly apparent that Lefty had needed a moment of thought before replying to this latest sentence—Lefty, who had ever been as a roaring lion in the camp; Lefty, whose strong right hand and ready gun had flashed terror into so many eyes since the moment of his first coming into the employ of Jarvin! They expected to see him leap through the doorway and tear the cripple limb from limb. They expected to see Dan Buttrick come shooting from either hand beside or behind his brother.

Instead, they heard Lefty saying: "Come through the door and get shot down one by one as we come? We ain't fools, Hale!"

It was the crown upon the climax!

No, there was another thing to come, for they heard the cripple say: "I don't want to make any trouble with you fellows. I'm going back to Jarvin's house, and I'm going to wait there for half an hour. That ought to give you a chance to move your things out of your place. At the end of the half hour I'm coming back and, if you haven't started, I'll throw you out. This is Jarvin's property. He orders you off. You stay after a half hour at your own risk!"

And he left the veranda and walked back to the house of Jarvin—not straight away, but with a peculiar sidelong hitch, his face turned back toward the window which watched him from the Buttrick place, and his right hand swinging steadily beside the holster on his hip.

There was no burst of shots from that window. There was only silence. Then Jarvin's door closed and the cripple was gone to safety.

"What'll happen?" asked the cook, in an agony of delighted anticipation.

"Lefty'll cut him to pieces!" said the mulatto through his teeth. "Don't I know what Lefty is?"

"We got to wait!" said the cook. "We got to wait and

see. I told you that queer things was gunna start happening around this here camp!"

Chapter XX

A STRANGE SCENE

Of all those breathless watchers of this odd scene
there was not one so interested as burly Soapy. He
knew the Buttricks just a shade better than any other
man in the camp. As a matter of fact, they had caused
him to spend more than five months in bed. That
enforced rest had been divided into two periods of
almost equal length. Because after he had tackled
them the first time and been literally shot to pieces, he
was no sooner patched up and on his feet again than
he tried his hand with the Buttricks for a second set-
to. It was most strange that he was not killed in that
second battle royal. The doctor who came to see him
gave him an hour to live, at the most. But he lived out
the day. The appalling vitality which was living in the
deeps of his vast body kept him still alive at the end of
forty-eight hours, and the doctor said, shaking his
head:

"This fellow has used up a dozen lives already, but
since he *refuses* to die, let's treat him as though he
were going to get well. Give him some food. Give him
what would be a comfortable meal for an ordinary
mucker."

That food worked like magic upon the mulatto. No

127

matter how many bullets had pierced his body, there was no wound in his stomach, and in a week he was out of all danger. In a month those dreadful furrows in his flesh had closed, leaving only purple scars to mark them. And he was quickly back on his feet and robed in his full strength. The doctor stopped marveling. He declared that Soapy was simply a step back toward the primeval man.

But after his second encounter with the Buttricks, and his second long stay in bed, Soapy had learned discretion. He hated them both with an unabated rage. But still he knew that it would not do to presume upon his emotions. It would be infinitely safer to treat them with a distant toleration. They seemed to him like a two-faced god of war, watching in both directions at once, and so guarded from attack from the front or from the rear.

Either of them, alone, he would not have feared. He felt that he was just as quick in his use of a gun as either of them. He felt that he was just as straight in his shooting. If the fight ever came to closer quarters than bullets, he would willingly have taken a dozen men like the Buttricks and beaten their heads together, in perfect serenity as to the outcome of the battle. For the belief of Soapy in himself was an almost godlike confidence.

However, with all the faith that he had in himself, he regarded the Buttricks with a superstitious awe. They were not like the other men whom he had encountered. He felt that they were invincible. It was a part of their pride that they rarely or never fought alone. They moved together; they thought together; they worked together. Whenever one scanned the horizon which lay in front, the other was sure to have his head turned in order to observe any dangers that might drift into ken from the rear.

Yet here was a man who had dared to walk up to the door of the Buttrick shack, from which, like threatening deities, they had so often rushed forth and worked havoc in the camp among the enemies of big Jarvin. Here was a man who dared to walk up to that door and challenge them to step out and face him— only his lone, crippled self. Yet they did not come!

Said Soapy: "Killing with guns ain't good enough for him. That's the idea of the Buttricks!"

The cook regarded him askance. Then he said: "Now look here, Soapy, might it be that the two somehow is afraid of that gent?"

Soapy turned his round head. It wheeled upon his thick neck like the head of a bird, turning with a strange absence of effort, until he seemed to be looking almost squarely behind him.

"Tell me this, will you? Was they afraid of me?"

The cook was silent, but the remorseless Soapy continued: "And ain't I as good as any other one man in the world?"

Again the cook was silent.

"Is there anybody," said Soapy, with the slow earnestness of one who must be clearly understood, "that has ever stood up to me for one minute?"

"No," said the cook. "Not with the hands, anyway. I remember what happened to the big Polack that come up here special to bust you into bits."

At this, Soapy allowed himself to smile. The grimace sliced his face veritably in two and exposed a double row of huge, pointed fangs.

"Hands is one thing," said Soapy, "but did you ever know of a gent, either, that ever stood up to me with rifle or revolver or knife, or any other weapon that you can name down to a blacksmith hammer?"

The cook frowned reflectively. "Specially with the blacksmith hammer," said he in thought. "No, Soapy, I dunno that anybody has ever had better than an even break with you, except the Buttricks."

"No matter how they come, one, two, three, or four," said the mulatto, "there was never enough gents together in one group to lick me. I was too much for any one man. And I was too much for any two. And why wouldn't the boss give me the job as his guard, I ask?"

"Because that you snored too loud, maybe?"

"No, but it was only because that he hates a negro. And I'm a negro, cook. Know that?"

"Are you?" replied the cook in polite surprise.

"Yes, by Heaven," said Soapy with great vehemence. "I'm a negro, and I'm proud of it. I'm a negro and I want the whole world to know that I am, in spite of this here white face of mine!" And he pointed a thick forefinger at his yellow hide.

The cook did not smile. He would not have smiled

at a ghost, or at a tiger, within the reach of whose paw he stood. He merely nodded with the utmost gravity.

"Well, Soapy," said he, "I would never of guessed it!"

And only when Soapy had looked away to have another glance at the door of the shack of the Buttricks and make sure that it had not opened did the cook permit himself to wink broadly at a neighbor.

The wink was not returned by so much as a knowing glance, because that neighbor stood within the edge of the range of the negro's vision, and it would have been rash to take even the slightest chance, because the temper of Soapy was just a trifle more uncertain than nitroglycerin in cold weather in a closely stoppered bottle.

"No," said Soapy, turning back to the cook again, "the fact is the boss hates all negroes. Why? Because why, I ask you? Because they're too good for him, that's why! Yes, sir, I tell you that that's the reason! Too good for him! Why, when I think how he hates me, for instance, I wonder that you don't see me choke him one of these days!"

"What's made you so sure that he hates you?"

"I can tell by the way he treats me. What does he want me here for? To do dirty work. He pays me big. Sure he pays me big. I take his money, and then he's got the fun of seeing me do his dirty work, and while I do it, he says to himself: 'Ha! now I'm making a negro suffer!' "

"What sort of dirty work do you mean?" asked the cook.

"If he wants something and he wants it cheap, who does he send out to get it? I buy it if I can, but if I can't buy it, I got to steal it. Because I don't dare to come back and face him without it. His tongue would sure start working on oiled hinges if I was to do a thing like that!"

"Look here, Soapy, why don't you up and leave him, then?"

"Because I'm waiting for my chance at him, and that's the only thing under the sky that keeps me here, honey, and you can lay to that!"

"All right, Soapy, I can understand you feeling that way, only, what is there that keeps you from doing what you want with him? You're pretty near to him, most of the time!"

The mulatto cast an ugly glance over his shoulder.

"You tell me, then, why don't some of the others take a chance at him—and they's plenty of others right here in the same camp that would sure like to take a fall out of him so's he would never get up again, I guess?"

"Sure," agreed the cook instantly. "I'm one, curse his heart!"

"And what keeps you back? What's been keeping you back all of these here months?"

"The Buttricks," admitted the cook.

"And me!" said Soapy, rubbing his great hands together. "But now it looks as though the old man had gone crazy, and he's trying to get rid of the Buttricks. For why? For to be chopped up by the rest of us? Would you tell me that?"

The cook shook his head. "We're all wondering," said he. "But it don't look likely, does it, Soapy?"

"Likely?" said Soapy. "Son, the Buttricks'll come out and you'll see 'em *eat* that fool!"

"Will you?" queried the cook. "Then you tell me how you're gunna explain the thing that we're seeing now, if you can!"

For the door of the Buttrick house had opened, and yonder stood the terrible Lefty, but not girt for battle. Instead of that, his bag of dunnage was slung heavily over his shoulder, and under his other arm he carried a bristling canvas bag which contained Lefty's gun.

He stepped out onto the veranda.

"Well?" said the cook.

"It's a fake!" gasped the mulatto. "Lefty comes out this way so's to draw the other sucker out of his house, and then Dan will whirl in and eat him— No, by Heaven!"

For directly behind Lefty appeared the form of the second brother, Dan, equipped much like Lefty with a burden of luggage.

Chapter XXI

HARD-BOILED EGGS

There was a moan from the mulatto, a moan of pain, as twin gods fell from their pedestal in his mind and crashed into nether limbo.

"And all the time," asked Soapy, straightening upon

133

his feet, "was the pair of them yaller hounds only lucky in getting the drop on me?"

He received no answer, for the very good reason that among all those fairly hardy onlookers he was the only one really capable of speech at the moment.

They watched the Buttricks trail their luggage toward the stables and then they watched the Buttricks appear again, riding their best saddle horses, and leading their spares. It was noted with an increasing wonder that the great Buttricks, the men of blood, did not take the straight way, which led past the face of the house of the boss. Instead, they chose to circle around the shacks, close to the mouth of the mine and, in this fashion, they made their exit from the camp and started down into the valley.

"What does it mean?" asked the mulatto, sighing. "Well, ain't we all been kind of blind and stupid? I tell you, boys, that this here is nothin' more or less than hypnotism. That cripple, he got the two Buttricks hypnotized. Can anybody else give a better way of explaining the things that we just been seeing?"

No one could. That was apparent. They looked back from one to the other and shook their heads.

"Wait a minute," said the cook in a whisper. "Here he comes again. And now you take another look at him, he's pretty big! He looks kind of mean, even for a cripple!"

Soapy shook his head. Vigor of no mere physical dimension was capable of explaining the miracle which he had just seen. He needed more than that.

They saw Jarvin and his companion move slowly across the clearing and toward the stables behind the shack. In the distance they saw the monster stallion led forth. The cripple raised himself to the saddle with a singular dexterity.

The cook exclaimed: "What awful arms he must have! What awful arms, mates! Don't he sling himself around just as though he was stuffed out with feathers instead of flesh?"

There was no doubt that that was the case. They saw him fix his steel-braced feet in the stirrups and then they watched him guide the stallion back and forth in front of the stables. There was a raking big fence, crowned with a heavy beam, near by, and suddenly the cripple put his mount at that fence. The big horse cleared it flying, and landed with a wonderful rolling stride in the inside of the corral. In the next moment he had been turned and had jumped out again.

"Look!" said the cook. "Suppose that that hoss had fallen. No help for that cripple. He couldn't of moved himself! He would of been done. And that's what I call nerve, old sons!"

"Cook," broke in Soapy, "you don't know nothing. You think that that horse *could* fall, even if it wanted to? No, sir, it couldn't, and the reason why is what I'm gunna tell you plain and true, old-timer. There was something in the head of that gent that kept the hoss from falling. There was the power of something in his head!"

"What power?" asked some one.

"What power took the nerve away from the But-tricks?" asked Soapy, with a harsh violence. "Ask me, will you, what power it was that sent the Buttricks away like beaten dogs. Well, it was the same thing, just!"

"Spooks?" said the cook.

"You talk, son," said Soapy darkly. "I've said enough. I'm ready to listen to the rest of you giving good explanations of the things that we been seeing with our own eyes!"

There was such a world of conviction in the voice and in the manner of Soapy that the others banished their smiles at once and grew sober. There were few of them of sufficient education to be above the grade of low superstitions, and indeed, there had been something miraculous in the thing which they had seen, for they knew the Buttricks, and they had too often seen those hardy men in action in their midst. Many and many a one of them, indeed, had stood in front of the yawning revolvers held by the steady hands of the Buttrick brothers. And that was an experience to be remembered with chills through all of a long life!

And here was the pair of them, ushered forth like frightened children! Mere words could hardly explain such a thing as this.

After a time they could see the cripple dismount and go back with Jarvin toward the shack of the boss.

"That's it!" whispered Soapy. "That's it, sons! There he goes along with old Jarvin. Didn't I tell you that Jarvin was playing for something higher and bigger than ordinary? Didn't I tell you that he was getting ready to pluck something that was bigger than anything that he had ever taken before? And there's the proof of it. He gets afraid of the Buttricks. He brings in this gent to fire them. And then he uses that big hoss to bribe the gent! Why, you ask me?"

No one had asked, but Soapy had a way of conducting a dialogue in this fashion, filling in with his own mouth the little interstices in his talk.

"Why, you ask me?" went on Soapy, while the others watched him askance, as they listened. "It's because he knows that there's something in this here world that's a lot stronger than guns can ever be. A lot stronger! And this here stranger, he's got it. He showed it on the Buttricks, and he's gunna show it again. The cook, here, he was right. He knowed that some strange things was about to happen here, and we ain't seen the end of them yet!"

Undoubtedly the others agreed with this idea, and though they made no comments, there was a good deal of frowning and biting of the lip among them as they strove to work out the puzzle. The pause that followed had a suspense of its own, as though they all expected that something more must happen immediately.

They did not have very long to wait. Mike Jarvin came to the door of his shack and shouted: "Soapy!"

Soapy obediently, but with a snarl, raised himself and went forward.

"Soapy, you round in the boys. Everybody that ain't

working in the mine. I want 'em here!"

"Except the cook?" asked Soapy, as though knowing that that dignitary had special rights.

"Curse the cook!" said Mr. Jarvin. "You do what I told you and bring 'em in!"

So Soapy turned away, scratching his closely curled poll. He carried a terse message wherever he went through the camp.

"Show up at the boss' house, and show up pronto. Something queer is happening, boys!"

He gathered in the men who tended the horses at the stables, the chore boys who idled near the mouth of the mine at this time of day, and the half dozen others who had odd jobs about the camp. A considerable crowd was presently arranged, when Soapy rapped at the door of Jarvin with enough force to make the door shudder from top to bottom.

The door opened. And inside, Soapy saw Jarvin and the cripple sitting on opposite sides of a table, as though in the midst of serious converse.

"The gents is here," said Soapy. "What you want me to do with 'em now?"

"I'll do the doing," said Jarvin. "Go back with the rest of 'em."

So, presently, Jarvin stood at the door of the shack and turned his eyes back and forth over the group.

"Come here, Hale," said he. "I want you to look 'em over. Hand-picked, hard-boiled eggs is what you can see here for your own self. Nothing to come over this lot, old-timer. You could hunt a thousand miles north and south and east and west, and you would never rake in a worse lot than this here gang, I tell you."

He stepped aside. In the doorway appeared the big cripple. He had a mild but a steady eye as he turned it from face to face while Jarvin said:

"Now, boys, my friend, Hale, is gunna stay here with us for a while. I want to make him comfortable and at home. And the way that I'm gunna do that is to have one of you to take care of him.

"You can see that he ain't got all the control over himself that a man would like to have. Enough to herd gents like the Buttricks, you seen. But not enough to be without the need of somebody to fetch and carry and to run errands for him. Y'understand?"

There was a breathless pause. They had not objected to the beginning of the speech of Jarvin. They had not objected when he implied that they were a choice lot of rascals, for most of them were so far advanced in rascality that they were proud of that bad eminence and were glad to be classed so generously.

"And now," went on Jarvin, "what I want you to do, Hale, is to look over this lot and see which one of the bunch you would like to have as your man, to help you and make you comfortable, as I was saying before, because I want things to be dead easy and smooth for you in this here camp!"

The cripple thanked him with a nod and a smile. "Does it make any difference whom I choose?" he asked.

"Not a bit," said Jarvin. "They're my men and they

do what I tell them to do. And the pay that they get comes high. You pick!"

"Very well," said the cripple, "I think that I've made up my mind. There's the man who will suit me exactly."

Soapy looked behind him. No one was there, but the cook was a little to one side.

"Must be you, cook!" He grinned maliciously.

"No," said Peter Hale. "It's you, my big friend!"

Soapy whirled with a snarl. "Me?" he yelled. "Me to be a sort of a cursed valet?"

Chapter XXII

MAGIC

The others in the crew were thunderstruck. Such a thought had apparently never entered their heads—the mere idea that any man could wish to have around him such a wild bear of a creature as Soapy. Even Jarvin was staggered. He caught the shoulder of Hale and murmured hastily:

"You don't mean that mulatto, Hale. Change your mind and change it fast. I'd rather have a wild horse to wait on my table than Soapy around me. Change your mind, I say."

But Peter shook his head. He said calmly and aloud so that all could hear: "I'll have you, Soapy, if that's your name. I need somebody strong enough to handle me, and you look fit for the job. Will you try it?"

"I'll see you cursed!" shouted Soapy, reaching for his gun, as though he expected that he would have instant need of it.

But Peter Hale made no gesture toward his own hip. He merely said in the same calm tones: "Come inside with me, Soapy. I want to give you a few reasons. And this isn't to be the sort of a job that would shame you. An easy bit of work and a respectable life, I hope, is what I can offer you. Will you come inside for a minute?" He turned his back and swung himself into the house on his crutches.

Soapy remained glaring at the retreating back of the cripple. "He can bulldoze the white folks," snarled Soapy, "but he ain't gunna manhandle this negro! Go inside? Who says that I ain't gunna go inside of the house with him? Who says that I'm scared of him?"

He glared wildly around him. Fear of the unknown and wild rage made his face almost too terrible to be watched. There was no answer from those around him, who saw that he was only looking for a chance to find trouble closer at his hand. And he went on in the same savage murmur:

"I'm gunna go inside with him, and if I don't like the way that he talks, I'm gunna break him wide open, boys, and I'm gunna see what it is that makes him tick!"

So saying, he advanced upon the house with his enormous stride. He passed the door, closed it with an echoing crash, and left Jarvin walking nervously up and down on the porch, always with his eyes fastened upon the crowd, but with his thoughts obviously busy with the two men who were inside the room.

All that could be heard was the loud tone of the mulatto declaring as he entered the room: "I'm here. An' I want to know what in the devil you got to say to me that you can't say in the open, with other folks to watch?"

The reply of the stranger was as smooth as the current of slow water by night. They could not distinguish his words.

But inside the house Soapy was finding himself confronting a peril which, he felt, was more vital and certainly stranger than anything which he had yet encountered in his roving life. The cripple sat on the farther side of the table, nearest the wall, and with that table in front of him his useless legs were screened from view. Soapy was aware only of the erect body and the squared shoulders of the other—the most supple and formidable torso, he felt, that he had ever seen in his life—aside from his own swelling bulk.

It seemed to Soapy, also, as he faced this stranger, that he had been most foolish in his recent way of living. He should take more care of himself; he should make it a point to do a bit of sledge-hammer work every day and so strip the loose fat away from his body and harden himself for a test, as this stranger seemed to be hardened.

For the face of Peter Hale was as cleanly drawn as that of an athlete about to step into a prize ring. Perhaps the labor of swinging himself along on his crutches was enough to keep him fit. And yet Soapy felt rightly that that was not all. To be sure, the legs were nothing. They were worse than useless. But now all that Soapy saw were the long, muscular arms, with the swelling cords of strength bulging against the sleeves; at the points of the shoulders were hard lumps.

Above all this might of hand and shoulder there were thinking eyes buried beneath a deep brow.

From the shadow the eyes watched the negro, and Soapy felt more and more ill at ease. He wanted to bring this matter to a quick test; to have the battle over in one crucial struggle—and be out and away in the fresh, open air, because inside this house he felt that the breathing was not easy.

Said Peter Hale: "Now, sit down, Soapy, and tell me why you're so angry, will you?"

"Ain't it enough to make any self-respecting man mad?" said Soapy, making his teeth grit in fury. "Me to be a sort of a body servant. What d'you take me for?"

Said Peter: "Sit down, Soapy."

"Cursed if I will!" roared Soapy. "You hear me say it?"

"I hear you say it."

"Then what are you gunna do about it?"

"Are you afraid to sit down?" asked that quiet voice of Peter.

It was a new way of putting the matter. Soapy had only one religion, and that was that he was unafraid of

143

anything that walked the earth—except the two Buttricks! His religion made him sink into the chair opposite to Peter.

He regretted it the instant he was in that position—for he was much shorter than was Peter. The latter seemed to tower above him on the farther side of the table. No, Soapy wanted to be up and on his feet, but he did not see, at once, how he could scramble out of the chair and still retain any of his dignity.

In the meantime, there was a constant pressure being exerted upon him. He could never have defined that strain upon his nerves. But he only knew that those restless, working eyes of Peter were constantly prying at his own. He forced himself to meet that gaze; yet he could only manage the thing with a savage stare, while the white man was at ease!

The calm eyes of Peter passed through the burly roughness of Soapy and made his very heart quake. Hypnotism—did it not begin in such a fashion, with the commanding pressure of eye upon eye? The thought brought cold perspiration out, beading the glistening forehead of Soapy.

"Now here I am," said Soapy, "and what is it that you want out of me, and will you snap it out quick? Because I ain't one that can be worked upon the way that the Buttricks was. I'm up to your tricks, stranger. I tell you that I'm up to your tricks!"

He said it with a savage leer of cunning, jabbing his rigid forefinger at Peter, as much as to say that he had discerned the fiend behind the human guise. And he half expected that Peter, when he heard these words, would tremble and turn pale. To his amazement, Peter did nothing of the kind. There was an instant flash through his shadowed eyes; then a faint smile appeared and disappeared on the corners of his mouth. Soapy felt that he was being laughed at by the superior might of the spirit of evil which certainly resided in the heart of this white man.

Bitterly Soapy regretted that he had entered that house; terribly did he regret that he had settled himself at that table!

For now it seemed to him that invisible hands encircled him, and his strength was running out of him. Were not his great hands already shaking so that he could hardly have held a gun? Did not even the accusing finger which he had pointed at Peter quiver most uncertainly?

He turned still paler, and watched with fascination the smile of the big white man. He had quite forgotten that Peter was a cripple, now. The idea had melted from his brain. He was sitting in the presence of a giant of might and of cunning, also. And Soapy felt that he was lost—but not lost without a struggle. No, he was still prepared to fight for the honor of his manhood.

"Listen to me," said Peter. "I want you to understand that I mean you no harm. I offer you this work because I need some one with arms and shoulders like yours around me. In return for that, Soapy, I think that I can raise your position in the world a few degrees. I don't intend that you should have disagreeable or disgusting duties. Rather, like a friend on whom I can rely. Some one to watch my back, since in this camp it seems that a man's back *needs* watching.

"And on that understanding, I wonder if you wouldn't shake hands with me, Soapy?"

The fear of Soapy increased. He stiffened in his chair. "No, curse me if I will!"

"What?" said the other, with that same flashing hint of a smile. "You're not afraid, Soapy?"

"Afraid? I'm afraid of no man!"

And Soapy thrust out his long arm and his great hand was closed upon by the smaller fingers of Peter Hale. They were so much smaller that a sudden feeling came to Soapy that in one instant, now, he would crush the pride and the strength of this weird monster.

He closed the vise of his grip—a famous grip which had done prodigious things in the matter of crushing porous pine wood and other matters. He closed it now with all his might and he felt the grip of Peter relax slowly under the mighty pressure; relax and give and give, but always with an increasing slowness, until the point suddenly came when Soapy could crush no more.

The thinner fingers of Peter bit into his very flesh like narrow rods of iron. And though the jaw of Soapy set and his monstrous arc quivered with effort, he could not make the other yield.

"Magic!" thought the negro. For no mere human

hand, so much smaller than his, could have withstood that grip. "Magic!"

The instant that that idea came home to him the strength seemed to pass from his fingers. Or was it that the other with marvelous suddenness increased his own pressure?

The smaller, bony fingers bit hard into the flesh of the mulatto's hand—and suddenly his grip gave way; his great hand straightened and folded under the power of Peter Hale!

Chapter XXIII

UNRULY HANDS

That instant, the hold of the cripple relaxed and he said: "Now, Soapy, I think that you and I shall understand each other very well. We shall get on, Soapy, like old friends, eh?"

These words were only partially heard by the mulatto. He was staring down at his hand as though it were a diseased part of him or as though, like a traitor, it had refused its duty to its master. It lay upon the table, crushed and weakened and numbed, a fiery red except where four snowy-white bands crossed it—in symbol of the four fingers of Peter Hale which had done their work so well. Soapy had been beaten, though he would never have suspected it, not by a superior might, but simply by the fear of something supernatural.

The force which, it had seemed to him, had crushed his hand as though it were that of a child or a woman, had not been the might of the cripple, but the crumbling weakness in Soapy himself. Now, as he dragged that hand from the table, he moistened his shapeless white lips and looked at Peter like a poor martyr being thrown to the lions.

"And yet," Peter said again, "I don't wish for an instant to force you into a service which may be unpleasant to you. The fact is, Soapy, that I need a strong and brave and clever man to help me in this work. And it seems to me that you are the fellow for me. Am I wrong?"

Soapy pushed himself back in his chair and rose. "You got any need of me right now, boss?" he asked.

"No," said Peter, "no need of you at all."

Soapy slunk sidewise toward the door.

"But I'll expect you back here before dark, say?" called Peter.

Soapy marked that fact by rolling the yellow of his eye toward his new-found master, and then issued from the house. Those who still lingered on the outside looked with wonder as they saw him pass with staring eyes and drawn face. Soapy had aged by ten years, so it seemed. He skulked across the open part of the circle like one who glides away from a beating, inflicted by a superior force.

"He's killed Hale!" cried Jarvin. "Curse him, he's throttled Hale!"

He tore the door open. But there was Peter in the act

of swinging himself lightly to his feet.

"You're safe, Pete?"

"I'm safe, Mike."

"Curse it—then what did you do to Soapy? It's all right, boys!"

It was something more than all right. The point of the matter was that, from the bearing of the mulatto, they had felt that some desperate deed had just been done—if not by Soapy, then by the cripple. Those who wandered after Mike, filled with grinning, yet breathing curiosity, were just in time to see the great shining body of the stallion, Larribee, flash down the back trail from the camp, with the mulatto stooped low on his back, as though to avoid any random bullets which might be sent in pursuit.

That news was brought back to Jarvin at once, and it threw big Mike into a fury. He went storming to Peter Hale. "Now what in the devil d'you mean by that?" he shouted. "Have you throwed a scare into Soapy that'll make him run and never stop? Have you throwed away with your cursed college-made—thick-headed—"

There was a chair of formidable weight standing close to the wall. It suddenly lurched up and whirled over the shoulder of the cripple, darting straight at the head of Mike Jarvin, who leaped backward with a scream, from the path of the flying danger. It would be death if that heavy weight struck his head, he knew, and Mike loved life most desperately. As he leaped, he hurled the door shut with a slam.

It mattered not to Jarvin that he tripped and fell backward down the short flight of steps. It mattered not to him that half a dozen of his startled and grinning men saw this sudden fall of his. All that was of importance was to find out whether or not the sudden devil which had transformed the face of the cripple was now sending him in grim pursuit.

So he scrambled to hands and knees and made sure that the door was still shut. It was. But so terrible was the violence and the true aim with which that chair had been flung, that one leg had splintered the solid panel, and another, in the center, had thrust itself bodily through the door! Mike shuddered to imagine that, instead of the tough and senseless wood, his own tender, mortal flesh had been opposed to that thunderbolt.

Mr. Jarvin sat down on a distant tree stump and fanned his hot face for some time, until the tremor departed from his limbs. He considered various ideas, in the beginning. What seemed to him, at first, the only sensible proceeding, was to touch a match to the shack and let it go up in a mass of flames, bearing the soul of Peter Hale to heaven along with its smoke.

Later on, he felt that it would be an excellent thing if he called in some of his men to tackle this big fellow and give him a thorough disciplining. Jarvin decided that he would make an example of Peter Hale—an example which would be remembered through the rest of Jarvin's life. However, even this had to be paused upon. He recalled that most of his own men were only

150

waiting for a good opportunity to stick a knife in his back. And as soon as the shadows closed upon this day, would they not set about gratifying their wills on him?

The Buttricks were gone. Had not his own men welcomed the dissension which had begun between their boss and his new defender? Heartily did Mike Jarvin curse the day when he had had the Buttricks discharged. Most violently did he groan when he remembered the day on which it had come to him as an inspiration to replace the two hopeless scoundrels with one fairly honest man!

However, in the meantime the sun was riding down the western sky. If he were to make his peace with the cripple, it must be soon. And if he did not make his peace with big Peter Hale, what would happen? A murder before the sun of the next day rose over the cold eastern mountains? Jarvin had no doubt of that. He saw himself fallen, and none to lament him. Who would inherit his mine and all of its riches? Mr. Jarvin began to perspire. He decided that the thing for him to do was to saddle a horse and flee from the camp at once. Yet, if he went to the stable, would he not be placing himself in the hands of those fellows to whom he paid wages, and who hated him with such a cordial might?

Jarvin rose. He walked to the veranda of his house, cleared his throat, and then ventured a polite tap at the door. "Well, Hale?" he called gently.

A most cheerful voice responded: "Come in, Mike!"

He opened the door by inches until there was revealed to him the Herculean torso of Peter Hale reclining upon the Morris chair, the one luxurious article in the furnishing of that room.

"Come in, Jarvin! I'm glad that that chair missed you, really!"

Mike gasped, as he looked down at the shapeless mass of wreckage which was all that remained of the chair upon the floor. Peter, apparently, did not intend to stir himself to clear up the mess.

"Well, Hale," said Jarvin, "the main thing is for us to see that we both been sort of foolish, eh?"

"Not a bit," said Peter. "Little things like this will always be apt to happen, unless we know just how to treat each other, eh?"

Mr. Jarvin stared. There was something about this speech which he did not like. He ventured cautiously: "Matter of fact, Peter, that temper of mine, it sure does run away with me. I never know where it's gunna take me. You'll get used to that, won't you?"

"I don't know," said Peter. "The fact is, Mike, that when people talk roughly to me, my hands begin to do things without asking my permission. I really didn't know that I was going to throw that chair at you, however. And I'm sure that I won't do such a thing again—unless your tongue runs away with you, once more!"

Chapter XXIV

HYPNOTISM

That seemed to the mine owner a rather lopsided bargain—if he continued to talk with a flawless politeness to this young man, the young man would refrain from murdering him! However, he took a great breath, beginning to feel that there was in Peter even a greater value than he had at first attached to him. But it was most patent that the youth was an edged tool, to be handled with the utmost caution. Otherwise the master would himself be injured. Certainly, it would be foolish to throw away the services of this terrible fellow, until it were first known whether or not he could be thoroughly controlled.

He said: "Now, Peter, I ain't aiming to bother you none. But I got to say that Soapy was about the best man that I had working for me. And matter of fact, Pete, it would be a bad blow to me to know that he's sneaked away. Besides that—he's taken along that hoss of yours with him—"

"Why," said Peter, "that's nothing at all. I sent him away on a little errand, but he'll be back by sunset, you can depend upon it!"

"Why in Heaven's name didn't you tell me that before?" shouted Jarvin.

At that roar in his voice, the big hand of Peter stole out and wrapped itself around the back of a chair—but Jarvin leaped through the door with a grunt of fear and went off to sit in the sun, once more, and consider what was good and what was bad in life. What was of account as a good to Jarvin was that which gave him profit and pleasure, what was a bad, in his world, was all that gave him personal danger or discomfort.

He felt that this universe was a place where sweets and sours were oddly commingled. For instance, yonder was the black and gaping maw of the mine, swallowing the labor of toiling scores of men. And in return for the bitterness of that painful exertion, it rendered up rich ore which was trundled down the long incline by the rails which he, Jarvin, had built, until it came to a low road from which it could be hauled to the nearest shipping point. From the mine, therefore, came the shining jewel of wealth which increased and increased with such a steadiness that Mike Jarvin began to think not in terms of his present hundreds of thousands but in the scope of future millions.

On the other hand, the toiling scores who tore the gold for him out of the bowels of the earth were, one and all, his enemies. Was it because he had occasionally beaten them at a game of cards?

It seemed hard to Mike that they should take it so bitterly. Any one who sat down to a gaming table should have his wits about him. It was a deadly encounter, and if he were not trained for this sort of battle, he was a fool to ever undertake it, and he should be grateful for having his money taken away from him as painlessly and swiftly as Jarvin usually extracted it. But there was no reason in them; they hated him profoundly and ceaselessly. When a new man was brought up to the mine, it was not twenty-four hours before he had heard the stories of the others and loathed the big boss as cordially as any of the rest.

Mr. Jarvin, reflecting upon this, felt that the men who laid the treasure at his feet, deposited gold with one hand, and with the other, clutched a dagger behind his back. When would they have a chance to use it?

At this, fat Mike, in some tension, drew forth his revolver and blew a shining bit of quartz to bits. Then he saw the glimmer of a face at the dark door of the cook house. But no one moved suddenly at the sound of a gun near the mine. If a murderer, for instance, were to creep up and plant a bullet in the small of Jarvin's back, who would hurry to see him fall?

Indeed, at this moment, might not that dark-faced rat of a fellow who worked in the stables—might not he be worming his way up the slope, from rock to rock, ready to polish off his boss?

Jarvin whirled about and balanced the gun in his fat palm. The slope was still. But a little gust of wind shook a bush suddenly. Jarvin fired that instant. If there were a man there, let the fool take the result.

A thin scream came back to the ears of Jarvin. He listened to it with a savage satisfaction. Hereafter he would never distrust his premonitions; he would lean upon them, as a woman upon her instinct!

But no man's inert body rolled down the slope from behind the bush—only the light form of a jack rabbit which had been cruelly mangled by his bullet.

"Jarvin luck!" said Mike. "That's Jarvin luck, by Heaven!"

He carried the rabbit to the cook. "Nailed it with a snap shot at forty yards, cook!"

"Like the devil you did!" said the cook with a broad grin.

He took the rabbit and turned his back upon his boss without another word. So much for human sympathy! Mike sighed as he turned away from the shack. Not that he turned his back upon it; he never actually turned his back upon any of his men, unless he had a guard along with him. But he moved in a circuitous route away from the cook house and back to his own shack.

The work of cleaning out the Buttrick shack and making it ready for the occupancy of the new tenant was already under way.

An ex-sailor and a Polack miner were busily scrubbing down and sweeping out.

"Hello, Pete," Mike called. "That Soapy ain't showed up yet!"

"He'll be here in time," said Peter Hale.

"In time for what?" asked Mr. Jarvin.

"For all I need of him," said Peter, "and I suppose that's enough, since he's working for me, now?"

Jarvin heaved a great sigh. "I'm giving up the most valuable rat of a man that I ever had, if I give up Soapy," he declared with much feeling. "But if you want him, I suppose that you'll have your own way about it and take him, eh?"

Now all of this time, the machinelike stride of the big stallion had been sweeping Soapy away from the mining camp with wonderful speed, and when a mile or two had intervened the chills no longer chased themselves up and down his back. He felt sufficiently secure to ease the horse into a walk. But while he rolled a cigarette, he still paused and looked behind him from time to time. Why? There was nothing in the way of horseflesh, in those mountains, that could overtake the stallion, after the pace that Soapy had established; yet he felt that there was a pressing danger just behind him—just around the edge of the next curve!

He knew that he feared the power of the mysterious other world, which lies outside of the ken of most people. What hands might reach toward him from that unknown abyss? Poor Soapy strove to shake from his memory the recollection of all that had happened in the shack when he had sat at the table opposite to Peter Hale. Yet the more he tried to drive the thought into an obscure corner of his mind, the bigger proportions it assumed.

The fact that he had become a horse thief, on this day, and given up his old job at the Jarvin mine was no matter. He was glad to be clear of the place. And he looked down with a shudder to the bruised and aching hand which trembled even now as it held a cigarette.

Twice he reined in the big stallion, with a sudden resolve to turn back, compelled by a fear of he knew not what. The third time, seeing the sun roll softly through the trees on the edge of a western mountain, he remembered the time which Peter Hale had appointed for his return. The mulatto whirled the stallion around and sent him swiftly on the back trail, not pausing to reason, only knowing that he wanted most desperately to reach the camp at the correct hour.

Just as the sun, seen from this elevated plateau, dipped behind the lower hills, covering the sky with rich reds and purples, he came to the mine. Vastly relieved, he reached the stable and stripped the saddle from his big horse. The stableman growled at him: "What were you sent for, Soapy?"

"Sent for?" echoed the mulatto.

"Sure," said the other. "We thought that you'd beat it, but this Hale, he said that he'd just sent you off on an errand, that you'd be sure to come back. And here you are!"

Poor Soapy, standing with the bridle in one hand and the saddle in the other, gaped into the gathering dusk and wondered what was happening in this strange world. As to what had brought him back to the mine, he had no doubts, now. It was the silent will of the white man, which covered the distance of miles and reached at his soul with an invisible hand. He felt that he had been helpless all the while, and when Peter Hale had wished, he had brought the truant back.

"Hypnotism!" gasped Soapy. "I'm gone already! And how did he do it?"

There was no answer for this last question. He was only sure that he was utterly done for, and that no matter what Peter Hale willed to do with him, he would be helpless to resist.

He went into the shack. A bed stood in one corner of the room; there was a bunk in the other. The negro found that all his possessions, which he had left behind him in his hasty flight from the devil, had been distributed on pegs near the bunk. Around the bed were the belongings of the white man, and near the head of the bed, a long rifle leaned against the wall of the house.

Soapy took it up with rather frightened hands, noting how well worn the stock was, and how the barrel showed the effect of frequent polishing. The mechanism slipped frictionlessly beneath his touch. All was clean and neat as a pin in the lock of the weapon. And Soapy told himself that this was the gun of one who knew well how to manage it, though it seemed to the negro that guns were hardly needed by such a formidable person as this same Peter Hale.

A metallic clattering on the narrow veranda of the little house, and here was big Peter Hale at the doorway, with his crutches under his arms. He nodded most cheerfully to Soapy.

"There is news already, Soapy," said he. "We are going on a trip tomorrow, all three of us. You, Jarvin, and I. Will you be ready for that?"

"A trip where?" asked Soapy, grown sullen.

"A trip away from the mine, to gather any sort of deviltry that looks comfortable and pleasant to Mike Jarvin. Have you ever been out with him when he was harvesting that sort of grain, Soapy?"

Soapy, in spite of himself, grinned broadly, showing two semicircles of flashing teeth. Those excursions were an old story to him. He began to wonder if the hypnotist might not, after all, prove a not-altogether-deadly burden to him.

Chapter XXV

PLANS

The great Mike Jarvin did not often descend upon the world. In the days of his prime, when his waist line was slighter, and his gun hand faster, Jarvin frequently showed himself abroad in the company of strangers. There was this great advantage. In the first place, he would thus find himself among strange faces, and above all, his reputation could be shielded behind an assumed name. In the second place, even when men resented him, in those days, they were not so apt to express their resentment with guns.

Times had changed sadly. With profound melancholy great Mike Jarvin regarded the world upon which he looked down, from his fastness of the mine. There, seated among a rebellious garrison, he kept his fort, as one might have said, against the constant assaults of fear. It was like sailing a rotten ship through a sea filled with reefs. Jarvin had seen the waters lapping upon the stones so often that he was almost grown accustomed to the pale face of peril.

When he looked forth and wondered where he could go to seek diversion among strangers, and so escape from the more constant and almost more terrible dangers at the mine, he was in a quandary.

He had once been slim enough to pass almost anywhere and melt easily into a crowd. But there was now a certain dimension of his jowls and a certain fullness of his waist that called too much attention his way. And no sooner did he show his face than men were apt to say: "There's Mike Jarvin!"

After that, there was sure to be a reaching for guns, to make sure—each of them—that he was properly heeled for the approaching event. One would have thought that honest Mike was in the habit of taking money from others like a bandit, at the point of a Colt, whereas, as a matter of fact, he always used well-oiled, soundless and painless methods at the gaming table. It made Mike sigh and shake his head, when he thought of the viciousness with which other men regarded him. He almost wished that he could open his heart to them and let them see how many virtues were harbored therein.

However, on this day he was filled with a new hope. To his buckboard there were attached two strong-shouldered, gaunt-bellied mustangs, capable of unrolling a hundred miles behind them in the course of the day, and yet be fresh enough to kick the hat off a man's head at nightfall. With these powerful animals, he proposed to cruise farther afield than usual.

As a rule, he had never dared to get farther away

from the home port than a single hot ride, at full speed, would carry him—unless he had the Buttricks along, like a company of soldiers. But even with the Buttricks, there was a distinct limit to the distance over which he could cruise. The mine was comparative safety for him. The rest of the world was filled, as one might say, with dangerous, cruising sharks and submarines, all aware of the past of Mike Jarvin, all ready to tear him to pieces or to swallow him whole.

But now, he was filled with a new confidence. The Buttrick boys had been famous and gallant fighters, to be sure. But they were not like Soapy and the cripple! For many and many a month, he would really have preferred the single hand of Soapy to guard him, rather than the troublesome Buttricks. But he had not dared to approach the mulatto. He knew that the negro's hatred for him was of a well-ripened variety and that nothing in this wide world could be so thoroughly pleasing to Soapy as to have a chance to fasten silently his thick fingers in the throat of his master.

Now, however, there was found for Soapy a master whose influence possessed such a mysterious strength that Soapy could actually be kept in hand. It amazed Jarvin and delighted him to his heart's core. Here was he, Mike Jarvin, reasonably capable as a fighting man, but preferring that his enemies should come at him one by one. Behind him now stood the strange form of the cripple who was not a cripple—the wise, calm, terrible strength of Peter Hale. And behind Peter Hale there was a ravenous beast, a madman; one who breathed terrible danger as another breathed the freshest and the purest mountain air. They made a powerful triangle. Was it any wonder, then, that he thought that he might safely venture down into the rich lowlands for another piratical cruise?

From those lumber camps, those distant mines, those swarming towns, those populous cattle ranges, and those teeming farms along the river bottoms—from each of these sources there was a steady current of wealth flowing forth. To be sure, in these days of much banking, the rivers of wealth were apt to flow invisibly. But, after all, wise men were usually able to detect the presence of the invisible streams and sink a well to tap them. Men no longer carried about with them a great amount of gold dust or large sheafs of treasury promises to pay. On the other hand, they could sign IOUs for much fatter amounts, and their courage was the greater in the dealing with high sums, just as their resources were the greater behind them.

This was the way in which Mike Jarvin looked upon the fattening world beneath him, rubbed his hands together, and smiled, so that his eyes disappeared.

"Ah, well," said he, "who can tell? By night, we may be in a part of the country where they've never seen me before!"

Jarvin proposed to cut straight across the domain of his mine to the purple hills against the horizon. On the farther side of those hills, he would have a chance to drop down among new men. There, perhaps, he could perform enough interesting exploits to warm his heart for something to come—enough rascality to let him chew the cud of evil joys in the deadly quiet of the mine.

And if danger should suddenly rear its head against him, he had gathered to his side the two most formidable men that he had ever encountered in all of his busy life—so much of which had been spent in rubbing elbows with expert fighters of one brand or another. The mustangs, he knew, would see them safely to the conclusion of their journey—in a single sweeping march. But they were not to be trusted alone. Besides the mustangs, there was Soapy's long-striding, patient, untiring mule. And there was Jarvin's own pet horse, of powerful build, yet fleet enough to stand off most challengers on the road. Besides these resources, they had the giant form of Larribee to carry their fighting ace, their Peter Hale, into the teeth of danger and out again!

On the whole, Mr. Jarvin was contented. He spent some moments carefully looking over the luggage which had been prepared. When that was all arranged to his complete satisfaction, he added one little item which happened to be an old traveling companion and favorite of his.

"I may be queer," said Jarvin to Peter. "I may be sort of old-fashioned and out of date, complete. I see some of the boys have even took to the wearing of these automatic pistols, that you just pull the trigger of them, and they sluice out a half dozen bullets as slick and as neat as you please! Well, Pete, they may have all of their new-fangled contraptions, but I tell you that I'm exceeding partial to this here sort of an old gat.

"It ain't fast, and it ain't long distance, and it ain't very accurate. But satisfying? I'll say it's satisfying! With this here same gun, I got into the way of a bunch of cattle raiders that was heading back to Mexico. I didn't aim to interfere with them. I didn't know them. I didn't want to know them. But when I turned the corner of the trail, there I was, and there they was. They just had one thought—that I'd been sent out to stop them. Before you could wink, there was a gun glittering in the sunshine, and there was a pair of bullets humming past my ears.

"Well, it was sort of an emergency, you might say. I fetched up this here old pal of mine. I didn't have no time for aiming. They was just getting the right and proper range of me, and they was about to erase my face, Pete, as you might say.

"I hitched this here old friend up above my knee, and I tipped the muzzles of her—and I pulled one trigger—and then without looking, I just pulled the other. Son, it was a crime—the way them slugs had spread.

"A minute before, there was all of them bold, bad cattle raiders heading for Mexico. And the next minute, here was the same bold, bad cattle raiders all lying in the dust, some on their faces and some on their backs, and some praying wonderful fast, and some cussing wonderful loud, and all of them bound for a hotter place than Mexico.

"From that day to this, I've always made a point of carrying the old gun along with me. Even if drunk, you ain't helpless, if you got her handy.

"Hop in, Soapy. You're gunna drive. And I'll sit here beside you and watch your pretty face!"

Chapter XXVI

AN ARRANGED GAME

The mustangs jerked the buckboard steadily along. Before they had dropped into a walk, they had spun out the long leagues which lay between them and the northern hills. When these hills rolled from blue haze into brown reality, and when the road was winding up the steeper grades, Peter Hale was indescribably weary. He was tired of the racking in the springless seat of the buckboard, tired even of sitting on the smoothly gaited stallion. Most of all he was disgusted with life itself, which had tied him to two such companions.

For it had not been a dull trip to Mike Jarvin. He only made sure that Peter was not looking at him from behind, and then he produced a capacious whisky bottle. It was filled with moonshine, colorless as water and terrible as gunpowder. It passed from him to Soapy and back again all of the long, dusty day, and though he knew well enough that the negro would have enjoyed nothing more than a chance to wring his neck, still with Peter in the background it was safe to make a boon companion of Soapy.

Mr. Jarvin reached a state of reeling hilarity when the hills were reached. He was bellowing forth noisy songs while the mustangs toiled upward; but when they reached the crest of the rise, honest Mike pulled himself suddenly together with a great effort. Soapy, as sober as though alcohol had not passed his lips on that day, sent the horses onward at a smooth trot, while the buckboard jolted and rattled over the bumps on the downward way. Presently, his hat off, and a tin cupful of water poured over his head, Mike allowed the cooling breeze of the sunset to blow through his hair until his wits cleared.

His singing ended, and his red eye brightened and cleared, as he stared down upon the valley beneath him. It was plain that he was laying his plans rapidly. The sunset reddened, darkened, and then through the evening shadows they could mark two groups of twinkling lights, one to the left and one to the right. To the town upon the right they steered their course.

It seemed that instinct had guided the fat man aright. Even before they reached the bridge across the little river, Jarvin knew that he was right. For there were other vehicles journeying toward the town. Carts and buggies whirled along past the tired mustangs, and gay voices floated back to the journeyers. When they crossed the bridge over the creek, they could hear the widespread bellowing of hundreds of cattle.

Lawson Creek was celebrating its fair. The streets were lighted; every window showed a lamp, and an unusual activity stirred up the dust of the winding lanes. At the hotel, one room was vacant. It was enough—a little corner room with a single cot in it, but some extra blankets could be rolled down on the floor for the second and the third members of the party. So Soapy shouldered the baggage and carried the entire mass of it up the narrow stairs at a single journey. Peter, negotiating the stairway dexterously, saw that all possible arrangements were made for their comfort, but fat Mike Jarvin was concerned about a greater matter than this. His first act was to open the window, not for the sake of more fresh air, but to scan the slope of the roof beneath them. It descended fairly close to the ground, and Mr. Jarvin asked the advice of Peter soberly.

"Could a gent jump to the ground, yonder, without busting his leg?"

"Yes," answered Peter.

"All right," said Jarvin. "We want a place like that. A lot better than a front room with thirty feet between you and a hard street. I tell you what, Pete, when you get ready for fun, there's nothing like having the way clear for your retreat, eh? That's generalship, Pete, ain't it?"

Peter said nothing, but it was not necessary to give an answer. Jarvin continued:

"The hosses is fagged out, Soapy. Go spot a good

tough span of mustangs somewhere. Trade in my pair and get the others. A hundred dollars ought to be boot enough. Then you get those new mustangs sized up and have the buckboard ready. And see that the saddles are on the three horses. Maybe we'll have to start away from here sudden and fast. If we got the time, we'll go in the buckboard, but if we *ain't* got the time, we'll travel in the saddle. Y'understand? You be ready at that end with the life line. Pete and me is gunna be busy."

Afterward, while they ate dinner, the satisfaction of Mr. Jarvin increased by leaps and bounds. There was a swirl of noise and excitement and tobacco smoke around them. Somewhere in the distance, Soapy was finding a meal to his own satisfaction and seeing to the exchange of the horses. It left Peter and Jarvin alone, and the latter unburdened his heart freely.

"When I hear folks talking like this and joking and scraping chairs and hollering and laughing, it makes me feel pretty good, Pete!"

"You like to see people happy, eh?" asked Peter, raising his brows a little, for this was a touch of humanity such as he would never have guessed in the other before.

"Happy! The devil, yes!" replied honest Mike. "Because when I hear that noise, it sounds to me just like the rattling of money. Their change is loose in their pockets, and they're getting ready to get rid of it. Why, when that time comes, they don't have to ask anybody to hold out a sack to catch what drops. Old

Mike Jarvin will be there, to rake in the coin! Old Mike Jarvin will be there, ready to take what they got to spare! That's the kind of a burden that I love to take off of the shoulders of other folks, Pete!"

He laughed and rolled a little from side to side, so complete was his joy. "There's something fat coming in now. There's one of them chaps that's known as 'good' boys, Pete. Handsome, quiet, discreet-looking. But you lay to it that there's just as much of the devil tied up inside of him as there is inside of any man! Some of the neatest hauls that I ever made in my life was made from just such quiet boys as that! Sure, he's important, too! He's the son of somebody! Look at the two old gents get up to shake hands with him. Look at the way that they slap him on the shoulder! Why, son, that's a sign that he's too big for them to trim, and that's why they admire him so much! Now, Pete, I'd like to get that fish on my hook. Because the amount of coin that I'd get out of him would surprise you a lot! A whole lot, old son!" He grinned again.

Peter, not realizing why Mike had indulged in this elaborate description, ventured a glance over his shoulder. Then he knew; for he saw the fine, clear eye and the handsome face of none other than Charles Hale. He turned his head hastily back, and shuddered a little. Feeling that he had hardened himself against the opinion of the world, he had tried to tell himself that it all made no difference, and that he would go on his way, regardless of the manner in which others might look upon him. But now he shrank as from a whip at the thought of meeting Charlie and talking with him, hearing the hurrying questions and answering them with—what lies?

He would have to tell the truth, and a gloomy truth that would be. While he was brooding over this so deeply, he heard little of what his companion was saying in the interim. Finally he did hear Jarvin ask: "Now, Pete, did you ever take a hand in a little game of poker?"

"In a crooked game, do you mean?" asked Peter.

"It's a lot better to call it an *arranged* game, Pete. But I ain't the man to dodge facts. Crooked you can call it, if you want to!"

Peter raised his fine head and smiled. "I think that you're joking, Mike."

Jarvin regarded him an instant and blinked. "Sure, I'm joking!" And he turned his talk to other channels.

The arrangement was not difficult, after all. Peter was not to be asked to offer protection, except against the most imminent destruction. In that case, he would come to the rescue—but not otherwise.

He would not have to sit at the table. All that would be required would be that Peter take his place some-where in the room where his patron started gambling. Then he could keep an eye upon the events as they passed. Only in case of a crisis would he be asked to give help.

It was a bitter pill, but Peter saw that he would have to swallow it. After all, it was rather a nice point as to whether protecting a thief was not as bad as thievery itself. Peter tried to tell himself that, in the final outcome of the business, he could say that the thing in which he was interested, was not in the knavery of the fat man or in any of his acts of sharp practice, but merely in the preservation of Jarvin from danger. Consoling himself as well as he could with that thought, he prayed that there would be no need for his intervention.

There were a dozen places where games were running that night. The cattlemen and the miners, flushed with money, staked high. In the room where Jarvin selected a chair at a corner table—with a great, gaping window conveniently behind him—there was already a bustling crowd when they entered.

The chairs, presently, would not hold a third of the people who wanted to play. A shifting crowd began to pass back and forth, pausing to stare at the play, and then shift on. Behind that screen stood Peter, propped between his crutches and the wall, his steel-braced legs holding him up without effort on his part. Between the heads and over the shoulders of the others, he could look down and watch the progress of Jarvin's campaign.

Chapter XXVII

AN INNOCENT CARD PLAYER

It was a liberal education in roguery to watch the progress of Mike Jarvin. Having secured that chair near the open window, through which a single backward leap would carry him, fat Mike entered the game with a softness that amazed Peter. In his innocence, Peter expected wild exploits to begin at once, expected looks of wonder, envy, and, presently, of rage to be cast at the stranger. He found to his astonishment that Mike seemed the very least important person at that table. His bets were certainly not a whit larger than those of the others. Indeed, he seemed to stake his money unwillingly. As for cleverness at the cards, Jarvin surprised him by losing time and again. Whatever he did, was wrong. If he bet cautiously with a powerful hand, no one cared to stay. If he tried a gallant bluff, he was sure to be called after he had pushed a quantity of cash onto the table.

There was only one way in which Mike Jarvin began to be conspicuous at that table, and this was through his successive losses. Indeed, he began to be little better than a joke. They smiled faintly—poker smiles—as he lost round after round. They looked swiftly at one another as he attacked the dealing of the pack and, in the vigor of his shuffling, spilled the cards upon the floor. Then, as he dealt slowly and clumsily around the table, perspiring, some one could not help asking, in a mingled tone of contempt and amusement and pity: "What might your business be— when you ain't playing cards, stranger?"

General smiles were suppressed with difficulty. Mike answered gently: "Mining is my business, friends. That's what I do for a living. Not card playing, as you might suspect."

The faces of the others at the gaming table turned purple with suppressed laughter at this remark. And another rancher said dryly: "Matter of fact, sir, I was sort of thinking that maybe you made a regular thing of this!"

"Oh, no," said the innocent Mike, "I just have a fling at it, now and then!"

Laughter could not be held in longer, at this point, and there was a universal shout of joy at this simplicity.

However, he was a miner. And no one who digs his gold out of the ample wallet of the earth, is to be given much pity, when he sits at the gamblers' table. They looked upon Mr. Jarvin as sure prey, and to the bewilderment of big Peter, they had what they wanted.

He did not keep a very accurate score of the game, but he was sure that by the time it had proceeded an hour, Jarvin was at least two or three hundred dollars out of pocket. There was an interruption here, as one of the players plunged foolishly on three aces and was neatly and briefly trimmed by the florid lumberman who sat to the left of Jarvin.

"That's me, boys," said the loser. "I'm done, if you don't object!"

And he left the game.

"Who's next?" asked the red-faced lumberman, as he raked in the spoils of war. "Who's next, gents? How about you, sir?"

"Why," said the familiar voice of Charlie Hale, "I'm not much at this sort of thing, but I'll take a hand!"

And, being next to the vacant chair, he slipped into it.

Peter bit his lip in vexation. But after all, the chair of Charlie had its back turned to him, and there was not a great chance that his cousin should turn about and see him. At least, he profoundly hoped not.

His entrance made no great difference. It was plain by his very manner in holding his cards that he was not an expert at the game of poker, but it was equally plain that he intended to invest in the contest all his natural store of good sense and discretion. He lost his first two bets, but he recouped handsomely on the third round. And still Jarvin had not won a bet.

"You was down buying some of those Herefords of the Giveney Ranch?" asked a withered cow-puncher at the right of Charlie.

"Yes."

"They beat everything on the range, those Herefords," said the puncher with conviction.

"I believe that they do very well on this part of the range," said Charlie with a modesty which became his youth.

175

And there was a general nodding of heads around the table. They respected this young man a very great deal. That was plain. They respected him just as much as they were inclined to laugh at poor Mike Jarvin who, however, suddenly won a small stake.

"First win in the last hour, ain't it?" asked the lumberman with a broad grin.

"Yes"—Mike sighed—"luck has been agin' me a little. But maybe it'll set my way pretty soon, eh?"

And he looked about the table with such an open and confident smile that even Peter found himself shaking his head and smiling in shame and amusement at such a foolish confidence in Dame Fortune. As for the rest, they had now reached the point where they were beginning to pass the wink openly to one another, concerning Jarvin.

However, the game lapsed into its former drowsy quiet until Peter heard some one saying: "Here's fifteen hundred to see that!"

It was the voice of Charlie—and behold, Charles had lost! Two thousand dollars passed from his pocket at that one stroke. It was by some hundreds higher than any betting of the evening. There was a half-frightened look on the faces of most of the others at the table. Even the red-faced lumberman—who had won again—did not seem more pleased by his victory than he was awed by it. But Charles was sitting very erect in his chair, smiling cheerfully upon the others.

There was a world of battle behind that smile, and Peter could not help guessing that his cousin was in for a little elbow rubbing with misfortune that evening.

A moment later, Charlie was betting still more hugely. Three others remained in the pot with him. The bets climbed slowly out of the hundreds, into the small thousands—until one stopped—and only the red-faced lumberman and Mike remained with Charles. And Charles won.

He had recouped all of his losses, without much waste of time. It occurred to Peter that a level head and a sound set of active wits might carry a novice even over worse reefs than this. But Mike's behavior amazed him even more than this. For he was saying: "That's the way! Sort of tickles me to see the money trickling out like this! Win big or lose big! That's what I feel like this evening. What about it, boys?"

He was as good as his word. He dropped fifteen hundred in the very next pot, and Charles won again.

Said some one near Peter: "Now, I don't mind seeing a greenhorn plucked. But darned if there ain't a limit. Now that poor, old fat fool—whatever his name might be—he's had enough! They'd ought to get him out of the game!"

Peter bit his lip. If only they could know the name of yonder simple old fellow!

But the game had entered upon a new phase. The red-faced lumberman was suddenly out of the match. He had lost to Charles, and then a crashing stake had gone to Jarvin, his first big winning of the evening. The lumberman ran for shelter. The others had gone there before him. There was only Mike Jarvin and Charles. And the stakes were nothing but thousands.

It occurred to Peter that this was a crime against his own blood. He should step up and whisper a word to Charles and warn him that he sat at the table with one of the biggest rogues in the world. But he restrained himself.

For one thing, his Uncle Andrew had piled up enough money to stand a very severe loss indeed, and if there was any such wildness as this in Charlie's blood, it was far better that he should have it out before he came into all of his father's lands.

There was no question as to how the game would run now. Jarvin had begun to win. And he had managed it so that every one looked upon him with a sort of wondering sympathy. It was, in fact, that run of luck for which Mike had been "waiting" all the evening.

"Looks like I can't lose!" said honest Mike. "And a while back it looked like I couldn't win! Now, stranger, I'll tell you what. If I was you, I wouldn't play any more tonight. It ain't your lucky night for winning."

"Never mind that!" snapped Charles. "It's your deal, I believe!"

Oh, yes, it was the deal of Mr. Jarvin. His fat fingers seemed to have grown more clumsy than ever, as they struggled with the recalcitrant pack of cards. Even so, it was a strangely lucky pack for him.

Here was Charles writing on a scrap of paper: "I

owe you ten thousand dollars. Signed—Charles Hale."

"Is that good with you?" he asked.

"Why, man, I dunno your name," said Jarvin, "but your face looks honest to me. Sure your signature is good. Only—I would just like to advise you that since you have begun to lose—maybe it would be better if we quit now. You've lost pretty near twenty thousand dollars, Mr. Hale!"

It cast a hush over the crowd. This, indeed, was gambling upon a large scale! Charles, stiff and straight in his chair, played with perfect calm. Only, his face was a little pale, and his back was rigid. He was doing the usual foolish thing. He was plunging to recoup, doubling his bets. The minutes were dizzy ones which saw poor Charlie betting five thousand on two kings! And yet he had an excellent hand the next moment. The bets passed hastily back and forth—IOUs from Charlie; money and more of the same slips for Jarvin.

And then came the call—three sevens and a pair of deuces in the hand of Charlie, a pair of deuces and three jacks in the hand of Mike Jarvin.

"I congratulate you," said Charles as he pushed back his chair. "That's as far as I care to go this evening. I've finished!"

Chapter XXVIII

THE ROUGH LIFE

So Charles walked from the room with his head high and his eyes calm, glances of respect trailing after him, as much as to say: "There's a man!"

But when they looked back to Mike Jarvin they shook their heads and smiled. "A lucky old fool!" was the general comment.

"I hope," Jarvin was saying, "that that boy can stand losin' as much money as that. Who might he be? Name of Charles Hale. Can he stand it?"

"Is that Charlie Hale?" said a bystander. "Sure he can stand it. Or his old man can stand it for him. Got millions, I guess. Rich as the devil. It won't hurt them none!"

"Well, well!" exclaimed Mr. Jarvin. "Dog-gone me if I ever cleaned up like this before! I guess that I'd ought to shut up shop after that, eh?"

They entreated him to stay. They knew that his pockets were loaded with a fortune, and not a small fortune, at that. If only he would sit in at a game where the stakes were not rushed over their heads— they were willing and confident enough that they could take away the last penny of his gold, by easy degrees.

But nothing could persuade him to remain. He had played out his lucky streak. Some other day, perhaps, if they still wanted to play— He waded through the crowd, and Peter found himself following behind the other with a half smile upon his lips.

In the street, he came up with Jarvin and found the miner bursting with happiness. "I never done nothing so slick in my life," declared Mike. "Now, sir, would you ask me what I got away from that game?"

"Over fifty thousand?" asked Peter.

"Over sixty-five thousand, or I'm a sucker," said Mike. "I was too smart for them. I've took away lots of money out of a game before this, but I never managed to do it and have the folks standing around just hankering to have a whirl at me! I never was able to manage that before. Why, Pete, this here town is a gold mine to me! They got no eyes. I could teach a dog to sit up and beg in the time that they give me for shuffling the cards and dealing them and patting them into shape. I could run up the pack every time. I was doing it with two crimps, toward the last. And that sucker sitting there like a soldier. 'I will not leave my post,' says the soldier. 'Take this, then,' says I, and saps him for another ten thousand.

"Sweet? Oh, it was sweet, Pete. I never got into anything that was half so cheerful as that game. And now they're all in there pitying me! Heaven keep 'em from recognizing me before I get another whirl at 'em! There's still money in that gang. And now they're itching and anxious to pluck me! Well, I'll lose enough thousands now to stall them along, and then I'll clean up. You can't tell what'll happen the next time that I get a lucky streak!"

He clasped the muscular shoulder of Peter with his fat hand and laughed like one half-choked with joy.

"Let me see the IOUs," said Peter.

"Here they are," said Jarvin. "You count them over. They come to— Hey, son, what's the main idea?"

For Peter had slipped the bits of paper into his pocket.

"That's fifty-five thousand that you're rumpling up and smearing around!" exclaimed Mike Jarvin.

"It's too much," said Peter. "You'll have to get along with the cash that you stole out of that game."

Mike groaned. "It ain't possible! Are *you* gunna double cross me? And you an honest man? Is that the size of your price? Pete, are you gunna double—"

"Stop whining," said Peter. "Do you think that I can stand by and see you rob a cousin of mine with your dirty card tricks? No, Mike, this stuff goes back to him. Walk on—the game is up, so far as I'm concerned!"

Mike Jarvin uttered one long burst of curses; he even went so far as to reach significantly toward a hip pocket, but then he suddenly changed his mind and, whirling on his heel, he strode off down the street.

Peter started out in search of his cousin. It was easy to find him. If Charlie had been a figure of some importance before the game, he was a celebrity after it. The clerk in the hotel took Peter instantly to the room of Charles, and in answer to his knock the door was instantly opened by that pale-faced gentleman himself.

182

When he saw Peter he recoiled from him with a gasp of astonishment. "Peter! What in the world brought you? Come in!"

He dragged Peter inside and closed the door in haste. "You've heard about it, Pete?"

"Yes."

"It's the finish and the smashing of me, Peter!" said Charles huskily.

He began to walk hastily up and down the room. "I've put in a life of hard work—you know that. I've played exactly the sort of a game that my father wanted me to. And now I'm floored and done for!"

"Done for?"

"Done for with dad. He'll have no use for me. I tell you, there's one thing that he hates worse than poison, and that's gambling. He says that a man who gambles, deserves to take his medicine, because he's a hopeless fool. I could have committed a murder without breaking dad up as much as the news of this will. He'll have no confidence in me. No more than if I were a dog. After the things that have happened between us, I suppose that you'll be glad to see me down! But it's a life work that I've thrown away!"

"A third of a life," answered Peter gravely. "That's all there is to it. Why, man, you're a child. You've got plenty of years ahead of you."

"To start at the bottom—and climb?" said his cousin bitterly.

"You have something worth climbing for!" replied Peter.

"You mean Ruth, by that. I know that that's what you mean. But that's no good. I've never been able to get her to talk about the future with me. I never can get her to say 'Yes,' since she got to know you. But I know that it would be very easy to have her say 'No.' I've had to handle her with gloves, Pete. And now that I haven't a thing to offer her——"

"Why, Charlie, you're not disinherited yet!"

"Not yet," said the gloomy Charles; "not until my father hears the news, but five minutes after that, I'll be a gone goose. I tell you, he's iron. Absolute iron, and when he knows what I've done, he'll wipe me off the slate. He'll adopt some one. He'll give his property away."

It seemed to Peter that there was only one side to this grief. It was not for the broken and disappointed heart of his father that Charles had any thought, but only for the property loss which lay before Charles himself.

However, Peter could delay no longer in the business for which he had come. He drew the notes from his pocket and laid them on the table.

"As a matter of fact, Charles," said he, "that fellow was simply having his joke with you. He knew you all the time, and he didn't intend that he should rob you. The cash that you put in the game was enough for him. But he didn't want to steal your money!"

Charles, taking the IOUs one by one, examined them, and turned with a stare to Peter. "I try to make it out," said he, "but it's no go. I try to understand, but

184

cursed if I can! Did you hold that poor, old fat simpleton up and rob him?"

Peter shook his head. "Let me tell you the name of that fat old simpleton. Why you haven't known his face, I don't quite make out. But the fact is that he's Mike Jarvin."

"Jarvin?" gasped Charles.

"Jarvin the crook."

"My heavens, and I—what a fool I've been!"

"It rather looks that way."

"But what—"

"He didn't mean to rob you, Charlie. He simply wanted to give you a lesson, and that's why he took your notes."

"But Jarvin never gave back a penny he'd stolen. Not in his life!"

"Even Mike finds certain things which he can't do. Even he wants to play the game straight, in a way. That's a peculiar thing. I can't explain it. But I suppose that taking that money from you was a little too easy."

Charles struck his hands together with an exclamation. "I could have sworn that the fat man was hardly more than a simple old half-wit, who'd drifted into a bit of luck in a mine, somewhere. And now it turns out to be Jarvin! Why, Pete, I only wonder that he didn't come to tell me about it, himself. Why did he send you?"

And he fixed Peter with a cold and hostile eye.

"The fact is," said Peter, "that he had something else

185

on his hands. He knew that you'd be here. And he sent me along—"

"Sent you?"

"I'm working for him, Charlie."

"You're—working—for—Jarvin!"

"Yes. Since—"

"And that's why you disappeared? And that's why your father is nearly going crazy?"

"That's it," said Peter.

"But why, man? In Heaven's name, why?"

"I'll tell you," said Peter. "I've always had a touch of wild blood in me, Charlie. And I grew a bit tired of the dull life on the ranch. I hated to trouble father. But after all, the ranch is pretty well on its feet, now. And so I broke away and went up to Jarvin's mine, where there's a chance of seeing life rough and in the raw, you know."

A flash of contempt glinted in the eyes of Charles. "Very raw indeed, I suppose!" said he.

"Yes," said Peter, "very raw indeed!"

Chapter XXIX

THE CHAMPION OF THE COUNTY

The care which Soapy gave to orders was never unreasonably great. For he felt that if something was due to his master, still more was due to himself. So, when he had put up the saddle horses, he did not wait long before making a selection of horses. He merely rubbed down the tired mustangs and, having fresh-ened them with a swallow of water and a mouthful of crushed barley, he started out to make the trade. It was easily done. The town was filled with men eager for buying or trading. And in a few minutes he found a buckboard with a serviceable pair attached to it. He found the owner and offered Mike Jarvin's span in exchange. There was not much delay. The stranger liked trim-cut nags, and those of Jarvin were far neater about the heads than his own. A hundred dol-lars in boot had been permitted by Jarvin; Soapy got the new pair for forty dollars bonus, and he went back with fresh horses, and sixty dollars' profit in his pocket.

But money to possess was only money to spend, to the mulatto. He harnessed the team to the buckboard and gave their heads to a youngster to hold. Straight across the street from the hotel stable, there was the lighted front of a lunch counter, newly erected and glowing with bunting for this grand occasion. The stools in front of the counter looked like so many thrones to Soapy. And though the order had been specifically that he should remain in person at the heads of the team, his hunger spoke in a loud voice.

He crossed to the eating place and slipped onto the first vacant stool. Three cooks worked vigorously at a range of oil stoves. Clouds of steam from hot milk and fragrant, boiling coffee rolled out to bathe the soul of Soapy. There were columns of smoke ascending from hissing griddles, where hamburger steaks were siz-

zling and turning black and brown. French-fried potatoes, too, bubbled in little tubs of fat and were drawn
out, dripping hot grease and exuding a delicate aroma
to the quivering nostrils of Soapy.

"*And* you?" asked the waiter, as he swept the dishes
of the last customer from the oilcloth before Soapy.

"Me?" asked Soapy, half closing his eyes to consult
his sense of smell.

At that moment a gruff voice said at his side: "White
folks before colored, man. Gimme a pie!"

Soapy rolled his eyes. It was almost the first time in
his life that he had failed to snatch up the opportunity
to make trouble with his fists. But now his brain and
his senses, all save one, were benumbed with delight.
There was all of sixty dollars in his pocket. What with
the recent gain on the big horse, and now this second
profit, he felt like a millionaire. So he let the insult
pass.

The words merely brought a suggestion to his mind.
"Pie for me, too," said Soapy.

"Apple, blackberry, peach—" began the waiter.

"Apple," said the stranger.

"Apple," echoed Soapy.

Two plates, with a generous wedge of pie upon each,
were rattled upon the counter.

The deep voice of the man beside Soapy said: "Ain't
there no hope of more'n this? Is *this* what you call a
piece of pie, waiter?"

"Leave it be!" snapped another man, with a sharply
rising nasal twang. "How can you expect to fight in

the ring in another hour if you got a whole pie in your—"

"Leave me be!" snarled the first, seizing the piece.

Soapy was growling at the waiter, "This'll do to start. Now, a pie. A *whole* pie!"

He had gobbled up the piece in a gulp or two and now he extended his great hand and gripped the big apple pie as it was brought toward him. As he ate, he rolled his little eyes upward and to the side. He saw a dark-brown giant sitting beside him, glowering down.

"Now curse my heart," said the big man, "but I think that that negro is eating that pie just to get a rise out of me, Bill."

Bill, flaming in a crimson necktie, set off with a sparkling diamond stickpin, gripped the bulging shoulder of his charge.

"Now, you come on, Bud, will you? You come on, will you? They'll be hankering for a sight of you before the fight. Then let 'em see you!"

"Oh," said Bud, "I would like to take one pass at the neg—"

But he let himself be dragged from the stool, while Bill frantically growled: "Would you be busting up your hands on that head? Like hitting a marble dome! You come on along with me!"

So they disappeared, and Soapy, as the last of the pie flowed down his throat, cast yearning eyes after them. He wanted to take big Bud apart and examine his interior. Rarely in his life had his passion for fighting waxed so hot and high in him, but on the other hand, the pie had merely awakened his appetite, and the leading aspiration of his life was consuming the mulatto. From the corner of his well-occupied mouth he had been bellowing for hamburger. A great portion of it was brought for him. He reached for the nearest loaf of bread, hurling the contents of a pitcher of water into the street, then extended the pitcher to be filled with coffee and hot milk for his use. And that was only the beginning.

At the end of some thirty or forty minutes, he wiped his pale-purple lips and sighed.

"If this here was a restaurant," said Soapy regretfully, "I might be able to make sort of a meal out of it. Hand me that lemon pie."

It was handed. Cooks and waiters stood before him in an awed but grinning circle.

"Where's the folks gone?" murmured Soapy, around the disappearing pie.

"The fight," said the waiter, mopping the counter with an anxious hand, in hopes of a tip.

"Oh," said Soapy, as his mind traveled back to an earlier incident in the evening. "The fight, eh?"

And his recollection surmounted fried potatoes, jam, two kinds of pie, hamburger steak, strings of luscious sausages, and other minor incidentals in this light lunch. His thoughts arrived at the departed form of big Bud.

"That sap—that one that they call Bud—he fights, I guess?" asked Soapy.

"Sure, he fights with 'Canuck Pete.' And a darn good licking he'll get."

"From Canuck, eh?"

"Yep."

"Well," said Soapy, "maybe I'll go and see that fight."

"I dunno that you got time to get to it. You hear 'em hollering, now?"

The noise of the shouting guided Soapy through the night. He arrived at a high board fence with a flare of light and a dense fragrance of tobacco smoke inside. Parting from a dollar at the gate, he stepped inside the fence in time to see his recent acquaintance, Bud, climb through the ropes of the ring which had been arranged on a rough platform in the center of the field. And the crowd roared again.

It was easy to see that Bud was the county champion. And when he stood up in the flare of the great gasoline lamps he looked worthy of their betting.

Thick muscles padded his hairy chest, and his dark arms swept down almost to his knees, rippling with ponderous strength from the shoulders down. His black hair bristled above that cramped forehead, and his mouth was stretched in a grin of confidence.

But still the hope of seeing him licked swelled high in the mulatto when he saw the other warrior rising and shaking off his bathrobe. Canuck possessed every whit as much bulk as Bud. In addition there was a taper finish to his limbs that promised speed as well as power. He stepped forth into the light, showing a lean, cadaverous face, shadowed with unshaven beard, and furnished with a great bony jaw, built to defy battering. What chiefly interested the mulatto was the eye of this man, thoughtful, deep-sunk, and filled with a keen fire. It reminded Soapy of another eye that he knew well—the eye of big Peter Hale, the worker of mysteries.

What mysteries, then, would this warrior enact in the ring? He was a man of some fame, was Canuck. He had already risen some distance up the ladder of ring fame, and perhaps he would rise still farther. That natural fighting heart and fighting instinct which had made him celebrated through the hardy Canadian lumber camps had, for some months, been directed and polished by a clever manager. This manager was of the old school, letting his protégés fight their way into the acquisition of greater skill. What he taught five days a week, he liked to see his man show in the ring on the sixth evening. And so the Canadian was taken touring through the countrysides, taking on all comers, and winning usually with consummate ease. There would be plenty of time to take him East after the big purses and the famous fighters, when he had acquired a trifle more skill with that long left arm, and a bit more snap in his deadly right.

It was plain to every man in the field that the battle would not be long, as Bud, with all his brute strength and confidence, squared off before the fiery eye and the well-poised body of the other.

The cries were only: "I bet on you to stay three

rounds with him, Bud. You stick to him. Don't you let him spank you with that right, Bud. Hang on and get my money for me, kid!"

But no one was prepared for what actually happened. Bud, scowling with a tense battle fury, rushed from his corner as the bell sounded. He swung with either hand. The other slipped beneath those flailing hands and then dipped up and smote from beneath with his left hand.

Perhaps he had not intended to strike quite so hard. Perhaps he was not able to gauge the power of his own punching any too accurately. At any rate, the terrible Bud flung his hands high above his head, reeled blindly, and dropped stunned upon the floor of the ring.

The crash of his fall sent a wide echo over the field.

Chapter XXX

BRUTE FORCE

There was no question of counting, on the part of the referee. He took the head and shoulders of Bud, and the timekeeper took his feet. After he was dragged to his corner and a bucket of water poured over his head, the crowd realized that their dollars had been paid for no more of a show than this. And then a grumble began in the rearmost ranks—where crowd commotions always start—and it spread to a mumbling in front and then to a whisper of discontent toward the ring. Another wave of sound immediately recommenced from the rear of the host. It was a snarling that brought an ugly murmur toward the center of the field. Then, as at a universal signal, a great howl of rage and disgust went up.

The deputy sheriff left in haste. To try to find his chief, he said! The promoter of the match started to find the gate, but before he had gone half a dozen steps he was recognized, and violent hands were laid upon him. He was carried in a forward wave and deposited with a heave in the ring, while two or three sturdy cattlemen clambered in beside him.

"Now you tell the boys what the main idea might be!" said they to him.

The promoter was a shifty-eyed gentleman. He may have wanted to talk, but his mind was diverted by two distractions. One was the furious noise of the crowd, and the other was the heavy holsters adorning the hips of his new companions in the ring.

"Why, gents," he whined, "you all know that Bud is a husky sort. He's never been licked, and Heaven knows that he's had fights enough. He said that he'd eat Canuck!"

"Leave off what he said," growled one. "The boys want to know why they shouldn't get their money back. That's all. They're plumb anxious to find out why Bud thought that this here was a swimming pool and why he tried to do a high dive so quick. You call that a fight?"

The promoter perspired more profusely than ever,

194

but convincing words failed him. At this moment, by the grace of good fortune, he was rescued by help from an unexpected quarter. The mighty form of Canuck stepped forward, waving a gloved hand. At once, silence fell over the assemblage.

"Say, fellows," said Canuck in a voice ridiculously high and thin, contrasted with his imposing bulk, "I'm sorry that the show ended so quick and that I happened to hit Bud so soon."

There was a wail of laughter and derision. It ended at once, and Canuck went on: "I ain't here to rob you. I see a lot of husky gents out yonder. Maybe some of them would like to come in here with me. There's a pair of gloves handy for the first gent that wants to try them on. And, as far as I'm concerned, I'll keep on fighting till you say that you got your money's worth!"

On the whole, this was a good sporting proposition. But who would be apt to select himself to stand within the circle of the ropes and confront this swarthy monster who carried poison in the tip of either glove?

There was a sudden backward movement through the crowd. Faces turned, searching for a hero. There was a figure moving toward the ring, leaving a narrow wake of confusion behind him—a short, heavily built man, whose hat was brushed from his head as he struggled forward. His long, ponderous arms swept men from before him.

"Lemme get in there at him!" said the stranger.

The crowd parted before his voice and gave him a

clear path to the ringside. In another moment he had laid his hold upon the ropes and hoisted himself with a swing of the body into the ring.

"Gimme them gloves!" said he. "I'll take on this here fighting man!"

It was Soapy!

A wild whoop followed. Every voice in that crowd was raised with joy as with cunning eyes they calculated the bulk of Soapy's body and the length of his arms. He looked very much like business. Perhaps, after all, this would be a double show and very much worth while.

The promoter seized opportunity by the forelock. "There's fifty dollars in this for you, kid, if you stick out four rounds with him. Here's the togs and Bud's shoes."

Soapy drew the shapeless boots from his feet and contrasted the unshod bulk of his foot with one of the tennis shoes which had been drawn from Bud—poor Bud, who was now beginning to sit up and take a sick sort of interest in the proceedings.

"I don't want no togs," said Soapy. "And how'm I gunna get even my toes into them shoes? Stockings is good enough for me. And I got clothes on my back right now!"

He stripped himself of coat and shirt and was revealed in flaming red flannel. Two men on either side were now tugging onto his hands the largest gloves which could be produced. They had to be sliced open at the sides, and still they cramped the formidable knuckles of the negro.

In the meantime, there was a time of earnest and low-voiced conversation in the farther corner of the ring, where Canuck had lost some of his martial ardor. "Who is this bloke?" he asked his manager. "He looks to me like Sam Langford, multiplied by two."

"It's fat, kid," said the manager, peering anxiously at the mulatto's vast bulk.

"Fat nothing!" said the Canuck. "That's muscle—all of it. A ton of it inside of that red shirt. What've you led me up to here?"

"Aw, look at him," said the manager. "He knows nothing! Look at that!"

Soapy, equipped for the combat, tried a few practice swings that whistled in roundabout fashion through the air. Canuck looked and then grinned suddenly.

"All right," said he. "It ain't old Sam, after all. You tell them that I'm ready!"

The ring was cleared. The groaning Bud was half led and half carried to the ground. Silence succeeded the excited murmurs of the spectators.

"Are you ready, gentlemen?" asked the referee, yanking his cap lower over his eyes.

"Ready," said Canuck.

"Start the music," said Soapy. "I'm ready for dancing."

"Are you ready, Mr. Timekeeper?"

"Ready, doc!"

"Then swat that bell."

The bell clanged, and Canuck slipped gracefully to

the center of the ring. He extended his open gloves, to shake hands. But Soapy saw the wide opening and swung mightily for the jaw. There was a roar of mingled laughter and hisses. Soapy had missed by a yard or more as Canuck danced back.

And now—how beautifully Canuck was working! His arms flashed forward—twice with either hand he smote and stepped back, to let the colossus have room to pitch forward on its yellow face, stunned.

The colossus did not pitch forward. Neither was he stunned. For Soapy did not even shake his head at these punches, but started blithely in at his enemy with both ponderous hands ready for action. The crowd shrieked again. Certainly the mulatto was not made of tender stuff, for the sharp, spatting sound of those blows had been heard throughout the gathering.

The general plan of Soapy was to crowd his foe into a corner of the ring and there hit him—only once! But how strike a floating feather with a sledge hammer? He rushed with might and main, but suddenly the poised form of Canuck dissolved into a blur, and from the side a pile-driving glove landed upon Soapy's ear.

This was different. That blow, which might have felled a bullock, did not daze him, but it split the rim of his ear and hurt like a hornet's sting. He wheeled with a growl and smote with the full sweep of his right arm. Surely that blow drove straight through the glistening body of the phantom! Or had he, indeed, been able to slip deftly back and avoid the whistling ruin?

The solid crack of a heavy glove lodged against his

jaw, at the point called the button, and a dim mist scattered not unpleasantly over the brain of Soapy. He smiled and, reaching out with his great left arm, he gathered in his opponent. This was no phantom, after all. No; it consisted of two hundred and thirty-odd pounds of magnificent muscle, writhing and struggling and snapping short-arm punches against the body and head of Soapy.

Well, these love taps were no matter. He drew his foe closer to his breast. With half the power in his left arm he crushed the other to a sudden gasping feebleness. And then he poised his terrible right hand to smite Canuck senseless.

But a voice, piercing as a sword of fire, stabbed at his ear. "Leave go! Leave go of him, kid, or the mob'll kill you! There ain't any hitting in the clinches. I told you that!"

"Is this here a clinch?" asked Soapy sadly.

He flung the other from him. "This ain't a fight. It's only a dance!" said Soapy in disgust.

And he started to rush, just as the bell clanged the end of the round. The heavens rang with the cheering of that joyous throng.

Kindly hands drew Soapy backward. "Kid, ain't you dazed from the way he soaked you? This'll freshen you up. You hurt him when you hugged him! Man, man, you got a fortune waiting for you in the ring! Here—"

They doused him with water.

"Leave that water be," sputtered Soapy, "or I'll

break a couple of you in two, I say. Leave it be, and gimme a nip of gin—will you?"

Chapter XXXI

"HIT HIM!"

In the opposite corner, a voice complained: "Why didn't you hit him, kid? What're you doing in there?"

"You *sap!*" gasped Canuck. "I hit him enough. What do you call hitting?"

"Oh, you hit him. But you didn't set yourself. You got to *soak* him, Canuck. You're losing a lot of prestige letting a tramp like that stick out a whole round with you!"

"He's busted a rib for me, I think," groaned Canuck. "He ain't a man. He's a bear. He squashed me, I tell you! They ought to disqualify him for that."

"Disqualify? You think that a disqualification would go down the throats of this gang? They'd fill us all full of lead! No, Canuck, but the first thing that you do in the next round—you tear his head off!"

"I'll kill him!" snarled Canuck.

And as the bell clanged he was out of his stool and across the ring before Soapy had so much as straightened up from his place.

With the might of that long run behind him, with the impetuous sway of two hundred and thirty pounds of trained and hardened muscle—with the snap and precision of the good boxer, Canuck smashed his fist straight against the point of Soapy's jaw. And the lunging force of the blow toppled the mulatto to the side against the ropes, snapping his head back across his shoulder.

Soapy was not down, however. He rolled heavily back from the ropes, and Canuck, his mind bewildered because he had failed to knock the other straight through the ropes and among the crowd, met the negro with hammer strokes with either hand.

He smote his terrible straight-driving left into the pit of Soapy's bulging midriff. It was as though he had struck an India-rubber cushion, with springs beneath it! He hammered his right again to the jaw, but the blow glanced futilely away. He smashed once more with the right for the heart, and he felt as though he had sprained his wrist, beating against a stone wall.

And before him there was a smooth globe of head and face, split asunder by the widely grinning lips. "My, *ain't* you in a hurry, mister!" remarked Soapy, as he smote at the phantom in haste.

It was a descending punch. It missed the jaw for which it was intended—missed by a foot, but it grazed along the ribs of Canuck, and he felt as though he had been scraped along a sharp reef of stone! He drew back, gasping, dazzled by this miracle.

"Kill him, now that you got him started, Canuck!" shrieked the familiar voice of his manager.

But Canuck knew better than that.

The whole crowd was seething with a terrible joy in this carnage. It looked to them as though the mulatto were being torn to shreds. But, as the yellow face rolled toward Canuck, the champion chattered from the side of his mouth to the referee:

"You better stop this. I don't want to kill him. I can't afford to pay funeral expenses!"

The withered face of the referee puckered with interest. But then he shook his head. "You ain't hurt him yet, Canuck."

"I could cut him to ribbons. He ain't got a guard. Look at this!"

He stepped in and struck twice suddenly across the flailing hands of Soapy. The blows landed on either side of Soapy's head. But his forward progress was not halted. He rolled closer, and Canuck braced himself to block the driving punch.

It smashed through his erected guard, flinging away his right forearm. It dashed the back of his left glove glancing against his jaw. A thoroughly well-blocked blow, surely, and yet the head of Canuck rang, and he was shaken to his feet, while he heard the voice of the referee drawling:

"I dunno that I can stop the fight while he's still coming after you, Canuck!"

There was no more blocking of punches, after that. The thing to do, obviously, was to avoid the rushes of the mulatto by lightness of foot, and that was what Canuck intended to do. He sped about the ring with wonderful lightness, striking out when an opening offered.

But suddenly here was the mulatto standing still in

the center of the ring. "You stand up and fight, you sneaking, low-down skunk! This ain't no foot race! It's a fight!"

That, after the battering which Soapy had been taking, brought a roar of sympathetic delight from the crowd. They began to look closer and they saw, as the bell clanged and the men went to their corners, that the face of Soapy was apparently unmarked! In spite of the dreadful punishment he had taken, he was still without a vital injury. And he was actually grinning.

Now he sat on his stool and, waving his eager handlers away, he leaned over the ropes to ask: "Ain't there none of you gentlemen that can make that sucker stand up and fight? Speaking personal, I sure want to give you your money's worth!"

It brought a shout of approval from them. And when they stared up into that shining, yellow face they saw that this was not meant for waggery.

A stern-faced gentleman raised a handful of bank notes. "I got five hundred dollars, boys, against any man's hundred that the yellow boy lasts out the four rounds!"

Soapy stood up with a roar. "Look here, white man, d'you think that these folks is foolish? Don't they know that I'm gunna kill Mr. Canuck the minute that he stands still?"

The bell clanged in an uproar of laughter and cheering. And Canuck rose with no undue haste from his stool.

"My arms are numb to the shoulders!" he had told

203

his manager. "I soaked him with everything that I had when I first went after him that round. And it didn't matter. My fists just bounce off of him. What'm I gunna do? What'm I gunna do?"

The manager growled through his set teeth: "If only the newspapers don't get hold of this! Looks like your wrists are made of mush. Looks like you was only playing with him. Well, keep away from him. You keep away and pepper him from a distance!"

It was all that Canuck could do. He went back into the third round and danced until his knees sagged with weariness. For, after all, there was hardly fifteen pounds less bulk for him to carry than Soapy trundled around the ring. And with the passage of every moment Soapy was growing more active. The meal which he had stowed away had settled now. He felt lighter and more at ease, and he was growing momently more accustomed to a setting with which the other had been familiar for so long! He was faster afoot, now, and twice as fast with his hands. He followed with half punches, making easy play, his head up, yellow fire in his eyes, as he skipped forward, waiting for a chance to strike. And the game was still sledge hammer against feather, except that there was less wind to buoy the feather from moment to moment.

Luck, however, had something to do with the matter before the end. Canuck, ducking out of the way of an over-arm swing, slipped a little, and the blow glanced from the top of his head. It was enough to make his knees spring beneath him. He staggered back until his shoulders struck the ropes and he recoiled. The recoil threw him out of the way of flying destruction.

He wheeled to strike again. The lurching, low-built body of the mulatto glided in under his punch, and a lifting blow struck big Canuck on the breast. It lightened his feet and hurled him back. He strove to regain his balance, but it could not be managed. Canuck staggered, reeled, and fell headlong against the lower rope on the farther side of the ring. As he sat up, dizzy and sick, he heard the deafening roar of the crowd.

He knew what that sound meant. Always, before this, he had heard it as he was beating an opponent into submission, but now it was, for him, like an avenging roar of the sea, and the heart of Canuck sickened and grew weak within his breast.

Then came the mercy of the bell, clanging out like silver music to his ear.

He dragged himself to his feet. And here was his manager at his side, drawing his arm across his shoulders and helping him to his corner.

"Kid, what happened?"

"Shut up. Don't ask me! He shot me with a cannon ball. It wasn't no fist. What a man he is!"

Canuck sank with a gasp on his stool and heard a voice barking from the side and beneath him: "Five hundred says that the negro knocks out Canuck in the next round. Who takes that? Or a thousand, if you want it!"

"What odds do you offer, Jerry?"

"Two to one—"

Canuck closed his eyes.

Suddenly he was seized with a great nostalgia for the deep glooms and the cool silences of the Northern woods. Let others climb the flaming ladder of ambition. But only to be freed from danger and from pain!

So thought Canuck, and then came the crisp voice of his manager: "Kid, you're done if you don't duck out of this! You got to foul him. Understand?"

Chapter XXXII

THE HAND OF DESTRUCTION

To the desperate mind of Canuck, the clang of the bell seemed a solution. His wind was more than half exhausted. There was a telltale tremor in his knees. And along the ribs and in the back of his neck there was an ache and a numbness from the shock of the glancing blows that Soapy had dealt him. What would happen if one of those terrible strokes landed full and fair upon head or body? He thought of crushed bones and shrank with a shudder. Then he saw the yellow face of the mulatto coming toward him, grinning and eager.

"You come along, white man! We're gunna have a good time, this here dance! Will you stand up and fight? Or do I have to keep right along playing tag with you?"

And he launched a glistening, flashing, terrible length of arm at him. The torn edge of the glove flicked and cut the lip of Canuck as he flinched backward. Canuck struck with both hands at the wide-open target in front of him, but if his might had been useless when his strength was still fresh upon him, and when his confidence was like strongest steel, what was it now—now that his self-belief was so dreadfully diminished?

Two hundred and fifty pounds of monstrous humanity shook with terrible laughter, as Soapy mocked this effort and sprang at Canuck with a renewed energy.

There was no weariness in this inhuman creature. He thrived upon blows. They were like the breath of life to his nostrils. And Canuck was barely able to spring back out of the way of lunging danger.

"Ten to one," a voice was bellowing above the tumult of the throng. "Ten to one on the negro!"

And another voice: "Ten to one on Soapy!"

Who had learned that name?

Soapy himself heard, and his battle frenzy left him long enough to allow him to turn his head and scan the throng. Who knew his name in that crowd? That knowledge meant danger to himself and double danger to his master. If there was some one here who recognized him, the same man would be most apt to know Mike Jarvin.

And recognition would probably spell disaster.

It flashed upon the mind of Soapy that, after all, it

would have been far more discreet in him if he had obeyed the instructions of Mike and had remained in charge of the horses—waiting for a crisis in the evening's affairs. Now—who could tell what might happen?

These thoughts raced through his mind and then were gone. There remained before him only the knowledge that he had chosen pleasure first. So Soapy turned to the joyful duty, forgetting consequences and Mike Jarvin.

Already there was a babel of voices from curious questioners around the ring, as Soapy chased his flying foe back and forth.

"Who knows the negro? Who *is* he?"

"Soapy. Old Mike Jarvin's trained man-killer!"

"Jarvin's?"

"Yes."

"The devil!"

"That's what he is!"

"Where's Jarvin now?"

"I dunno."

"Stop betting, boys. If the negro belongs to Jarvin, it means that the fight will go the way that he wants it to go!"

"Stop betting? I've stuck up a hundred and fifty already!"

"A hundred and fifty? You lucky dog, I've backed the mulatto for twelve hundred. We'll kill Jarvin and the coon too if he don't polish off Canuck."

To all of this chatter Soapy was deaf. He had fixed

his mind too ardently upon the work that was before him. He started a swing—and he saw Canuck, unhit, drop to one knee—it would be a foul to strike him now, and Soapy strove to check his blow. It landed only softly on the side of Canuck's head—but instantly he collapsed along the floor of the ring!

Beside the ropes sprang up a frantic figure, and a clarion voice rang in the ears of the referee:

"Foul, Mr. Referee! Foul! Foul!"

"Curse the foul!" shouted a tall cattleman near the ring. "Is Canuck quitting? *I'm* gunna see fair play here! Get up, you Canuck skunk!"

The eye of Canuck, rolling to the side, saw the flash of a long-barreled revolver. It brought him scrambling to his feet, and yet there he stood, staggering as though badly hurt by the last punch.

"Look here, boy," the referee was saying, shaking his finger in the face of Soapy, "one more trick like that, and you're done, you understand? Now you go in and finish this fight fair—and polish him off if you can! Don't you get foolish and excited—even if Mike Jarvin *has* told you which side he's bet on!"

The referee knew that name, then? But Soapy, staring at him, hardly knew what had been said. His eyes were glaring over the shoulder of the official and at the unsteady figure of the other fighter.

When he was loosed, he charged like a maddened bull. He missed Canuck with a first punch. But the second, a roundabout left, grazed the forehead of Canuck and flung him flat on his back with a resounding smack of his shoulders against the canvas.

The screech of the crowd pronounced this the final stroke.

But Soapy prayed that his foe might rise to be struck once more—a little—only a little more solidly!

That prayer was to be answered. Canuck was drawing slowly together, bunching himself, raising his knees.

"Five!" counted the referee, and Canuck drew into a close bunch.

"He's done!" shrieked the crowd.

"Six!" barked the referee.

Poor Canuck rolled over and strove to push himself up on hand and knee. But his whole body trembled—not with pain or weakness, but with fear. He dreaded that waiting hand of destruction which the mulatto had poised in the air.

"Seven!"

And now the sharp voice of the manager yelled across the ring: "Are you crazy, Canuck? Is this the end of you and your big money?"

"Eight!"

He rose suddenly to his feet, and in a nervous frenzy drove both hands rapidly into the face of Soapy. But he could not beat back that machinelike brute.

And in despair he resolved upon the last and the lowest expedient of the prize fighter, he hit low and foul.

The mulatto, with a snarl, dropped into a deep crouch.

The referee cried: "Are you hurt, Soapy? D'you claim a foul?"

"Claim a foul? No; I'll kill him!" cried Soapy, and he leaped at Canuck.

The hoarse screech of the crowd was like the very voice of Soapy himself as he flung himself at the other.

And Canuck's last cunning deserted him. He struck out blindly, his blows recoiling from the padded body of the mulatto.

Then two great hands seized big Canuck. Through the masking canvas of the gloves he could feel the bony fingers grip his flesh. He strove to struggle free, for there was a paralyzing power in the hands of the other. Where his clutch closed, it turned the body of Canuck numb.

Gathered into the grip of Soapy, Canuck found the breath crushed from his body. He thrust feebly back at the yellow face of Soapy. And here was the referee, screeching:

"I'll disqualify you, Soapy. You hear me, you wild fool? I'll disqualify you—and the crowd'll kill you if you foul him. Let him go, Soapy!"

He might as well have spoken, to a dumb beast. Soapy raised his dreadful right hand, poised it, and struck. The shining body of Canuck turned limp and senseless.

Then in both his giant hands Soapy lifted his enemy and hurled him, face downward, upon the floor. He saw the head of the senseless man rebound from that terrible shock. And he leaned to pick up Canuck and repeat the dose.

A meager shadow of danger stepped before him and his purpose. It was the referee, shouting: "You're done, Soapy! You've lost this fight on a foul, you fool. Either a fool or a crook. Now keep back from him, or I'll shoot your head off!"

And in his hand, to back up the threat, there was a glittering Colt.

So Soapy drew back, panting with murderous desire, his great hands twitching. And he heard a thunder of an angry sea of voices. And a hundred hands were brandished at him.

"Kill the crooked negro. He threw the fight for Jarvin!"

Chapter XXXIII

THE MOB

The brain of Soapy cleared a little as he heard that murderous shout. When he looked down to the utterly flaccid form of the defeated boxer, he knew that there was some reason for the anger of the mob. He had been a little "rough." And now he most sincerely hoped that he had not killed the man. However, he had wit enough to know that, for the moment, the chief concern was not the condition of Canuck, but the loss of the sundry bets which had been placed so liberally upon Soapy when once his fighting prowess was beginning to be revealed.

They had wagered much money, and now they saw the rich odds, which they had been about to collect, snatched from their hands by the reckless fury of this yellow fighting man. And they wanted to make trouble; they were most sincerely bent upon making it.

Here and there a scattering of voices shouted something in the favor of the mulatto. A doctor near the ringside had leaped in and clapped his ear to the heart of the fallen boxer. Then he had leaped up, shouting that Canuck was not seriously injured—only stunned. And there were others—chiefly those who wanted to collect the bets which they had placed upon Canuck—who called to the crowd that Soapy must have a fair deal.

But the others were deaf. They proceeded from shouts and cursing and fist shaking to more vigorous efforts. Presently a dozen hands reached for Soapy. But he turned himself about, and their hands slipped from his perspiring body.

There was no handier person than the referee—and there was hardly any one for whom Soapy had so great a grudge. He picked that touchy little gentleman up by the ankles and flung him in the face of that wave of angry cattlemen.

Half a dozen went crashing to the floor. A revolver exploded. "He's coming, shooting!" yelled some one, and instantly the entire crowd was thrown into the greatest confusion.

But Soapy, his fighting temper roused, did the very

best thing that he could have attempted. Instead of running away from this attack, he turned and ran straight through it. He had knocked a hole through the head of the attacking wave. Now he leaped into that hole, found the ropes, and catapulted himself through the air at the heads of those beneath.

An ever-ready gun exploded, sending a bullet whistling near his body. But those in the distance foolishly attributed that bullet to a gun in the hand of the mulatto. And there was a fresh wail of fear, rage, and nervousness.

Soapy, like a hard-flung projectile, crashed through the crowd and found the ground. He recoiled from it and waded ahead. In the confusion before him, he was hardly seen before he was striking. Yonder in the ring he had been at a disadvantage. He had had to attend a dancing lesson, with a man close by to make sure that all his steps were according to law and custom. But this was far different! Here were men wedged so closely together that they could not escape. And Soapy smote with a tireless zeal. His very elbows, as he drew back those ponderous arms, brushed against bystanders and toppled them backward. He cut through that mass like red-hot iron through butter, followed and surrounded by a stream of oaths.

The confusion grew worse and worse. Here, there, and again, guns exploded in that overarmed mob, and with every explosion there was a fresh shout that the negro was killing mad! That confusion caused a great horde to rush toward the gates, and through them, as fast as they could push away from the danger point. All could not escape at once. More backs than faces were turned toward Soapy, however, and perhaps he would have been quickly away to freedom, across the fence, had it not been for a most unlucky accident.

Yonder in that crowd were a dozen woodsmen who, in their time, had worked in Canadian lumber. Moreover, every one of them had seen some of the earlier battles of Canuck, and all looked upon him with an immense pride, as a sort of shining glory brought forth out of the shadowy glooms of the Northern forest. He helped them to respect themselves a little more. He was like money in the pocket or a drink under the belt.

So they had come to this prize fight, not to see a battle, but to see big Canuck win again. They placed a few dollars apiece on the strength of what Canuck would do to that rough fellow, Bud. And afterward they watched Canuck step lightly forth and smite big Bud into nothingness, exactly as they had desired. They saw a fresh victim brought forth to the slaughter, and they settled back in their places, chuckling and nodding and talking with a good deal of unnecessary warmth about their days in the Northern woods with Canuck.

And then they were forced to grow silent. All was not going quite so well with Canuck. He was striking his blows at a creature of rubber from whom all punishment slipped away. They stood amazed, a mute and stricken row of beholders, while Canuck was felled. Finally, in the concluding round, they saw him taken as in the embrace of a bear. They saw the dreadful right hand of Soapy raised and they saw it fall. They saw their fellow woodsman raised like a helpless child and dashed violently against the floor.

While other people yelled and shrieked with excitement, they said not a word, merely drew instinctively together and stood shoulder to shoulder. They had come from the land where war is war, and they would not flinch from the consequences of it. Their favorite, their pride, and their chief had fallen. The luster was stolen away from the Canadian timberland, but, nevertheless, they were determined that they should stay and see what this thing would come to in the end.

Something should be done. They hardly knew what. In a deep silence they stood their ground while the crowd pushed for the narrow gate. They did not have to shoulder and fight that crowd away, either, but from before their stern faces and their wide and lofty shoulders the turmoil of men divided at once, washing about them like water around a strong rock.

In the meantime, it happened that the progress of Soapy was taken in a line which led directly toward them, and the tallest of the Canadians noted this fact with a little flare of inspiration.

"Boys," said he, "you might notice that there seems to be a need for somebody to stop Soapy—if that's his name. Now, suppose that we hold him and see what he's wanted for!"

Grim, glad faces looked back to him from either side and thanked him in silence for this suggestion.

The next moment a lurching, low, vast-shouldered form appeared before them, brushing through the last skirts of the crowd. He saw the group of lumbermen and lurched for them.

Two of them went down, one crushed by the hammer fist of Soapy, and the other involved in the fall of his friend. But Soapy, leaping into the breach, found hands like iron vises closing on him—and more hands were vindictively reaching.

He tore himself away, and half of his clothes came off in rags under their clutches. Attacking them again, left and right, he downed them, made a staggering path through them, and lurched away toward the fence once more.

Two of that stalwart company were down and would not rise again in a hurry, but the others had tasted vengeance, and they wheeled like a hunting pack and rushed after the fugitive.

It was well for Soapy that he possessed speed of foot along with his other virtues, but it takes a rare engine to give wings to two hundred and fifty low-built pounds. Soapy began to fail in that race. They were drawing up on him fast when, luckily, he saw that the fence was just before him. He leaped for it, drawing his heels up just clear of their reaching hands. A gun flashed in the grip of one of the group, but a comrade struck it down.

"We'll tear him to bits, but we'll do it with our hands!"

They swarmed across that fence and rushed into the

mounting dust cloud that masked the roadway. They could see Soapy just ahead of them, jogging along, with the crowd giving ready way to him upon either hand. After him they went in a compact charge. It seemed to Soapy almost like the charge of horses. He turned around his head with an owlish ease and regarded them with a fierce eye.

He recognized that group. Any one who had seen them together before was not likely to forget, and now he knew that a grave danger was come upon him. However, he was still confident. He had beaten a fine prize fighter on this night, and then he had cut his way through a whole hostile crowd. Why, then, should he fear this single group?

So argued Soapy. When he turned about to strike down the leader of that flying wedge, he beat that man down and out of sight, to be sure, but the others came rushing in like a moving wall of stone. He was battered before them and carried back to the side of the street.

He fought like a lion. Again and again those mighty fists of his brought down a foe. But still they drove him. His foot slipped, and he was down in a cloud of dust.

The first who dropped upon him declared afterward that it was like dropping upon a crouched tiger. He was fairly twisted into a knot the instant that he came within the grip of the fallen mulatto. But there were still others in that formidable group. And they caught Soapy with many hands. Legs and body and head and terrible, twisting arms, like two great pythons, were grappled—and he was ground back into the dust.

Some fifteen hundredweight of brawny muscle had been cast upon Soapy, and therefore it was no wonder that he struggled more or less in vain. But fight he would and did until the last gasp, though there was dust in his eyes and a cloud of it stifling his lungs— and this vast burden of hands tearing at him.

Then across his blurred vision something like a great sword flashed. He heard howls and yells. Hands released their grips. He twisted to his knees.

"Get up, Soapy, and come with me!" said the voice of Peter Hale.

Chapter XXXIV

DANGER AHEAD!

Soapy looked up, and above him he saw the cripple standing, braced upon his ruined legs and upon one crutch that was propped under his armpit. The other crutch, rimmed with strong steel as it was, had become a formidable flail in the ample grasp of Peter. With it he had beaten some of the grain of discretion from the chaff of the lumbermen's fury.

Still, as he flourished the long crutch about his head, the crowd drew farther back, like a ripple spreading from a stone cast into the pool. And like the running ripple, so the awe and the wonder rushed through the mind of Soapy.

He himself was a man of might and a man without fear, and yet this power of numbers had overcome him, at the last. How dreadful a fate might have been in store for him he dared not even guess; yet here was the crippled white man who had ventured forth and with a single stroke had scattered the assailants, releasing Soapy from the vast peril.

It was not mere power of heart and hand. Of course, it was much more. It was the touch of the magic hand, the enchanter's way of solving a difficulty. The old belief in those occult powers of Peter rushed back upon the brain of Soapy. He feared those powers as much as ever, but now, in the place of naked dread alone, there was an added something of love.

In a heat of doglike devotion, he could have thrown himself in the dust and embraced the knees of his rescuer. For Peter had been exalted from hell to heaven. He was no longer an evil genius. He was both divine and good. So thought Soapy, but he found a more useful way of showing a bit of his devotion. Behind his idol a crouched monster of a man lurched out to take Peter from the rear, dodging under the dreadful sweep of the crutch.

Of course, he could have warned Peter, but words were ever slower than deeds to the mulatto. He leaped from his crouched position. The other man flung up his arms to guard the threatened blow, and vain was that guard. Home crashed the mighty fist of Soapy, and the other lay motionless in the dust.

From the upper regions of calm and mercy he heard

the voice of Peter Hale: "Turn the poor fellow over, Soapy. He might choke in the dust."

Soapy obeyed, trembling with wonder. How clear it was to him, now, that this man was a veritable god! Certainly he was the master preordained for Soapy's guidance through this world! With wisdom, with gentleness and charity, with a dreadful might, also, he ruled and reigned. And the heart of the mulatto confessed his power in every way. He followed at the back of the cripple, to guard him from any attack from the rear.

But there was no danger of this, in the meantime. For there had been quite enough fighting to satisfy even the crowd, this evening. There had been enough bloodshed and broken ribs and noses. And here and there one could hear a groaning or a snarling from the rear.

Peter and Soapy were left to go slowly on toward the hotel.

"Walk beside me, Soapy. I want to talk to you."

"Some son of a gun might jump you from behind, Mr. Hale."

"Why would they jump me and not you, Soapy?"

"Why, what good would it do them to get me down, as long as you was left, sir?"

Peter turned with a little laugh. "Don't take that too seriously, Soapy. I simply took those fellows by surprise and clubbed them away from you. They weren't expecting anything like that!"

Soapy merely smiled, and a light glistened fitfully in

his eyes, for he understood it all perfectly. When a god performed a deed of heroism or of might, he referred to it thereafter not at all, or else with easy modesty. And so it was with Peter Hale. To have scattered those raging Canadians—that was a mere nothing!

A sort of dizzy joy flooded the childish heart and soul of the mulatto. For, having lunged about the world from the days of his childhood, from one mischief to another, he now felt that he had found a haven and a refuge. Thereafter he need fear nothing. For he had met with a savior and with a guide. Indeed, when he looked back upon his first meeting with Peter, he could remember that there had been a singular gentleness in the manner of the white man, always.

Only he, Soapy, had forced on the contest. He fairly shuddered when he thought of it. How well it was for him that the mighty man of wisdom had not chosen to blast him and shame him forever! Poor Soapy, having entered into this trance mood, hardly knew where they were wandering, until they arrived at the flare of the big gasoline lamp in front of the hotel.

"Now," said Peter, "suppose that you go back to the horses—and get the buckboard ready—and get the saddle horses ready, too. I'll find the governor and bring him out as fast as I can. But be ready, Soapy."

"Mr. Hale, I'm gunna be right on the spot, now and always!"

"I'll tell you this one reason to make you hurry: The thing that made me start down the street was just a breath of rumor that Mike Jarvin's Soapy was in town and raising the devil. If they have coupled you and Jarvin together—and if some people are guessing that Jarvin is in town, this may be a very serious affair! Jarvin is not supposed to risk taking the air so far away from his home!" He said this with another smile.

Soapy blinked and ran away toward the stable. He was beginning to see the other sides of this unlucky matter, and there were so many of those sides that it fairly made his head spin to contemplate them. They had linked him with Jarvin, then. They had recognized him. He recalled some of the ringside shouts. Yes, they had accused him of throwing the fight away on a foul, so that his master could win crooked bets.

It seemed that one could fall into other dangers than those which one actually deserved, and, for the first time in his life, a feeling of innocence went through the soul of the negro.

He found the boy he had paid to watch the horses soundly asleep at the edge of the fence, with the horses almost trampling upon him. Some of the new-found virtue melted from Soapy, and he raised the boy by the nape of the neck and kicked him into outer darkness. Then he secured the heads of the team, which had so luckily been kept from falling into some mischief or other, and he went to the saddle horses.

They were refreshed enough by their few hours of rest, to all appearance. And Larribee was lying down—a sure sign that he would be practically as strong as ever when wanted. He prepared them hastily for immediate use and returned to the buckboard, to find that the cripple was waiting for him there.

"Have you seen Jarvin?" he asked.

"Not here," said Soapy.

"He's not at the hotel," said Peter in some trouble.

"Let him go and be cursed," said Soapy. "This here is a time for us to be saving our own hides, Mr. Hale."

He saw the hand of Peter raised to check him, and therefore he pointed anxiously toward the street.

"What's that crowd of folks gathering out yonder for, Mr. Hale?"

"I understand you," replied Peter. "But I won't budge from the town without another search for Jarvin. Perhaps the old scoundrel has got into some new trouble and had to vanish suddenly."

He went back to the hotel, and the mulatto waited in great concern at the heads of the horses. For the crowd which he had pointed out in the street had now grown. And yonder was some one on a bench, making a speech to them. Only an occasional word reached the ears of Soapy, but he knew that when a crowd stands patiently to be harangued by a leader, there is danger in the air. So it seemed to be gathering now, and he could hardly watch them without turning cold with bitter fear.

In the meantime, Peter had found a clew, as he was turning onto the veranda of the hotel again.

"Have you seen," he began, addressing a passing cow-puncher, "a fat fellow, rather oldish, with big—"

"You mean Jarvin, don't you?" asked the other,

turning upon him with a cold eye. "You're one of Jarvin's men, ain't you?"

"Perhaps," said Peter, growing a little red. "Do you know where he is?"

The cattleman had already turned away, letting fall over his shoulder: "No, I dunno that I know where he is."

The hand of Peter caught his shoulder, and he spun around—and did not draw his Colt. He was very near to the verge of drawing his gun, but he changed his mind, for certain wild rumors were now flying thick and fast about the manner in which the cripple had rescued the giant mulatto from the hands of numbers. One of those rumors had lodged in the ears of the cow-puncher. So, though he hated Jarvin with the clean man's loathing of the unclean, yet he looked upon "Jarvin's man" with more respect.

"He's back yonder at the other hotel. He's sitting in at a poker game—but maybe he won't be sitting long."

And as he spoke he pointed with a somewhat malicious grin in the direction of a cluster of men who were hurrying down the street.

Others trailed behind them, and well to the rear came the less aggressive element in the crowd. Just what they were headed for Peter did not know for certain, but he very shrewdly guessed. And he knew that this pack had been already fought and rebuffed. So he feared for the worst, if a crash came!

Chapter XXXV
ON A RAIL

Now that the grip of big Peter had relaxed, the cow-puncher withdrew his shoulder deftly and hurried on into the hotel. But Peter watched events maturing with a wonderful speed down the street, where the crowd was formed in a thick mass before the hotel. Some of its leaders were entering. If they were indeed bent on the capture of big Mike Jarvin, how sadly would events go for that worthy, captured by such a throng, in such a humor!

Peter, himself, was in no little danger. Behind him he overheard a murmur of voices:

"Are they overlooking the big stiff on the crutches?"

"What about him?"

"He's been wandering around the town, bashing gents over the head with that crutch of his. Besides, he's one of the Jarvin outfit!"

"The devil he is! Is Jarvin picking up his men from the hospitals, maybe?"

"Jarvin has him, and that's enough to make any man with good sense lay odds that he's a crook and a bad one. I'd like to know how he got wrecked. That's what I'd like to know, old pal! I'll lay my bet that it would make a story that would interest some of us, including the sheriff!"

"If he belongs to Jarvin, why don't they round him up?"

"Yes, and it was him who pulled that Soapy out of the hands of the boys—when they was about to give him a lesson that his yellow hide would never forget."

These remarks were never intended to be heard by Peter, but his ears were supernaturally acute on this evening. He heard this, and he heard, moreover, that there was much talk of taking big Mike Jarvin and riding him on a rail, after his capture—and then trying him for various and sundry crimes which were laid against him, including even that old but unforgotten death of Sam Debney! Assuredly, the air of this town was growing hot for Mike and for his protégés.

Peter waited to hear no more. It was reasonably certain that that crowd meant the torment of Jarvin. And, richly as Mike might have deserved trouble, still he was the patron of Peter, and Peter had been hired to protect his skin. So he swung himself about on his crutches and he went back behind the hotel to the stable, where Soapy waited with the horses—a very nervous Soapy, whose teeth glinted in his wide mouth as he spoke.

"It's the boss, ain't it, Mr. Hale?"

"It's Jarvin, right enough. They've gone down there to get Mike at the next hotel. What can we do, the pair of us, to help him?"

It amazed Soapy to hear his master ask such a question—he who had shown such godlike powers. But apparently here was something beyond even the hands of big Peter Hale.

So Soapy said with much fervor: "Mr. Hale, it looks

to me like the right and reasonable thing for us two to do is to get right out of this here town. As you say, what can we do for old Jarvin by staying in here? Nothing but get throwed into the same jail that's he's put into. Or get our necks stretched on the same rope alongside of his. Because these folks is fractious. I heard some cow-punchers going by a minute ago and talking big and bad about a lynching—laying down that it would do a power of good to the town to have a real, first-class lynching here, y'understand?"

"I understand." Peter sighed. "And that's exactly the atmosphere that I've been guessing at in the place. And so, Soapy, of course, we can't desert him."

"Jarvin?"

"No."

"Curse him! He'd desert us quick enough!"

"We didn't hire him to take care of us," said Peter mildly. "You must never forget that."

"Humph!" said the mulatto. "I dunno that I foller your line of thinking, Mr. Hale, but I'd just as soon be throwed into the corral, yonder, with that flock of wild Nevada hosses, as to get laid hold of by that crowd again. They was only playing when they first met up with me. But, believe me, they'd be in earnest now!"

"They would, and they'd be in deadly earnest. However—something—"

His voice died away. For, down the street, they could see where the crowd had surged with a sudden violence straight into the hotel. In another moment there was a distinct sound of crashing and splintering.

"There goes a door down!" said Soapy through his set teeth.

Instantly the crowd pressed back from the hotel into the street—and there was the form of a bulky man dandled high and light upon their shoulders, with many an angry hand reaching for him. It was Jarvin; the angry roar of the crowd testified to that. Jarvin! Jarvin! They would have the truth of his wickedness out of him, and they would tear him to rags and to tatters.

But who needed to wait for his confession? Did not every sensible man really sense the truth about this matter? Of course—and, therefore, let them live up to the standards which their ancestors set when they had brought law and order into a wild land! So thought the crowd, and Peter Hale, reading their minds, watched their numbers and their fury grow with every instant.

Now that Jarvin was in their hands, every one wanted to join himself to the list of the men of justice. And yonder was a rail for the taking. It was of new, strong wood. And it was nailed into oaken posts with strong, new spikes, countersunk.

But so many hands laid hold upon the three-by-six beam that it was torn away as though it were nothing. And now Jarvin was mounted a little higher, perhaps, than any horse had ever carried him; certainly upon the most narrow saddle.

Twenty willing shoulders crowded under the stick. And Jarvin was brought along with a swelling voice of triumph that made even the wild Nevada horses tremble and quake in their corrals. They were a grim-looking lot of horses, having been brought down by some venturesome horse dealers for men who wanted tough saddle animals—tough in both spirit and flesh. But there was too much devil in these creatures to make much of a sale possible, and there still remained fifty of the brutes in the corral, rolling their eyes and flattening their ears as they heard the roaring voices of men. Peter, observing them, felt that here was a chance for him to either kill his employer outright or else to set him free.

He said to the negro: "Soapy, stand by on this side of the road. I'm going to let those horses out. When they come piling through the gate, start shooting and yelling—shooting with both hands and yelling as loudly as you can. Do you understand?"

"Mr. Hale, you ain't gunna fool with those wild horses, are you?"

"Will you do what I ask?"

"Yes, sir, I will!"

Peter left him and reached the lofty corral fence, while the throng of horses shrank from him and then rushed closer along the fence with a perverse desire to catch him with their teeth. He shot back the bolt and let the gate swing wide with a screech of rusty hinges, as their breasts pressed it back. Instantly they had bulged out into the street.

There stood Soapy. From either hand issued a series of rapid explosions as he waved his flaming guns above his head, and from his throat was poured out a

230

dreadful series of wails and yells. The mustangs recoiled from this fire-breathing monster. They swayed this way and then that, and finally they surged, with snorting and squealing, straight down the street toward the avenging crowd which was riding Jarvin on a rail to a just trial and a quick vengeance for his ill deeds. With their heads and tails tossing, and the dust flying around them, the horses ran.

Peter saw Mike Jarvin disappear from the rail on which he was carried. No doubt he was dropped straight into the dust as the men who had carried him bolted for their lives.

And now Peter shouted: "Back to the buckboard, Soapy! Back as fast as you can fly, man!"

Soapy flew. He reached the buckboard fast and leaped into the seat. But he had hardly gained it before the cripple swung past him on the crutches. The saddle horses were tethered at the back of the buckboard. Two of these—Larribee and Jarvin's own horse—were detached by Peter. He swung into the saddle on Larribee just as the wagon gathered headway. And Soapy did not need to be told what to do. He knew that Peter intended to take a most desperate chance, and to take it right at the heels of that fighting, smashing herd of wild horses. Therefore he loosed the reins on that fresh mustang team and gave them the whip. They flew forward at a gallop, into the thick dust cloud which the wild horses had raised.

Peter himself was not far behind, gaining with every

sweep of the long legs of Larribee. And now, before him, he saw a thing that he had half expected but had not wholly dared to believe might happen. A solitary man was waddling toward them, up the street, as fast as he could leg it, with a swinging glimmer of steel shining from either hand.

That was none other than big Mike Jarvin, rushing for safety up the street, and ready, now, to be killed before he would let himself be taken.

Chapter XXXVI

"YOU CAN'T FAZE HIM!"

There were no figures of men lying in the street; Peter Hale could thank the Providence which had whisked them out of danger as the herd of horses roared by. But that charge had accomplished its purpose admirably. The crowd, so solidly formed and so intent on its purpose, had been torn to shreds and scattered here and there in doorways, on verandas, and behind picket fences.

In the meantime, here was Jarvin, who had torn himself clear and was bolting for safety. He saw the familiar buckboard with Soapy at the helm and started for it with a shrill scream of satisfaction. But others had seen the coming rescue and had fixed their minds on the destruction of Mike. Even wild horses could not tear the idea away from them.

A big man ran out from a doorway—a tall, clean-cut

fellow, poising his gun. Peter spurred Larribee ahead, and the great horse took wings, leaving the buckboard behind. The big man ahead fired. Mike Jarvin's gun flashed in response, and then Peter struck the tall fellow and rode him down—not under the hoofs of the great stallion, but striking him in straight-arm, football fashion. And as his victim went down with a shout and rolled headlong in the dust, Peter saw that it was his own cousin, Charles, whom he had felled in this summary fashion.

He had time for one mental commentary—which was that it was very odd that Charles should be so hot for the death of a man who, so far as Charles could know, had most generously returned to him a whole fortune won at the cards earlier in the evening. However, there seemed to be many qualities in Charles that were a matter for wonder.

In the meantime, people were pouring out into the street in increasing numbers, but Mike Jarvin had reached the buckboard and had pulled himself up into it. And now Soapy was whipping the mustangs into a frantic gallop.

Peter reined hastily back to the side of the flying wagon, for in the hands of Mike he saw the short, terrible, two-barreled shotgun. If that weapon were ever discharged into the faces of such a crowd as this, there was no telling how many men would go to the last accounting. It would be hanging for Mike, afterward. It would be hanging for Peter and Soapy, also.

So Peter shouted in stentorian tones: "Mike, if you

233

fire that gun, I'll drive a bullet through your head. Remember!"

Mike, his face convulsed with fury, cast one dreadful glance at Peter and even waved the muzzles of his weapon toward the big rider. He returned no other response, but, standing braced in front of the seat, like a sailor who defies the lurching of his ship, Jarvin turned his shotgun first to this side and then to that.

This crowd that had regathered was not composed of fools. They knew what such a gun meant, and they scattered back toward their houses with yells of consternation. There were perhaps half a dozen shots fired, but they were wild. Only one weapon was being fired by a steady hand, and that was held by a man who was posted on the steps of the general-merchandise store. His hat had been lost in the confusion, and the wind fanned back his silvery hair. Peter had only a glimpse of it through the same dust clouds which were doubtless saving the lives of all three from this marksman. Twice bullets whistled from the man's gun close by the head of Peter; three times leaden slugs tore through the body of the buckboard, luckily missing man and horse.

But that was the last danger, as they hurtled around the next bend of the street and headed out onto the road toward the creek. That was the last danger—for the moment. In a few seconds they would be mounting and riding hard behind them.

In the meantime, here was old Jarvin, tilting the

familiar black bottle at his lips and then passing it to Soapy. Yet Soapy, standing up to lash the horses to a great frenzy of speed, disregarded liquor for the first time in his life. He was literally garbed in flying tatters, rather than in clothes. And the bellow of his exultant voice came back like a dim thunder to Peter.

"I smashed 'em! I made 'em take water! I backed 'em into the last ditch and made 'em holler when I jumped in their faces. I was ten wild cats. I was a roarin' grizzly! Oh, Mike, you should of been there to of seen what I did to them."

And the booming voice of Mike Jarvin roared in answer: "I'm glad you trimmed 'em, kid. But what was that compared to what I did to 'em? Made suckers of the lot of them! I would of quit after the first time. I had enough cash after that bout—but that sucker Hale sneaked it away from me! So I went back, Soapy. I sat in on another game. Why, it was taking candy away from babies. Except that these here babies wore whiskers and packed tons of Colts. I fished the coin out of their pockets and made them like it.

"Dog-gone me if they didn't think that I was losing, for a time. And then they begun to tumble to the fact that my 'luck' appeared in the losing of the small bets and the winning of the big ones. I'm salted down with money, Soapy. I got forty thousand in my wallet, pretty near. A hundred thousand, by rights—but that sucker Hale—" He broke off to take another drink, and then, forgetting his anger at Peter, his voice pitched into thundering song.

For all their exultation, Soapy was still lashing the horses, and Peter rode half turned in the saddle, constantly watching the winding bit of road behind him.

Now that the dust of the town was gone, and they had clean countryside behind them, the moonlight flooded everything with its own brilliant silver. The town, in the distance, was a mean huddle of shadows, surprisingly small to have held all the excitement which had been foaming up and down its streets that night.

Out of the larger darkness of the village other, smaller shadows crept out and wound down the trail behind them. Peter knew what those creeping shadows were. They were raging, cursing, spurring horsemen, mounted on their best nags and determined to ride them into the ground, to capture the fugitive trio.

How vast would be the disgrace of the town if it were to be told, hereafter, how three men had dared to beat up their best citizens and then had been able to rescue one of their members from the hands of count-less odds and whisk away to safety!

They were spurring hard for matters of personal honor—and for the honor of their town and the range around it. Besides that, how many in that scurrying party had felt the weight of the negro's fist or had lost money to the hated Jarvin? They had motives in plenty, and presently Peter could see that they were gaining fast. The mustangs ran well, rattling the buck-

board over the rough road. It was not in the horses'
power, hampered as they were by harness and the dan-
gling, banging weight behind them, to match the
speed which their pursuers were showing. Watching
the rate at which the townsmen gained, Peter sent Larribee swinging up beside the wagon.

"You hear me, Jarvin?"

"I hear ye, Pete, me lad," answered Jarvin, "and I
drink to you, too. I thought, after you trimmed me of
that money which I'd earned by a lot of honest, hard
work at the cards—I thought that you and me would
never be friends again. But, curse you, Peter, you
knock a man down one minute and you pick him up
the next—pick him right away from a thousand pairs
of hands, at that! Oh, lad, that trick of the wild
horses—that was better than any that I've ever worked
at cards, and yet I've trained and worked with the
pasteboard all my life."

"Will you be quiet, Jarvin? Look back down the
road, if you think that you're out of this mess. Look
back and see them coming. A hundred of them if
there's one. A hundred lions, at that!"

The fat man braced himself in front of the seat and
stood up, the better to scan the scene behind them.

"It's true." Jarvin shuddered, and he shook his fist at
them. "They'll get to know the insides of this pal of
mine, before the night is over. They're hungry and
hankering after it, and they're bound to get it, I tell
you!"

"Do you think that would do anything except hurry

up your hanging by a few seconds? Look again and try to see the facts. Those fellows are coming too fast for us to get clear of them."

"Then we'll take to the horses. What have we got saddles along with us for?"

"Fast horses for two of us—but what about Soapy on his nag?"

"Curse it, Hale, would you put my neck inside of a rope for the sake of a negro? Keep your hands from me, Soapy, or I'll blow you to the devil!"

As the great hand of Soapy darted to Mike's throat, Jarvin pitched the double muzzle of his terrible gun into the midriff of the negro—and Soapy's hand gradually relaxed and recoiled.

"There are three of us here," said Peter. "There's going to be three of us saved, or three of us who go down together. That's flat and final. Do you hear me, Jarvin?"

The other turned a desperate face toward Peter and then leered down the road at the group of streaking shadows. They had grown rapidly in clearness. Now across the face of a little hill they streaked in a rapid procession—an endless string of clear-cut silhouettes against the moonlit sky.

"All right," said Jarvin. "I'll stick by you—if you'll stick by me. But God knows what we'll do."

The hoofs of the horses beat hollow on the narrow little bridge, and beneath them they caught a glimpse of the river, like polished ebony, with the high light of the moon striking across its surface.

"Pull up, Soapy," shouted Peter. "Pull up, man, do you hear?"

Soapy obediently drew rein.

"Are you crazy, Pete?" yelled Jarvin.

But Peter was calmly dismounting from his horse.

"Listen to me, Soapy," gasped Jarvin. "He's lost his head. I'll sink a bullet through him. Then you and me—on the two fast horses—for the sake of our necks, Soapy—"

"You fool!" Soapy sneered. "D'you think that you and me—yes, or that whole crowd back there—could faze him?"

Chapter XXXVII

OUTWITTING THE PURSUERS

Of one thing in the world Mr. Jarvin was sure—that Soapy, the mulatto, was the incarnation of all that was wicked in the world, of all that was hard and self-centered. But this speech seemed to indicate an almost superstitious respect for the will and the opinion of big Peter Hale. It was most strange to Jarvin. He could not make it out. In the meantime, as the panting mustangs came to a halt, he could distinctly hear the flints in the roadway ringing under the volleying hoofs of that approaching mob of destroyers.

"Get out of that buckboard!" came the order of Peter.

Jarvin started—as though a gun had been pointed at

him—and he obeyed. Soapy was already on the ground, and Peter herded them back to the edge of the bridge.

"He's going to hold us up!" murmured Jarvin with a groan, at the ear of Soapy. "He's going to hold us here under his guns and then turn us over to that lynching gang—to pay for his own sweet hide."

"Shut up!" snarled Soapy. "You're drunk!"

And he faced his master in silence, turning his massive shoulders upon Mr. Jarvin.

"Now," said Peter with a maddening deliberation, "it's plain that we can't ride away from those fellows. And since we can't ride away from them, we've got to stop them. And the only place where we can stop them and insure our escape is at this bridge."

"Hold 'em at the bridge. Sure, the three of us could hold them all night!" cried the cheerful Soapy.

"And be shot to pieces when the morning came?" put in Jarvin. "You're talking a fine brand of sense, Hale!"

Said Peter: "This is our only chance. We stop them at the bridge, or we're dead men! Now let's see if the bridge won't do a little work for us!"

"What the devil are you talking about, Hale?"

Even Soapy was staring at his master now, bewildered and rather frightened.

"Come down under the bridge with me," said Peter and swung himself down in the lead.

They followed. By the slanting moonshine, they could see that the bridge rested, at this end, on two massive boulders.

"Now," said Peter, "we roll away one of those boulders and let the bridge slide into the river—or else we hang before morning. Is that clear?"

They looked at Peter, raised their heads and looked back down the moon-whitened strip of road at the approaching shadows, and then they laid their hands upon the boulder. They were three mighty men, to be sure, but the time-lodged and rugged weight of that great stone merely shuddered under their effort.

There was a snarl from Soapy.

"Lemme get under there and get my back agin that stone!" he said.

He lay flat, his feet against the bank, his legs bunched slightly, his heavy shoulders against the stone.

"Now!" said Soapy.

And as they tugged in unison, at the first strain he drove his great feet deep into the soft dirt. There they found firm grip. Then all the might of his body gradually came into play—not suddenly, for he was not one to bring all his forces to their highest development in a single effort—but little by little his power increased. The rugged face of the stone was grinding through his shoulder muscles and cutting against the bone; and they could hear him groaning with his agony, but still he heaved relentlessly. And the other two, inspired by his patient might, redoubled their efforts.

The stone trembled; there was a slight sliding, and

suddenly it bulged straight out from its socket, hurtling down the slope. It barely missed Peter, it brushed past Jarvin. And the bridge sloped and settled with a jar on this side, seemingly straight down upon the prostrate form of the negro, while the great rock leaped from the edge of the bank, crashed against the farther rock wall, and then fell with rebounding thunders, until it raised a mighty crashing in the water beneath, and they saw a white leaping of the foam where it had struck.

But Soapy?

"He's done!" cried Jarvin. "And good riddance. You and me, Pete, my lad—"

But Peter held him to the work. Their united strength budged that edge of the fallen bridge a little. And forth from the darkness crawled Soapy, snarling and gasping:

"I think there was a spider that dropped down my throat. Gimme a drink, Jarvin."

"We have something else to do besides drinking, Soapy," said Peter. "We wanted your hand to start the bridge sliding. Look there! All the planks that fastened it have been torn loose by that fall—now heave together!"

Together they heaved with a will. The bridge strained with a great groaning; then it slid forward, and Peter, losing his foothold, dropped fairly into its path. He had no chance to raise himself, and the sliding, ponderous mass of the bridge would have swept him straight into the dizzy void of the cañon.

But there was a stronger hand than his own that reached for him and plucked him lightly out to safety.

And Soapy chuckled. "Bridges, they ain't afraid even of you, Mr. Hale!"

So Peter, with his hand fixed in a kindly grip upon the bulging shoulder muscles of Soapy, watched the bridge stagger and then slide past the edge of the ravine. With a great tearing and rendering sound, the farther side of the bridge tore loose from its anchorage and kicked high in the air. Then the whole ruin shot down toward the stream.

The three of them hurried back to their horses. But there was no hurry. Three jumps of the horses brought them into the screening shadows of some low-growing trees, and as they jogged up the hillside, they could look back and see the dark mass of the riders raging up and down the brink of the ravine. And there were no means of crossing. No horse could ever have lived, going down that rigid-faced cliff.

All the pursuers could do was to wheel away, with a yell of hate and rage, and speed toward the nearest bridge, many a long mile away—or perhaps to some closer crossing. They would never catch the fugitives on this night; that much was perfectly certain. By the time their racing horses had completed the circuit, the three would be far, far away—toward the mine and the safety which awaited them there.

It was a jovial journey for both, but not for Peter. All the way, with his head bowed, he listened vaguely to the stream of wild language and of thundering praises which issued in his honor from the lips of the pair. As Soapy diligently pointed out, both Jarvin and he had been more than once saved during this expedition by the might of their new ally.

Toward morning, Jarvin dozed on the seat. He wakened in the gray of the dawn with a start. "Hey, Peter!"

Peter Hale rode closer to the wagon.

"Peter, I dreamed that I was fighting off snakes—and your hand reached down—a thousand miles out of nothing—and yanked me back to safety. Peter, bless you, what would have happened to me without you?"

It needed no answer, and Peter did not attempt one. So they journeyed on. In the middle of the morning they made a halt to rest the staggering horses and to sleep themselves. It was late in the afternoon before they reached the mine.

Telegraph and telephone had done their work, in the meantime.

They found a tall, spare-bodied man walking up and down in front of Jarvin's shack. And they found a grinning, excited group of miners waiting and watching.

"It's Will Nast!" gasped Jarvin, when he saw the stranger. "What does he want here?"

But Will Nast was not in an ugly humor, apparently. He waved his hand to them most cheerfully and then stood with his hand dropped on his hip, while the wind fanned his coat open and showed the sparkling face of his sheriff's badge beneath.

"Well, boys," said he, "it was a pretty good party, eh?"

They nodded to him in silence and waited like pupils before a teacher.

"As for you, Soapy, I s'pose that you'll be heading for the regular prize ring, before long. Matter of fact, I've often wondered why you didn't land there before. Easier money than this in the ring, Soapy—and not so crooked, either!"

Soapy grunted and stepped back—highly pleased to be dismissed in this fashion.

"Jarvin," said the sheriff, "you card sharper and sneaking rat—you miserable low hulk and scoundrel, I've been hoping that the time would come when I could get my hands on you, with any fair excuse. And when the first reports of this mess came in, I thought that the time had surely come.

"But it seems that I was wrong. All wrong! There are no dead men back there, after all. You're only a shade more famous. And there are only a few more shadows connected with you—a few more suspicions that you've been cheating at cards, eh?"

He turned his back on Mike Jarvin—a most daring thing was that, considering what he had just said. But Mike Jarvin was one who never struck in the day—when there were witnesses standing by. Though his face swelled and turned purple, he did not budge his hand.

"Now," said the sheriff to Peter, "I think that it's time for you to go back home with me, Peter Hale. What do *you* think?"

"I have a working agreement with Mr. Jarvin," said

Peter. "Are you willing to let me go, Jarvin?"

Jarvin snapped his fingers high above his head, with a brutal laugh. "Let you go? Say, Nast, when did you ever hear of Mike Jarvin throwing a handful of diamonds into the sea? And what's diamonds to me, compared with Hale. Will you tell me that?"

Said the sheriff: "Ah, Pete, what the devil has come over you? Why did you do it?"

"I'll tell you in one word," said Peter. "It's a thing that would land me behind the bars, sheriff."

The keen eye of Will Nast sharpened and shone. "Is it really as bad as that?"

"Yes."

"Then I've heard enough. But walk along here with me. I've some things to tell you about your father."

Chapter XXXVIII

A LETTER

The screen door of the McNair house slammed loudly as Charles Hale stepped out onto the front veranda. There sat Mr. McNair, with his chair tilted back against the wall and his heels hooked over a lower rung. He did not turn his head, but he said:

"Well, Charlie, you had some luck, today?"

"Ah, sir," said Charlie, "how did you guess that?"

"I see that you're full of talk," said McNair. "So go ahead."

"Why, sir, she's set the day."

"Who?"

"Ruth, Mr. McNair."

"You don't tell me!" said the father, and while he yawned, his eyes wandered carelessly over the face and form of his prospective son-in-law.

"Yes," said Charles. "If it meets with your approval—for next Friday."

"Quick, ain't she, once she sets her mind on a thing?"

Charles coughed. "Unless you have objections—"

"Me? Why should I have objections? *I* don't have to marry you."

Charles, very red, fell silent.

He said at last: "I'll be going along, then."

"So long, Charlie."

"But," said Charles, turning suddenly back, "it's wonderful that she should have changed her mind so suddenly when—" He paused.

"When you thought she was setting herself to marry Peter, eh?"

"Why—" began Charles.

"I'll tell you," said the rancher, "your cousin has gone and got himself so famous that she's proud to marry into his family. I guess that that's the reason for her change of mind. Eh?"

"As a matter of fact," said Charles, "I presumed—I mean, I guessed—"

"That Peter had shut himself out of the picture by raising so much deviltry over at Lawson Creek? Is that what you thought?"

"You might know, sir."

"I know a little about my girl," said McNair. "But I don't know that she's so measly and mean as to turn down a he-man, just because he's proved that he can fight better on wooden legs than most folks can on their own pins."

Charles, abashed, withdrew straightway, for he felt, somehow, that this was not his day to draw pleasant speeches from the father of Ruth. He mounted his horse and, as he rode up the road, he encountered Ross Hale riding hard toward him. They drew rein with a jerk.

"Is there any news with you, Charlie?" asked his uncle wearily, his eyes turning impatiently forward to the McNair house.

"Not much," said Charles, "except that I'm to marry Ruth on Friday."

And he rode on, smiling at the white face of Ross Hale. The latter remained for a moment, stunned. Then he let his horse wander slowly on until it paused automatically at the McNair hitching rack.

"You got a touch of sun, Ross?" sang out McNair.

Ross dismounted and went to the veranda.

"Now what's on your mind?" asked McNair. "I hear that you been thinking of buying the Weston forty acres next to your black land?"

"I was thinking about that, maybe." Ross Hale sighed. "Matter of fact—" He fell again into his sad daydream.

"Set down and rest yourself," said the rancher gently.

But Hale did not appear to understand.

Said McNair, still in the same, soothing tone: "Have you been hearing any news, Ross?"

"No news. He stays up yonder."

He turned his eyes toward the blue hills and squinted through the heat waves, while his hand slowly drew a letter from his pocket.

"That's from Peter, then?"

"Yes, it's from my Peter."

"He's making out pretty well, then?"

"He says that he's feeling fit."

The heavy silence fell between them again. Mr. McNair stirred in his seat. "Perhaps it's Ruth that you want?"

Hale started. "Matter of fact, I do."

"Ring the bell and send one of the negroes for her."

So Ross Hale rang the bell, and still like a man standing in a dream he gave his message to the servant. There was a little pause, and after a minute, feet hurrying on the stairs inside—and then a drawling voice:

"Miss Ruth, she says that she's mighty sorry—she's got a terrible headache. Can't even stand up. Would you give me a message for her?"

"Hey!" yelled McNair.

The servant jumped. "Yes, Mr. McNair?"

"Go up and fetch down that fool girl, will you? *I* want her, y'understand?"

Footsteps scurried away inside the house.

"Why," said Hale, "I ain't wanting to drag down Ruth if she's sick, old man."

"Don't you talk foolish, Ross. Set down and rest yourself. Have a chew? No? You still keep to them cigarettes, eh? I tell you what I got against cigarettes. So dirty. Always spilling tobacco dust all over a man while he smokes. A good, clean chew—that's what I take to. I been watching that hawk, over yonder, hanging over the Mitchell chicken yard. Ain't it a pretty thing, Ross, the way that it sails up agin the wind?"

There was no answer from Ross Hale. Still like a stricken man he turned his worn face toward the distant blueness of the hills, and where their lower ranges turned brown as they advanced nearer. There his gaze fastened, and he sighed again.

Other footfalls sounded, and then the screen door creaked.

"Did you send for me, dad? Hello, Mr. Hale! How's things over your way?"

"Fair," said Ross Hale, looking blankly at her.

"A terrible headache—" began the girl faintly.

"Shut up that fool clatter, Ruth, will you?" broke in her father. "Here's the dad of the mightiest he-man and two-gun fighter that's been in the range for a long time. Here he's given you the honor of coming over to call on you, and you let a headache stand between you and a talk with him? You fetch him into the house and give him a cup of coffee, and set him down where it's cool. He's got something terrible important to say to you, and terrible private, too!"

There was nothing left for the girl to do. She ushered

Ross Hale into the dim coolness of the parlor and obediently brought him a cup of coffee. But he let it steam unregarded on the table beside his chair. The letter was still in his hand.

"Is it something about that letter?" asked Ruth at last.

"Ah?" murmured the other. "Letter? Well, well!" His mind drifted away again and returned to him with: "I been seeing Charles—" He paused and looked wistfully at her.

"Yes," said Ruth McNair, coloring a little.

"Why," said Ross Hale, "Charlie is a right fine boy."

He was silent again, and suddenly Ruth stood up and slipped into a chair close beside his chair. She took his great, gnarled hand in both of her tender ones.

"You didn't come all the way over here to talk about Charles, I think."

"Why, honey, no, I didn't. But you see—"

He stumbled again and paused to search the brightness of her eyes and to wonder at the tears in them. "Now, the truth of it is that I once had hopes. No matter about what. I've come over here, wondering if you'd help me, Ruth?"

"Yes," said she, "with all my heart!"

"Would you tell me, first—was it that affair over to the creek?"

She nodded, and looked down. But then she forced herself to meet his gaze.

"Oh, I understand," said Ross Hale. "The things that

he done there would be enough to scare any girl."

"If he would write to me," she broke out. "If he'd give me any explanation—but just to go away—and suddenly begin to go rushing around the country with that beast, that Jarvin; oh, Uncle Ross, how could I stand it? Sitting here at home—and not knowing—and eating my heart out."

"Ah, yes," said the rancher. "That's it. Eating the heart out. Good heavens, how lonesome a house can be! Worse than a grave, a lot! There was a time when I was sorry for the dead folks. But that was when I was young. But speaking about Peter, you know, there's no power that I got over him. I've wrote and I've wrote. And back comes the answers, always gentle and nice."

He paused again.

"Yes?" whispered the girl.

"Well, sir," murmured the father, "it's a funny thing, what a bad hand he writes—and him a college graduate. With honors, you know! You look here how bad he writes down this address!"

He showed the envelope.

"Yes," gasped Ruth. "Oh—"

And she burst into a flood of tears.

Chapter XXXIX

"HIS FRIENDS"

Ross went back to the veranda and sat down, in more of a stupor than ever. For half an hour no word passed between his host and him. Finally McNair remarked:

"You didn't have a long talk with Ruth, old-timer."

Said Ross Hale: "You can't ask a girl to cry and talk at the same time, can you?"

"Cry about what?" said Mr. McNair.

"I don't know," murmured Mr. Hale. "I was showing her this letter, and just remarking on how bad my boy writes—"

His voice trailed away, and Mr. McNair offered no further comment. But for another hour, his keen eyes rolled from time to time toward the face of his guest. Finally the other rose. And leaning a moment against the wooden pillar which supported the veranda roof, he remarked:

"This here is the first good, long talk that we've had in quite a spell, Mac. I'll have to be going."

"So long," said McNair and fell to whittling a stick. "Come over and tell me all the news again, some time soon," said he, as Ross Hale mounted his horse.

But he did not look up from his whittling until his friend was a small dust cloud disappearing down the road.

"Watching a gent out of sight is bad luck," said Mr. McNair.

That night he sat at a silent dinner table.

When he came to pie—there was always pie for Mr. McNair at least twice a day—he remarked:

"You been going outside without no hat on, Ruth. That's what I call throwing away money."

"I don't know what you mean," said the faint voice of Ruth.

"Your eyes is all red," said McNair, his voice muffled by his mouthful. "Chop me off another wedge of that pie, will you?"

She obeyed.

"Why do you say it's throwing money away, father?"

"Which?" he snapped.

"Dad, I mean," she corrected herself.

"Why, you send away for a fancy lot of cold creams and smear 'em all over your face and get good and greasy, and start in to turn white like bleached cloth. Getting complexion, is what you call turning sickly, like that. And then here you go out in the sun and get reddened up again—waste of time and money, I call it!"

"It wasn't the sun, really," said the girl.

"Hey?"

"I was—I had a headache," said she.

"Does a headache make red eyes?"

"Perhaps it was neuralgia," she suggested hopefully, looking down at her plate.

"Not in this here weather—not neuralgia. Guess again."

"The fact is, dad, that I was a little upset."

"By what?"

She was silent, biting her lip in thought.

Her father smashed his great hand on the table and roared: "Upset, how?"

"I—I think I may have cried a little."

"Ho! Cried? About what?"

"Mr. Hale upset me a little."

"He did, hey?" said the father, pushing back his chair. "Dog-gone me if I ain't gunna go to the telephone and ring him up and give him a piece of my mind."

"No, no, dad!"

He rose and turned toward the door. "I'm gunna let Ross Hale know what I think of him!"

There was a flurry of skirts; a hand caught his arm. "No, dad, please!"

"What the devil does Ross Hale mean?" he cried.

"It was only a letter, really."

"What business has he writing letters to you?"

"Not from him—I mean—he showed me a letter."

"About what, then?"

"From Peter," whispered the girl.

"What did Peter have to say, Ruth?"

"Nothing. I don't know. I only saw the address."

"Go back and sit down," said her father. "I understand all about it."

She returned willingly enough to her chair, and he to his second piece of pie.

"I see just what's been bothering you, honey. Here

you go and get yourself engaged to a fine, upstanding young gent like Charlie Hale, eh?"

Her head bowed suddenly.

"And then along comes somebody and reminds you of all the bad blood that there is in the Hale family—"

"Bad blood?" interrupted the girl, lifting her head in surprise.

"Oh, I know all about the way that you feel," said McNair gently. "A girl, when she wants to marry, has got to begin to think about the sort of children that she'll have. And now suppose that your children, they was to turn out like you and Charlie. Why, that would be fine and we wouldn't ask for no more than that. But what's the facts? That behind Charlie there is a lot of bad blood that might be inherited, and the first thing that you know, you would be raising children so dog-gone mean and wicked and bad that it would about bust your heart. I know that's what you're thinking about, Ruth."

"No, no!" she protested. "That wasn't—"

"Don't you tell me," said her father, "because I know! I can see right through that wise little head of yours. Thinking about nothing but the future. That's what you're doing, old girl! And suppose that one of your sons was to turn out like Peter!"

He threw up his hands, rolled up his eyes, and shook his head in great consternation. But when he looked at her again he found that she was sitting stiff and straight with a certain fire in her eye which he had often seen there before—in her—and in his own mirror!

Said she: "I don't see just what you're driving at. Because I don't really see what's wrong with Peter Hale."

"What!"

She sat stiffer than ever. "Well?" she snapped.

He relaxed into sneering irony. "You don't see anything wrong with him? Well, honey, I do! In a gent that stands up and shoots down other gents—"

"Who has he ever killed?" asked his daughter sharply.

"Look here—would you deny, Ruth, that he's a gun fighter?"

She hesitated, and her eyes shifted. "He is not the only man who wears guns in this range, and you know it, dad!"

"Guns? Ornaments, that's all that they are," said her father with an airy wave of his hand. "Friendly ornaments. That's all. Look at the way I'm peaceable and plumb—"

"Dad! Why, it was only three years ago—"

"You mean that Indian from Okla—"

"And before that, only two years, when you—"

"You mean that overbearing, cross-eyed, mean, trouble-making gent from New York? It was only because—"

"And every time that you went away when I was little—wasn't my mother frightened almost to death? And just for fear that you would get into a gun fight before you—"

"Now, your ma was a good woman, Ruth. But flighty and scary was no name for what she was. Just naturally, she had more nerves than she could use."

"Besides," said Ruth, "what Peter did in Lawson Creek was just—just—brave!"

"Oh, it was, was it? Just brave to scare a whole town pretty nearly to death? Just brave, was it, to make hundreds of good, law-abidin' citizens climb fences and dive for cellar doors? Is that what you call just brave?"

"He—he really—killed nobody," said the girl, some of her color leaving her face.

"Turnin' the hair of folks white—I seen Jud McCruder. Plumb gray—effect of that terrible lot of inferno that Peter, he raised in Lawson Creek!"

"Nonsense! He's been gray for three years."

"And besides, herding up and down the streets of a town—and even knocking down his own cousin, real rough."

"Charles is large enough to take care of himself!"

"And then seeing a whole crowd of two or three hundred gents that had hold of a crook and was going to lynch him—and save the law a lot of time and trouble and expense—and snatching that crook away from them, and saving him—and then ripping along and knocking down twenty or thirty other men, all good, strong, hard-fighting gents, and taking a worthless negro away from them, just as they was about to wring his neck. You call them actions good, do you?"

She was standing on her feet, her hands clenched at

her sides. "I defend every one of those actions!" cried Ruth McNair.

"And then smashing along through the night and tearing up a bridge and pitching it down into a river just to keep back them same peaceable, law-abiding gents."

"Who would have lynched poor Peter! You know it! You know it!"

"And don't he deserve lynching, I ask you?"

"Dad!"

"Don't you yap at me like that! I tell you that I'm looking right inside of your heart and telling you what's really there!"

"Dad, you don't know one single thing about what's in my heart!"

"And raising all that deviltry in Lawson Creek for the sake of just amusing himself!"

"No, no, no! But to save the lives of two friends—"

"That's it! You're naming it now! For the sake of two friends! The worst, most sneaking crooks in the range is one of them friends, and a man-slaughtering, worthless negro is the other."

"Dad, you said yourself that Soapy must have fought like a hero to get through that wild crowd."

"A crook and a murdering negro. Those are his friends!"

"Dad, I won't listen!"

Chapter XL

A CROSS-EXAMINATION

Leaning forward, Mr. McNair beat upon the table with his fist so that the dishes jumped and clattered. "What is the actual fact, honey? Birds of a feather, they hunt together. You can't get behind that."

"Dad, will you listen?"

"You can't get behind what I've said."

"Ah, there's no wonder that poor Peter is misjudged!"

"Misjudged, eh? I tell you what the womenfolks do over to Lawson Creek. When they want to throw a scare into a naughty kid, they just say: 'Peter Hale'll get you, if you don't watch out!' "

"They don't!" cried the girl. "It's no such thing!"

"Ain't it? It was told me first hand by a gent that was in Lawson Creek."

"I don't care, and I won't believe a word of it! Of all the gentle, quiet, thoughtful men in the world—"

"Hypocrisy!" said her father. "That's the worst part of him! Hypocrite!"

"No!"

"Sure, soft and smooth speaking. Must take in a lot of folks. But thank Heaven, we know the facts about him!"

"You won't open your eyes to the facts—the real facts, dad! You just won't! You know perfectly well that Peter came back from college—a cripple—a poor cripple—"

"Having his father think for three years that he was a regular athlete."

"He *had* been, and a grand one, and you know it! And he didn't want to break his father's heart, because poor, dear, silly, muddle-headed Ross Hale thought that football was more important than studies."

"What studies?" asked her father. "What did he learn?"

"I don't know—except that it was something fine. Because he wouldn't learn cheap, low things."

"Cheap, low things that would make his bread and butter, eh?"

"Can you really say that? You know that you and everybody else expected poor Peter to sit down on the ranch with his father and slowly starve to death. But he *didn't*. He went to work. He made things. He made everything. He got money. He started the ranch booming along. Until—you've said yourself that he made that ranch so perfect that nobody—not even Ross Hale—could run it without making fine money out of it! You said that yourself!"

"He worked to pull the wool over our eyes. All the time the wildness was inside of him, and busting to get out. And now it's busted and we know what he really is!"

"I say that it will all be explained. You just won't wait for an explanation to—"

"And that man—didn't he dare to talk to you like he was sort of fond of you?"

"Yes!"

261

"By Heaven, when he knowed that you was as good as engaged—yes, you *was* engaged to Charlie! The skunk!"

"I won't stay in this room to hear you speak like this!"

"You got to stay! A fine, clean, hard-working, industrious gent like Charles, that nobody has anything against."

"Has he ever been tested? Has Charles ever been through the fire?"

"Mind you, nobody can speak a word agin Charlie! Except a mite of a word about him gambling high over in Lawson Creek."

"I tell you," cried the girl, "that that's the only really good thing I've ever heard about him!"

"Ruth, what're you sayin' to me?"

"I mean it! I mean it! I despise a man that wouldn't risk his life—or his money—just for nothing, sometimes! It shows that he has a heart! And that's the first flash that I've ever heard of from Charlie!"

"Ruth, you're talkin' about one of the most respected young gents in this here county! Nobody got a word—"

She stamped with fury. "I don't want to hear about the good things that they say of him! Nobody with any fire and flesh and blood in him was ever able to get along, really, without making enemies! Look at you, yourself! Haven't you got three enemies for every friend, and haven't you always gloried in it? Haven't I heard you say that you have friends that would

262

follow you to—to—"

"To the devil and back, yes, and they would. And so would I for them."

His whole manner changed. He settled back in his chair, smiling faintly at her. "Now, you set down, Ruthie. You and me is gunna have a talk!"

She sat down on the edge of her chair, staring in a rather frightened manner. "What—what do you mean, father?"

"That I been stringin' you along, honey, and now I know pretty much what I want to know. This here Peter, he told you that he let on to be fond of you!"

"He did more," said the girl. "He told me—I wish that the whole world knew it—that he loved me; that he loved me; that he loved me dearly. And that's the most beautiful thing that ever happened in the world."

"I think," said Mr. McNair, "that maybe I would agree with you, Ruthie!"

"Dad, do you mean that?"

He said steadily: "I think that maybe I could agree with you about that, because, from one way of looking at things, you might say that this here boy Peter, he come back from college with his head full of book knowledge, and nothing else. And he found the old ranch busted and done for, loaded with mortgages. And he found his father just a wreck of a man—run all down like his ranch—and what did he do? Why, it looked like he got together and lifted that ranch right up. First we smiled, and then we started in wondering. And pretty soon, we seen that this here boy had brains. And we seen that a man didn't live in his legs, but in his wits, eh? And more than that—in his heart!"

"Yes," said the girl faintly, but smiling through tears. "Dear old Peter! How he did work! And how cheerfully! Do you remember—"

"The fool way that he looked at you that day out in the shed where he was pretending to be fixing up furniture? Yes, I remember all of that. But what I was working toward saying is that, by the looks of the thing, this here Peter was a fine, honest, brainy gent— and with the sort of a heart that made him friends and kept them."

"Yes."

"And by the look of things, you would say that he *couldn't* go up there into the mountains and throw himself away on a crook like Old Man Jarvin without having a pretty good reason, that was stronger than Peter."

"No, no, no! You couldn't! You couldn't!"

"And then, after he got with Jarvin, he showed that he would fight like a hero—not for himself or for a good friend, but just for the sake of a sneaking gambler and a yaller man!"

"He did. Oh, he showed it!" said Ruth, and the tears of excitement and happiness began to stream down her cheeks.

"Very well," said the voice of her father, raised from its gentleness and from its calm, "then why in the devil ain't you engaged to marry that man?"

"God help me!" whispered Ruth. "Do you mean that?"

"Ain't you my daughter?" thundered McNair. "Ain't you mine? Ain't it my honest, mean blood that's inside of you? Why, no, it ain't. It can't be! Because here you sit whining like a sick cat. Why? Because this here Peter—this heart of oak, this clean-eyed, two-handed fighting man, this modest, kind, gentle, straight-shooting gent—this here Peter that tumbled you all in a heap of excitement when you seen him first, in spite of his crippled legs—why, you turn your back on him just because he ain't been writing to you!"

"Dad—he left and gave me no word."

"Girl, if there was something so terrible strong in his life that it sent him to Old Man Jarvin, how could he come and explain himself to you?"

"But—do you mean that I could write to him?"

"Ruth, didn't you learn how to do that when you was in that fool school?"

"But if I wrote—what could I say?"

"That you love him, you ninny!"

"Dad!"

"Sure, tell him that! Tell him that you love him. That you cry when you see his handwriting. That you lie awake at nights thinking of him. That you worship the ground that he walks on—that he don't have to explain nothing about his devil-raising actions to you."

"Dad, dad, I'm engaged this day to Charlie."

"Charlie? Who's he? I dunno who you mean, unless

it's that stiff-backed son of that miserly Andy Hale!"

"Oh, and you *let* me become engaged to him!"

"You rattlehead! How was I to know that you was capable of loving a real man and not an imitation one?"

"Oh, I *shall* write. I think—"

"To who—"

"To Charles, first."

"Curse Charles! Let him read of it in the papers! That's the best way for him. But don't you start to fooling and wasting time. Because you got hold of the finest thing in the world. Love, honey. You got hold of that. And you take it quick and put your mark on it and make it yours for keeps! No, letters won't do. You got to go straight to Peter yourself!"

"To Peter! Dad, I'd die!"

"The devil you would! And if you won't go, I'll go myself!"

"You don't mean that!"

"Don't you fool yourself about what I mean! I say that I'm dead in earnest! Now, you mind that if you don't go, I'll go in your place, and when I get there—"

"What would you do?"

"Get down on my knees and beg Peter to come marry my fool girl that's crying for him at home!"

Chapter XLI

THE END OF HIS PATIENCE

Although Will Nast had an eye for men, he had an eye for agriculture, also. As he passed through the lane, he looked on either side of him and admired the acres of greenery. He could remember, and so could every other man who traveled that road, a time when these had been dusty fields. He could remember, also, when these fine fences had been tumble-down, patched affairs, hardly strong enough to contain the few starving cattle in the fields. Now there was a veritable breath of wealth and contentment coming up from the soil. As he came closer to the house, he noticed the newly planted trees which surrounded it.

They had been brought in by Peter, at much cost of money, time, and toil—because he could not wait until the front of the old ranch house was properly dignified with a veil of fine trees, as it had been when he first went away to college. The stumps of the others had been removed, all saving the butt of the largest of them all. This remained in the midst of that flourishing little plantation of trees, and the reason for it was plain to the mind of Sheriff Nast, because, in the first place, it was men that he knew; agriculture was second.

He understood that the single stump was left there as an undying sign of the heroic self-denial of a father who had starved himself and ruined his land for the sake of a single son. Peter, when he looked at that stump, would remember, and never forget. And those in the world who were gifted with something more than half an eye could guess also.

Mr. Nast gazed for some moments on that stump and, after he had tied his horse at the hitching rack, he opened the gate. It was new and cleanly painted, like all the red fence that went around the Ross Hale place. He walked slowly up the path toward the house. Thinking of the ways and the methods of other men in his recollection, he was deeply amazed by all that had been done on this place, and in so short a time. There had been others who had raised themselves and their fortunes, and notably, there had been the case of Andy Hale. Andy had gone on putting one to one until he had two, three, then a hundred, a thousand—and finally he had arrived at a notable state of wealth. He would keep on growing, also.

But after all, Andy had used natural means. A little wit, much patience, a sharp eye and a ruthless hand in a trade, a careful watching of the market—these had caused the growth of Andy's fortune. Besides, he had had the steady industry of his son to help him. With Peter Hale, it was different. There had been no long and painful training in the ways of the range. He had stepped in from the outside and by the force of a natural genius he had done this thing. Not so great as the achievement of Andy Hale, if bulk were considered—but greater by far, if the time and the circumstances were considered.

What would Peter go on toward? Or rather, what

would he have gone on toward, if he had had a chance to develop in a natural manner toward all of his potentialities? This thought being on the tip of his tongue, the sheriff was on the verge of murmuring something aloud, when he saw the tall form of Ross Hale issuing from the house. Nast paused and waved his hand. The rancher started. And the sheriff hastened to say:

"I haven't come for you, Ross."

"Nor for Peter?"

"Would I be looking for him here?"

"No. And that's true."

The head of Ross Hale fell.

"I see that the beans are coming on big and fine and strong, Ross."

"Yes, getting pretty thick."

"Who would ever of thought of raising beans in this here county, Ross!"

"Aye, who would of thought of it! Never me!"

"But is there money in the fool things?"

"More than you could shake a stick at!"

"Old Sargent is putting in a hundred and sixty acres in them, I hear."

"Yep. Peter rode over and looked at his work and tried to tell him how his system was all wrong. But Sargent is pig-headed. He said that he knew, and that was all that there was to it. Peter says that the first hot summer will burn Sargent's crop right out!"

"Well, experience is the only thing that'll teach Sargent. But there's a few of us that don't need so much experience for learning, Ross."

"Like who, now?"

"Like Peter, for an example."

"Aye," said the father, "there was brains, for you. They worked out the reasons for things without no help! Was you—have you—" He paused.

"No," said the sheriff. "Peter ain't been pulling up any more bridges by the roots."

"Then what's happening over Lawson way?"

"About Peter?"

"Yes. I heard that a lot of men was getting together to raid him."

"They won't do it," said the sheriff. "Folks will talk a lot about what they'll do when they get together and take the law into their hands, but they don't usually do it. Not unless they have a handy chance, like finding a crook right in the middle of their town, or some such thing. A mob is lazy. It don't like to ride a hundred miles for its honey. It likes to have the fun easy and quick. And take it by and large, a mob is a pretty cowardly thing, Ross. It does fine when it sees a helpless man with no guns on him. But it ain't half so bold when it has to consider that same man with a pair of gats ready to kick in his hands. And the same thing goes with those boys over to Lawson Creek. They talk a lot about how their town is disgraced and made a laughingstock. But it'll be a long time before they turn in and hunt down three men that can tear up a bridge and chuck it in the river!"

Ross Hale listened with large eyes of wonder. "Then they ain't going to shoot up Peter?"

"No danger in the world. I tell you, old son, that son of yours has made himself so feared over yonder that he could swing down the street of Lawson Creek on his crutches, and there wouldn't be nobody that would dare to raise a hand against him!"

"But the law, sheriff, ain't it got something against Peter and the rest?"

"What'll the law do?" The sheriff grinned. "Accuse him of shooting? He didn't kill anybody! And he really didn't fire a shot! Disturbing the peace? He can say that he was being mobbed and that he had to fight back in self-defense! No, sir, Lawson Creek ain't going to ask into a law court the three men that made such a fool of the town. They know that this thing has gone far enough. They don't want any more air given to the story of what happened over there the evening of the fight!" He broke off with a chuckle.

"That's tolerable good news." Ross Hale sighed. "I just been sort of waiting. The other day, Will, I had an idea of something that might bring him back. But it didn't pan out, you know!"

"An idea for bringing Peter back?"

"Yes."

"Now," said the sheriff seriously, "that's what I stopped in here to talk to you about. I wanted you to know, Ross, that the thing for you to do is settle yourself down and get ready for a lot of time to pass before Peter comes back." The rancher sighed and looked at the ground.

"It's bleak, living alone," said the sheriff. "But it's

271

what you got to do. Because, between you and me, Peter ain't going to be here in any hurry!"

"Will you tell me what you mean by that, Will? And how could you know?"

"By the fact that I been up there talking to him."

"Ah, you been there!"

"Yes. And the last thing that he said was for me to drop around and to cheer you up. But what I wanted to say first was that Peter ain't changed. You might think that he's gone sort of wild."

"But he ain't?"

"No. He's just the same. Even a mite more sober and silent, maybe. But just the same, steady as a clock and as strong as iron! You would laugh, Ross, if you could see the way that that big negro waits on him!"

"I wouldn't laugh," said Ross Hale with a trembling voice. "Only—in the name of Heaven, tell me what I done that drove him away!"

"You? Why, man, you didn't do a thing! Not a thing! The whole point was that there is some sort of a pull that Old Man Jarvin has over him. That's the fact, and Peter as good as told me so. He has to stay there with Jarvin for a while. I don't know how long. Of course, he's useful to Jarvin. But Jarvin is sure to let him go, sooner or later. What the hold is, I dunno."

"Will, if Jarvin has a grip on him, Jarvin will be the death of him."

"Why?"

"Because Jarvin is poison, as you know."

"He hasn't poisoned Peter, and he won't. The only thing is patience."

"Patience? Patience?" The rancher groaned. "Ain't I had plenty of patience all of these years? But there comes a time when the patience is all burned out of a man, sheriff. You understand that?"

"Yes," said the sheriff, "I understand!"

So well did he understand that he cut his visit shorter than he had intended, and when he went away, he paused beside the bean fields and wondered again at the glistening acres of beans. A great work had been accomplished here.

He looked back and could see the distant form of Ross Hale striding up and down in front of the house. Some great resolution was forming in the mind of the father, for the sake of his son. When the sheriff remembered what great things this same man had done in the past for that identical cause, he wondered now what strange deed would come from the hand of the rancher. But even his fondest imaginings were far short of the resolution which had formed in the brain of Hale.

Chapter XLII

HAUNTED

The resolution which had formed in the mind of Ross Hale, was simply that he must reclaim Peter from the hands of Mike Jarvin. Sheriff Nast was not apt to be wrong. If the sheriff said that Peter was with Jarvin—not from any wish of his own, but because of some power which Jarvin had over him—then, of course, Peter would return to the ranch and to his old way of living as soon as the influence of Jarvin was cut off.

How, then, could that influence be removed? There was one simple and effective means, of which Ross Hale thought at once. There was no sweetness in his life, he had discovered, except through Peter. He had spent so many years laboring for the sake of his son that he seemed to have lost all taste of enjoyment except through Peter and Peter's accomplishments.

Even the richness and the beauty of the farm were nothing to him, except that they exemplified the cleverness and the industry of Peter. To live in comfort again and in a growing wealth was nothing; but to hear strangers praise Peter was the delight of Hale's life.

He had done all that he could, except one thing. And he determined on that one thing, now. He would ride straight to the mine, ask to see Mike Jarvin, and then, no matter how the latter was surrounded by his hired braves, he would send a bullet through the head of that fat gentleman and bring his wretched life to a close.

That would free Peter. As for Ross Hale, of course, he would be blown to bits by Jarvin's men. But what difference did that make? None at all! At least, he had the grim satisfaction of knowing that Peter would never forget him and would never let others forget him. Perhaps it would be better, too, to close his life with one great effort, such as this—better than to drag out long days to no real purpose. So thought Ross Hale.

The sheriff, riding slowly off down the road, heard the familiar sound of a revolver exploding. He turned and looked back to the house of Hale, but he could see nothing except the blurred outline of house and trees, at that distance. The gun sounded again.

"Ross has seen a rabbit." The sheriff chuckled.

So, indeed, Ross Hale had. And that rabbit lay dead, first lamed and then with its head nearly torn off by the slugs from the gun of the farmer. It was a mighty satisfaction to him. He stood over the little animal for a moment and smiled. For, after all, there might be some chance that he could penetrate the camp of Jarvin, kill his man, and even fight his way out again!

He started at once to reach his best horse and saddle it for the long trail. It was a fine brown gelding with one white-stockinged foreleg and a white blaze down its face; a very good horse. Indeed, it was sure to be of the best, for Peter himself had made a present of it to his father, and when was Peter contented with anything other than the best?

On that same day, the sun was blazing hot on the mine and the shacks which were clustered around the mouth of the shaft. Ordinarily, there was a little breeze moving across the valley, carrying at the least a current of warm air around the buildings. But on this day, all was as deadly still and hot as an oven.

Jarvin was in great distress. He had taken off his coat; he had taken a rather greasy towel to mop the perspiration from his forehead and from under his chin. But still there was a working conscience, as one might say, which kept Jarvin to his labors. He sat at the table and shuffled the cards over and over again, and then dealt them.

It was a most bewildering thing to mark the dexterity of those fat, white fingers as they handled the pasteboards. Steadily, anxiously, with a puckered forehead, Mr. Jarvin worked at his art. As he dealt he would say: "I win!" Or again: "You win!" Or, "Third man wins!"

Having completed the deal, he would turn the cards face up, and it was wonderful to note that his prophecies were rarely wrong. Not more than once in ten times did he make a mistake. But the hand which he selected was always the most powerful one going into the draw. In the draw itself, he could do astonishing things. The top two or three cards remained in place, but dexterously from the center of the pack or from the bottom of it he drew out cards, and all at such a flying speed that the most careful eye could not have detected it.

He grumbled to himself, however. Half a lifetime spent in similar labors, it was plain, had not lifted the cunning of Mr. Jarvin to the point which he desired. Like all great men, he had established above himself a goal which he could never quite attain to. Still he struggled patiently toward that end.

Said Jarvin: "Hey, Peter! Did you ever see such a cursed day?"

Peter, lying in the hammock outside the window, turned his head and observed his employer calmly.

"Very close," said he.

"It's worse," said Mr. Jarvin with emphasis, "than a katzenjammer. Soapy, gimme a drink, will you?"

Soapy grunted: "I'm busy!"

It brought a roar from Mr. Jarvin.

"Say, Peter, ain't you going to let that negro of yours do what I tell him to do?"

"Why," said Peter, "Soapy can't really work for two masters, you know."

A brilliant crimson suffused the face of Jarvin. Words swelled in his throat and made his fat lips tremble, but then they were suppressed again. He heaved himself from his chair and went to the side of the room, where he poured out a glass of tepid water and swallowed it, still looking terrible askance at the pair beyond the windows.

They had not altered their position. Peter lay with his eyes closed, again, and beside him squatted Soapy, with a tattered remnant of a newspaper, yellow with time, made into a fan, with which he set up a steady current of air. Now and again, he stretched forth his enormous hand and brushed away a fly which threatened to settle upon the face of his master.

In the beginning, Jarvin had hardly been able to refrain from gigantic laughter, when he saw Soapy adopting toward Peter the attitude of a mother to a child, or of a worshiper to a saint. However, the days had crept on, and still there was no change. Others, who looked on, ceased to smile, also. In the first place, it was always dangerous to smile when Soapy was near. Furthermore, it began to be apparent that this was no passing fancy in the mind of Soapy. He regarded the cripple with a strange species of veneration. Automatically, he followed him about through all the day. He was like a dreadful shadow lurking behind Peter wherever the latter went. And his anxious eyes continually studied the face of his master, striving to discover the will of Peter before it could be spoken.

Some observing people thought that Soapy was going mad. But others contented themselves with observing that Peter was a very strange fellow and that he might accomplish queerer things than this, before the end!

Said Mr. Jarvin, as he scowled upon this peaceful picture: "The darned cards won't behave."

"Look here," said Peter, "what's upset you so much?"

A great oath ripped from the throat of Jarvin. "Who said that I was upset?"

"You've acted like a nervous child since last night," replied Peter.

At this, Mr. Jarvin actually reached for his gun. But then he hesitated. The bright, round, unwinking eye of Soapy was fixed upon him. Jarvin changed his mind. Nothing could be quite so discouraging to rashness as that unwinking eye of Soapy's!

Peter asked: "Have you been sleeping badly? Or is it indigestion?"

And Jarvin groaned suddenly. "Peter, it's a ghost!"

The broad nostrils of Soapy flared; his eyes opened wider and rounder than ever.

"A ghost!" Jarvin moaned. "As I was riding along through the brush with you and Soapy, I looked back, and it sort of seemed to me that I could see a gent there behind the shadow of a bush—a gent with his hat off—and pale, silver-looking hair—that reminded me—of—somebody else."

His voice trailed away into a little gasp of emotion. Plainly Jarvin had been badly frightened.

"And I remember," said Peter, "that when we were getting out of Lawson Creek in such a hurry, there was a fellow, such as you describe, standing on the steps of the general merchandise store.

"His hat had been blown off, and his hair was long, and the wind was blowing through it. And he was shooting after us a great deal straighter than the rest of them! More dangerous than the whole crowd put together. He was the one that crashed those bullets through the body of the buckboard, you know."

Soapy cried: "Dog-gone it, Mr. Hale, by the way that you and the boss talks, it would sound like old Sam Debney had come back to haunt—"

"Curse you, you fool, Soapy!" screamed Mr. Jarvin, leaping to his feet. "I'll smash your skull in for you, if you say that again."

He relapsed into another groan. "I almost thought

that it was!" whispered Jarvin. "The same—sort of a—white face, too!"

Yes, when Peter recalled the figure of the man who had stood on the steps of the store in Lawson Creek with such an accurate rifle, he could remember that the face of the stranger had seemed to him to be extraordinarily pale. But he had simply thought that this must be due to the manner in which the lamplight was streaming across his shoulder from the open door behind.

"Hello!" said Soapy in a whisper. "He's back on that idea. He always said that Debney would come back to haunt him!"

Chapter XLIII

THE SPIRIT OF VENGEANCE

The evening of another day came softly down from the shadows of the mountains. But there was still enough light to pour through the window and illuminate the table of Mike Jarvin, where he worked patiently at his card packs. As the dimness increased, he thrice begged Soapy to light a lamp for him, but Soapy was as indifferent as a piece of stone, and Peter refused to interfere.

"Soapy works for me," said Peter, "and that means he doesn't have to serve other people, unless he wants to. That's final, Jarvin. You've heard me say it before, for that matter!"

"Well," said Soapy, "I'll light his darn lamp for him. Maybe it'll help him keep the ghosts away."

There was a half-angry and half-frightened snarl from Mr. Jarvin inside of the shack. But now as Soapy looked down the slope, he saw a rider approaching through the dusk—a rider who came out of the shadows and rapidly into his ken—and he knew that it was a stranger to the mine.

"And there's two more coming behind. A woman and a man coming up the slope behind, Mr. Hale. What might they be! Woman riding a mighty bright pinto hoss."

"A pinto horse!" echoed Peter, rising suddenly in the hammock. He gave the couple who were winding up the road, a single startled glance and then heaved himself to his feet. But now he started again. For he saw the horseman who was drifting nearer. "Father!" cried Peter. "What in the name of wonder has brought you up here?"

"Why, Peter," said the older man, waving his hand to him, "I've come up here to see how things was with you. There ain't any harm in that, I guess?"

"No harm," said Peter in a somewhat stifled voice. "No harm at all."

"But there's somebody else coming up the road that might surprise you, Peter."

"Tell me," gasped the son. "It can't be—it really can't be that—"

"It's McNair and his girl," said Ross Hale calmly. "I passed them on the trail a while back. I recognized them, but they didn't recognize me, I guess. I was cutting in from the side and looking back, with the light agin their faces. You'd best go meet them, Peter."

Said Peter in a shaken voice: "Do you hear, Jarvin?"

"I hear," growled Jarvin.

"Shall I go to meet them, or shall I stay here with you?"

"Let them be cursed! Well, I don't want to hear that McNair talk. Got no use for me, nor me for him! You go meet them, and let McNair know that he ain't welcome here. The fool had ought to know! And you might take your old man along with you."

"I'll wait right here," said Ross Hale as quietly as before. "There ain't any hurry about what I got to say to you."

Peter was already starting away with Soapy behind him.

"Hey, leave Soapy here!" shouted Jarvin.

"Go back, Soapy," said Peter. "Watch Jarvin for me."

Soapy obediently swung around and strode on to the veranda.

"No matches here for this lamp!" snarled Jarvin. "Soapy, got a match?"

"No," said Soapy.

"Go fetch me one, then."

"I ain't sent here to fetch things. The boss sent me to watch you, you fat swine!" replied Soapy.

"Here," said Ross Hale in genial tones. "Here's a match, Jarvin."

"Ah," said Mike Jarvin, "come in, Hale. You can see what I got to put up with," he continued, "from your son and his negro. Thanks!"

For Ross Hale had entered the shack and handed a package of sulphur matches to the miner. One of those matches spluttered with a blue light that steadied to yellow, and the lamp was lighted.

"Now look here, Hale," went on Jarvin more gently. "I suppose that you've come up here to get your boy. But that ain't likely! He's to stay with me, Hale. He gets pay enough for a major general. That ought to suit him. And he's able to pull me out of a good many scrapes. You've heard about what happened at Lawson Creek, I suppose?"

"Yes," said Ross Hale, "I've heard."

"So we ain't gunna have no argument, eh?"

"What I want to ask you, Jarvin, is just this: How long will Peter be workin' for you?"

"How long will I be livin'?" replied Jarvin. "That's a more sensible way of putting that question. And I'm tough, Hale, and I'm gunna last!"

There was a little pause, which lasted long enough to make Jarvin squint at his guest.

"I'd like to say," murmured Ross Hale at last, "that if you was to think things over careful, you might want to make a compromise with me, Jarvin."

"Compromise?" snarled Jarvin, growing ugly at once. "Why should I? I got Peter and I'm gunna keep him. I got him so's he *can't* get away. And that's the finish of it."

"Are you set on that? Is that final?" asked Hale.

"Soapy!" grunted the mine owner, "this here looks like trouble. Are you watching?"

"I'm watchin'," replied Soapy from the window.

"Jarvin," said Hale, "I've come here to have it out with you. And—"

His right hand went back to his hip; that gesture brought a snarl of fear from Jarvin. His own right hand went back to his gun and clung there.

As for Soapy, his own weapon was already bared and resting on the sill of the window. All of this, Ross Hale saw. He knew that, when he drew his own gun, a bullet would be through him. But still his courage did not falter. Life, for him, was not so sweet that he cared to linger it out. And before he died, he would be able to draw down Jarvin also into the eternal shadow.

But there was no chance for him to fire.

Suddenly Jarvin looked askance at the window facing Soapy. And Jarvin, with a shrill scream, threw up his arms before his face and cringed back against the side of the wall.

"No, Sam!" he shouted. "For Heaven's sake—"

It seemed to Ross Hale, as he looked in the same direction, that he saw at the other window a very pale face, framed with long, silver hair, distinguishable dimly under the shadow of a hat. He had only the faintest glimpse. A gun spoke from the hand of the stranger, filling the little room with sudden thunder. Jarvin crashed forward on his face and moved no more. The face at the other window was gone as

Soapy, his attention drawn from Ross Hale, fired a bullet vainly in that direction. When Soapy rushed around the side of the shack, there was no trace of any stranger. Perhaps he had run down among the big rocks that bordered the plateau.

Soapy hurried back into the little house and found Ross Hale on his knees beside Jarvin. He had turned the wounded man upon his back, but it was plain that nothing could be done. A crimson patch was growing in the very center of Jarvin's breast—and his eyes were closed.

He opened them at last with a faint chuckle, and then his voice sounded with wonderful steadiness and a note of exultation.

"A full house beats three of a kind, stranger!" said Jarvin cheerfully.

With the last word his eyes grew blank, and he was dead.

Jarvin was buried at the edge of the plateau. Some of the miners blasted a hole among the rocks, and he was laid away for the endless sleep. Afterward, he remained in the minds of men only as an ugly rumor, and no more. Perhaps he occupied less space in the thoughts of Peter Hale and his father than in any others—because there was too much, now, to fill the minds of the two.

There was only one point on which they differed—only one point of importance. Ross Hale was firmly convinced that it was actually the ghost of Sam Debney, Jarvin's murdered man, that had returned to work vengeance upon his destroyer. But Peter was just as firmly convinced that it must have been a brother, say of poor Debney, who had returned after these many years to give Jarvin requital for that foul murder.

However, they could not dwell on such ideas, and certainly there was never a trace of the destroyer. He vanished from the knowledge of men utterly.

As for Peter and Ruth—they were married before the week was out, and at their marriage every notable in the county was present, with one exception.

Andy Hale was there, stern, and with a forced smile which deceived no one. But Charles Hale, it appeared, had been called away to the East upon important business, and no one could say how long it would be before he returned. Indeed, he did not return for many long months. Not, in fact, until his father had gone for him.

There were ugly rumors afloat—that Charlie had fallen in bad habits while he was away; that the gaming table had a singular lure for him; that he had learned to squander money. And no one could understand how this could be, for certainly he had been raised according to a rigid rule of economy!

Peter passed on to a broader and a fuller life. He had the growing concerns of his father's ranch to occupy him. Beyond this, he had all the business of McNair's broad acres. McNair himself refused to lift a hand and left everything in the power of his son-in-law. As he said, he had been merely a worker on the old scale and scheme of things. He had merely sketched in the outlines of the picture, and now Peter could fill in the details. As for himself, he was fond of sitting at his ease with Ross Hale on the veranda of Peter's new house.

And he would say to his friend: "Now which of us has the most claim to Peter, Ross? You made him, I know. But I discovered him. And that's just as important!"

Center Point Publishing
600 Brooks Road ● PO Box 1
Thorndike ME 04986-0001 USA

(207) 568-3717

US & Canada:
1 800 929-9108